RETURN OF THE PRINCE

NANA MALONE

COPYRIGHT

This is a work of fiction. Names, characters, places, and incidents either are the product of the author's imagination or are used fictitiously, and any resemblance to actual persons living or dead, business establishments, events, or locales, is entirely coincidental.

Return of the Prince, Book one in the Prince Duet

COPYRIGHT © 2019 by Nana Malone

Cover Art by Hang Le

Photography by Wander Aguilar

Edited by Angie Ramey and Michele Ficht

Published in the United States of America

ONE

TRISTAN...

THE FIST CAME AT ME WITH STARTLING SPEED.

I was sluggish, slow. I'd had too many other things on my mind lately.

"Your Highness, you have to pay attention if we're going to do this."

I needed to get my fucking head in the game. Another round of fists, elbows, two knees. My blocks were faster this time, and my brain started to engage.

If I didn't block Frank, he was going to pop me in the face. And that was going to be a bitch to explain tonight on the red carpet. Frank Talbott had been on my personal guard detail since I was sixteen. I used to have two more guards, but now it was just Frank.

"Well," I muttered. *Jab. Jab. Right cross.* "If you weren't trying to maim me..." *Knee, twist, block. Front kick.* "Then maybe I could have a moment to breathe." *Knee, knee, elbow.*

Frank crumpled for a moment and then peered up at me. "Oh so, Your Highness thinks you can take care of yourself, do you?"

I growled at him. "I didn't say that. I'm just saying this is a bit of aggressive training."

"Didn't *you* ask for this?" He was on his feet again, lightning fast, bounding up as if that momentary respite was all he needed to dole out more beatings.

My brain clicked into that numb, automatic space. I knew how to deflect the blows. I knew how to block. I knew how to go on the offensive. I finally let myself engage, shut everything else out, and delivered.

I landed a jab to his face, the satisfying crunch pushing me on, driving me.

Frank was blocking at lightning speed. *Missed block. Gut punch.*

He *oomphed.* I delivered a front kick, then I was on him, twisting his arm in my grasp, and pinning it behind him with my knee in his lower back. "Say Uncle."

My voice didn't even sound like mine. It was cold, detached.

He gave two taps on the hardwood floor, and then he chuckled. "Well, I guess all I have to do is goad you into paying attention."

"I *was* paying attention. It was just taking me a second to get my head in the game."

He hopped to his feet and grabbed the face towels, tossing mine at me. "Are you burning the candle at both ends again?"

I rolled my eyes. Frank might have only been five years older than me, but he acted like a pensioning, agony aunt, always trying to feed me tea, make me eat, and get me to sleep 8 hours a night.

Granted, that was his job. But still... It was odd having

someone try to mother me. Especially since my own mother had been cold and distant at the best of times.

"Sorry, my mind was just elsewhere today."

He shook his head. "Your Highness, not to nag..."

I sighed. "Then don't nag. I beg you."

He pinned me with a glare. "Well, if I don't nag no one is going to. When we train, you need to be on. I'm the only guard you have."

I winced at that reminder. There'd been a shooting at the Vienna Opera House during a charity event a few weeks ago. I had felt the ghost whistle of the bullet as it whizzed by my ear. Yet still, the Regents Council didn't see fit to provide me any more guards. And I knew exactly who on the council was blocking my return. He wasn't the only one, but if everything went my way, there'd be nothing keeping me from going home soon. Or at least my plans would already be in place and it wouldn't matter what happened to me after that.

My cousin, King Sebastian, had been working with me to find alternatives, but the rules were clear, and since my uncle's death, they were being enforced. As a member of the royal family, I couldn't be guarded by civilians.

And given that my family was currently out of favor, however deserving, I was a sitting duck. My parents had one guard each. My sister, the same. All because my brother, asshole extraordinaire, had committed treason. We weren't necessarily in exile, but we weren't particularly welcome at home in the Winston Isles either.

I just needed this deal to go through. Then everything would change.

"No, I know you're right. I'm sorry."

He studied me. "How late were you up last night? I went to bed at one and I know you were still up then."

I made it a point to school my expression. I'd been working on my plans to go home and the plans for beyond that day, but I couldn't tell Frank that.

"Yeah, I was up a little late. You worry too much."

Ella, my fiancée, came out of her bedroom, all beautiful blonde hair cascading over her shoulders, her robe tied at the waist and a disapproving frown on her face. "Tristan, you're not ready?"

I sighed. "We don't have to leave for another *three* hours."

She blinked at me as if I had spoken Greek.

"You have to get ready, so stop playing *Mortal Combat* or whatever."

I laughed. "*Mortal Combat*? Please, you're going to have to update your references. Is that all you know about martial arts sparring?"

She shrugged. "Yeah. I don't really like action or violence."

The word violence was spoken softly enough to keep me from teasing her too much. "How in the world have you gone through life and not watched a proper Bruce Lee movie?"

She shrugged. "Too violent."

I sighed. "Right. Okay. We have plenty of time. Remember, all I have to do is shower, throw on some aftershave, and toss on a tux."

"Fine, don't listen to me. It's a lot better if we arrive early and show our faces. Then if we duck out, no one will notice."

She had a point there. But still, the idea of going extremely early to an event just to get as many paparazzi photos as possible was exhausting.

Frank inclined his head. "That's my cue to shower too."

I shook my head. "Way to leave me during a time of true strife."

He chuckled as he ran to his room. Once his door closed, Ella lifted a brow. "How is it going?"

I gave her a brief nod. "It's fine."

"He seems *concerned* about you."

"I'm fine. Just tired." No way was I telling her what was clouding my reflexes. We might not have a traditional relationship, but she'd certainly worry.

She studied me closely. Her gray eyes tracking every inch of my face. She was quintessentially beautiful and had an ethereal quality about her. From the moment I met her, I knew she was someone that needed my protection. But there was something *else* in her eyes now, something that I deftly ignored.

I knew just how bad an idea it was. We'd already gone down that road once, and it had been a disaster. Granted, that was what happened when you made love to one woman and called out another's name.

Not my finest moment.

So now, I pretended I didn't see her interest. It was the kindest thing I could do. We needed each other, and pretending we could be more than partners would only hurt her in the end.

"Are we still going to pretend that someone didn't shoot at us a few weeks ago? And that we might have poked the bear with what we've been doing?"

I shook my head. "Nope. But I have things under control, okay?"

She shifted on her feet. "Listen, Tristan, I've been thinking that maybe..." Her voice trailed off.

Shit. I knew that face. She was getting cold feet. "Ella, you can't back out of this now. We both agreed. Strangers on the train."

She swallowed hard. "I know. I just—the way you're training and the fact that somebody already shot at us indicates he's clearly onto us. Maybe I should just go back to him. This all stops if I go back."

I took her hands. "Look at me. Take a breath. We have no definitive proof that Vienna had anything to do with Max."

"What else could it have to do with? When we got engaged, he swore that he was going to make us pay, and what if this is it? He's trying to kill us."

She was scared, and she had a right to be. Her former manager was a psychopath. One that everyone in the entertainment industry loved. He was a star maker. He also terrorized his starlets. Everyone was too afraid to go against him, to expose him.

"When we met and I saw what he'd done to you, I told you I'd protect you, right? And haven't I?"

Her bottom lip quivered, and I prayed to God she didn't start with the water works. I had no idea how to deal with the overflow of emotions. At least not in some way that didn't ultimately hurt her.

"When we made this deal, I didn't think you would be doing something dangerous that could get you hurt. Jesus, someone tried to kill us already. I know you think it's not him, but—"

"It's not. He's a coward. That was too public."

"You don't know him like I do. He's dangerous. He already ruined my life. I don't want him ruining yours too."

"You need to have more faith. I won't be the one hurt. And I'm training so everything will go seamlessly. The other stuff with Frank is basic anti-kidnapping stuff. I don't have enough guards. I need to keep my training honed. I promise I'm going to be fine." I placed my hands delicately on both of her cheeks. It was rare that I touched her. I didn't want to give any mixed signals.

Like that one time.

"Ella, I made you a promise three years ago, okay? I'd protect you from Max and build you enough cachet so that you can have a career outside of him. And then I promised he would never hurt you again. Do you remember that day?" I'd been furious when I'd walked in to her flat and found her bleeding. When she'd told me her manager had hit her, I'd lost my shit.

She nodded. "Yeah, I remember."

"Do you believe I'll keep my word?"

She blinked rapidly. "Of course, but I don't know why you would even want to."

"Because it's the right thing to do. That guy is a fucking bully. The things he did to you... he's going to pay for all of it."

"You're probably the best friend I've ever had in my life. How sad is that?"

"Well, I'm your fiancée. I *should* be your best friend." I released her and stepped back.

"Tristan, do you ever think that maybe we should, you know... stop this?"

I stared at her for a moment. "What do you mean stop?"

"I just—you're doing so much for me. And I know this is the plan. This has *always* been the plan, but I'm worried. I don't want something to happen to you. Not to mention your whole plan to go home. You've said yourself there are barriers."

I shook my head. "Not insurmountable ones."

"Oh really? So your psychotic brother and the Council

member who vowed you would never come home are not insurmountable problems to you?"

Way to hit below the belt. The problem was when you were in the trenches with someone, it was difficult not to tell them your secrets. Ella and I had been through it. And she knew things about me I'd rather no one knew."

"Look, Gilroy's claim is false. He can't stop me from coming home. Not if I'm the returned national treasure." Which I would be if my current negotiation went well. "And you let me worry about my brother."

My psychopath of a big brother was in prison for crimes against the throne. That didn't stop him from sending me texts to remind me of the secrets he'd spill if I even dreamt about going home.

"I just worry that you're not taking this seriously enough. I don't want something to happen to you."

"Nothing is going to happen to me." And then it occurred to me that maybe she wanted to back out of her end of the agreement. "And listen, no matter what you choose to do, I will take care of Max. You will never have to worry about him again."

A frown marred her beautiful face. "What, you think I don't have the balls to take care of your brother?"

"That's not what I'm saying, Ella. You have the balls. But maybe this is too much. I never should have asked—"

She tilted her chin up. "We had a deal. *You* help me with Max, *I* help you with your brother. What you're planning on doing is the kind of thing that will get you hurt, or arrested, or *something*. All I need to do is get your brother's information. I think I have the easier end of the deal."

"Why don't you let me worry about that?" I'd agreed to help her with her twat of an ex manager long before I found out that her family had founded Banks Safes. Her great grandfather had been a bank robber. His son had wanted to restore the family name and built uncrackable safes.

Beautiful and ethereal though she may be, Ella had the magic touch. And it just so happened I had a safe I needed cracked.

She sighed. "One day, Tristan, you'll realize that relationships go both ways. It's a give and take. It's not you just riding in on your shining white horse being the hero."

"Well, today is not that day."

Once I was in my room, I leaned against the door. She had a fucking point. I was playing with fire. If Max *was* behind Vienna, it meant he was onto us, which meant he'd be on high alert and executing the plan I had for him was going to be next to impossible.

But I wanted to see it through. I had made her a promise to keep her safe and keep her secrets. And I was so close to making that happen, making sure that she'd be able to walk back into the world and never have to worry about Max ever again. When that was over, then I'd stop.

Then maybe you'll think about a life?

I winced as I marched into the shower and turned it to cold. Maybe I was thinking of home too much. I knew full well I couldn't go back to that time of my life.

Are you sure? Because you're still fucking in love with her.

Ariel fucking Scott. Going home, there'd be a risk I'd see her. But I needed to steer clear. I need to let her go, because if she entered into this equation, I was going to lose all my focus and ruin every plan I'd made in the last three years. Not to mention I'd promised Ella I'd keep her secrets. There was no way I could have Ariel and not betray Ella.

Later that night, next to me, Ella preened for the cameras. She was a natural performer.

Three years ago, when my agent suggested that I needed to increase my profile to cash in on endorsements and income, I had agreed. But this, our relationship, had morphed into something different.

I cared about her, but these days it was getting harder to pretend.

With every flash from the cameras, I felt like I was being stabbed with the white-hot metal of a sword, and I had to force the smile to remain in place.

But it had been worse since Vienna a few weeks ago. I was hyper-aware of the crowd size and increasingly conscious of just how small my guard 'team' of one was.

Is that why you declined the King's assistance? Admittedly, maybe that wasn't the smartest thing I'd ever done. I knew Sebastian wanted to help. But I had my own pokers in the fire, and I didn't want interference. If everything went according to plan, I'd be home sooner rather than later. And I wouldn't need as much guard presence.

I just had to make it through this stuff. When Ella felt me being distant or not present, she'd lean into me and place a kiss on my cheek and gaze up at me adoringly.

The press ate that shit up. It always sent them into a fervor and frenzy of more flash bulbs and questions. "Ella, Tristan. When will you two get married?" "Over here, Tristan. Will you be taking Ella home to the Winston Isles?"

When we were finally at the end of our death march, Ella squeezed my hand. "Are you okay? You seem out of it."

"I'm fine."

"Nope, this whole thing works when we both make each

other look good. When you're distant, or not in the moment, people start to ask questions. They will start to ask *me* questions."

I knew we were still being watched, and so I leaned forward and gave her what might seem a sweet kiss on the cheek. "I'm in this. We are tied together."

"Perfect. Then smile for the cameras."

So I did. And everything appeared exactly as it should.

Once we were inside, my shoulders relaxed. At least in there, we wouldn't be as tightly scrutinized. I led her into the ballroom and to our table and prepared myself for a long night.

I kept checking my phone. While I might be exiled, I still had friends back home, friends who would sometimes send me a photo or a snippet from a newspaper.

You're a masochist.

I was.

Just because I had a completely different life now didn't mean I didn't love her. That she didn't command half my dreams.

You have no idea what love is.

Maybe that was true.

And I honestly thought it was better for Ariel that I wasn't there. But after all the headlines from earlier this year, her dismissal, her leaving the Royal Guard, the big old scandal, now we were both collateral damage.

Granted, I could understand why the Council more officially sanctioned this exile for me. My brother was a traitor, and it seemed that my mother—well, she came from a long line of traitors.

I shook my head to clear my thoughts. Ariel wasn't my

concern anymore. It was fine. I could make our plan work. Pretend a little bit longer.

With all the negative publicity about the fallen prince, my endorsements had dried up. I had a contract negotiation, and it had been a bad time. My agents came up with a perfect solution. Find someone who could soften my image. Far from home, most people didn't even remember I was a prince until something bad happened, but they said I needed someone who was sweet and beyond reproach. Someone who could bring up my profile but at the same time needed me just as much as I needed her. And athletes and starlets together were money.

Enter Ella. She was beautiful and, most people said, talented. At the time, I'd never seen one of her movies. Her manager had wanted her in a showmance to increase her profile. Power couples in Hollywood were a thing.

But he hadn't anticipated how much the public would love our supposed fairy-tale romance. His jealousy got the better of him, and he demanded we stop. His request had been violent. I'd found her beaten and bloody.

I promised from that moment to always protect her, and we'd kept up the charade for three years.

The plan was for everyone and their mother to photograph us looking lovey-dovey and doing charity benefits. It was a fairy tale. People loved it. Thanks to the arrangement, I picked up four more endorsement deals. Contract negotiations had gone great. As for Ella, she had been cast in three movies despite her manager's attempts to blackball her.

After the benefit, we were ushered out the back to a side exit that no one else was going to use, and Frank was waiting for us there. "Your Highness. This way."

I paused at the door to wait for Ella, and I could see our limo waiting for us, as it should be.

When Frank opened the door for us, it was slow motion chaos. All I heard was an *oomph* and a gasp. In those frozen seconds, I watched Frank go down, and then there was blood everywhere.

He'd always been on me to train, to tap into everything I'd learned. And luckily, those years of training kicked in. The years of telling my body what to do and having it obey.

I hit the floor, dragging Ella with me and crawling back inside the door. When I shut it, the heavy metal clicking into place, I crawled over to Frank. "Frank, talk to me, man. Talk to me. Ella, hand me your shawl."

She sat there frozen.

I raised my voice. "Ella." Then she blinked into alertness, watching me. "Oh my God, someone shot him."

"Yes. Shawl, now."

She handed it over and I pressed it to his shoulder. "Hey mate, look at me. You're going to be fine."

He nodded and swallowed. "Your Highness, it's been a pleasure."

"Stop with that nonsense. You're not going anywhere."

I pulled out my phone and hit the emergency call button. "Ella, look at me. I need you to go back toward the benefit, call for help. Use one of the red phones. Hurry."

I applied pressure like I knew what to do.

I could have counted Vienna as an isolated incident. But I couldn't ignore this. And now Max had taken out the only bodyguard I had.

I was a sitting fucking duck. By hook or by crook, I was

going to stop him. The only way he was getting to Ella was over my dead body.

In the blur of activity with the paramedics, I was shoved back. I could only watch in dismay as they tried to help Frank. I looked up, but my vision was hazy. I was too raw, too tired.

In full crisis mode, I didn't even think as I pulled out the phone. I dialed the one number I hadn't allowed myself to call in ten years.

TWO

ARIEL...

A FEW MONTHS AGO, I'D HAD TO START FROM SCRATCH. With a little help from my chosen family, I'd been able to build new purpose in my life.

I'd never have been able to pull it off without them. And I could never say *thank you* enough. Royal Elite was up and running. I had six agents with varying skill levels, and I had every single one of them because Sebastian and Roone had bent over backward to accommodate me.

Any Royal Guard who left the service for some kind of family reason, or going to school, or anything like that, they funneled them my way. Any other security teams they'd worked with on travel missions that proved highly effective, again, they funneled my way. Two I had found on my own. So that felt like a good accomplishment.

But I'd been responsible for retraining everyone. I'd set the criteria, the business model, and I already had more business than I knew what to do with. Six months in, I was on my way to survival.

How had that even happened?

Well, it happened because of my family. I was going to have to get Sebastian some kind of insane present, or I could call Penny and just have her blow him on my behalf.

That was too weird. I owed them big though. And all I wanted to do was make them proud.

The phone on the bedside table buzzed. I ignored it. I didn't have anyone in the field at the moment, and I was tired. All I wanted to do was read my book. When I saw the screen said blocked number, I certainly wasn't going to answer it. Besides, no one in the islands had a blocked number from me, not with the encryption codes that Neela and I worked together to build.

I sat up and stared at the continually ringing phone.

Blocked number. *Bzzzt.*

Blocked number. *Bzzzt.*

My heart rate spiked with the hammering of my pulse. They rattled in my brain. Who could be calling so insistently?

How could it be so important that some unknown person would be calling me at eleven o'clock at night?

Finally, I gave in to the feelings of dread and picked up the phone. "This is Ariel."

There was silence. Even though all I heard was breathing on the other end, I knew who it was. Intrinsically, I knew. It was him.

I held onto my phone so tight, I was sure I was going to lose circulation in my fingers. The stupid tears pricked the backs of my lids and I fought for control. I was lying to Penny when I said I was getting over it.

I wasn't over shit. Just hearing him breathe evoked memories I wished were long dead. Memories that tore at the center of my chest threatening to break me apart. Memories that were sweet and bitter and painful and beautiful. Memories I couldn't exorcise.

Memories I didn't *want* to exorcise.

And then he spoke.

It was only one word.

But it was a word spoken with a man's tone, not a boy's. It was a word spoken with a mixture of reverence and pain, worry and sadness. "Ariel..."

The tear escaped before I could stop it, rolling down my cheek. Why now? I was finally back to my life. Back where I needed to be.

But of course, my past was never going to let me go. "Your Highness."

"I—I'm sorry"

I blinked. He was sorry? For what? Was this the apology I'd been waiting for half my life? It took me a second to realize his words had been slurred.

He's drunk. Had to be. "You're Highness, perhaps—"

"I know. I shouldn't call. But I had to. Just to hear... your voice. He's dying and it's my fault. I did this."

What? "Tristan, what in the—" But I didn't get to finish. He'd already hung up.

One Night Later
Ariel...

"WE ARE GETTING you laid tonight, my bestie, and you are going to enjoy it," my best friend, Penny, shouted in my ear.

I *wanted* to have fun tonight. I wanted to be carefree and light. I wanted to have a great time. I had to shake off that phone call. So what if the former love of my life had called me after nearly ten years of silence. It was *fine*. **Fine**. I wasn't going to let it ruin my night. This morning I'd very deliberately shut off my google alerts so I wouldn't be tempted.

Sure, you're not. Because you're having so much fun right now...

I glanced around the club at the meager pickings and lifted my brow. "Doubtful. Besides, my lady parts have shriveled. Nobody wants dry lady parts."

She jostled my arm. "Come on, this is supposed to be fun. You don't look like you're having fun."

We were out with the rest of the Princess Pirates, as we'd taken to calling ourselves, to celebrate my being knighted. Penny, Bryna, Jinx, and Jessa were all looking at me expectantly. I could feel them willing me to have a good time, but I just couldn't muster that loving feeling. But for my best friends, I tried. I forced myself to smile and dance and sip the champagne. After all, I'd been given back the keys to the kingdom. I should be thrilled.

Then why aren't you?

Penny tapped her glass to get everyone's attention. We were in the VIP area of the most exclusive club on the island, but several of the partiers down below quieted to hear what their queen had to say.

"A toast to the best friend a girl could have. Less than six months ago, after completing one of the hardest undercover assignments of your career and bringing home the lost princess, you made an impossible choice."

Oh shit. This bitch was not going to make me cry in public

with some damn emotional speech. I blinked rapidly. She knew how I felt about emotional displays. I was going to kill her.

Penny continued as if I wasn't giving here the death glare. "That choice you made led to the most badass move of your career. You run your own team of agents now, and I, for one, couldn't be more proud of you."

"Thanks, now if we could just—"

But Penny wasn't done. "And not only did you deliver the most recalcitrant princess in the history of princesses home—"

Jessa snorted. "Hey. That was not my fault. I am not recalcitrant. Besides, I didn't *know* I was a princess. If I'd known, I'd have come more willingly."

Penny continued. "And you were also the catalyst in getting me together with Sebastian."

"If I remember correctly, I feel like I distinctly told you *not* to bone him."

She rolled her eyes. "At any rate, you are strong, brilliant, and beautiful, and I'm honored to have you as a member of the King's Knights. As in everything else you do, I'm sure you'll kick ass and take names."

God, I fucking hoped so. To hear Penny tell the tale, I was some kind of epic badass. She knew me better than most, but sometimes I wondered if even she didn't have a skewed view of me.

Jessa leaned forward and squeezed my knee. "We're all really proud of you. Seriously."

I rolled my eyes and deflected the compliment. "If you bitches make me cry, I will be so pissed." The others laughed and ordered more drinks. But Penny watched me closely. She knew what I was hiding. Well maybe it was time to stop hiding.

Last night's phone call was an anomaly. An outlier. He wouldn't call again.

Are you sure about that?

All the girls around me were coupled up. Penny was the freaking queen right now. Bryna was engaged to Prince Lucas. And Jessa, well, I'd actually watched her fall in love with Roone. And even though Jinx was a member of single city like me, at least she dated.

I just worked too much and went to bed to ten-year-old memories of love. What if I wasn't even remembering that shit correctly? Did I really want to waste more time? I wasn't exactly lonely, but I'd eventually like sex with someone who wanted to know more than just if I liked how he used his tongue. I'd like someone who was interested in my name... my job... details of my life.

Out of the corner of my eye, I clocked Roone trying to look inconspicuous. As if. He was six feet four inches tall with shoulders wide enough to block the sun from view. He winked at me as he tried to sneak around to the back of the VIP area. He was trying to sneak up on Jessa. No doubt there would be kissing soon. And sure enough, if Roone was here, that meant Sebastian and Lucas weren't far behind.

Roone posted up at the VIP bar at the end of the section, still giving us space.

The appearance of five men dressed in black suits was my clue. Yep, the king was in the building. I glanced around and watched Sebastian's sure gait. They were just missing little brother. Leaning over to Bryna, I asked, "Aren't they missing one?"

She laughed. "Yep. Lucas had another last-minute trip to London."

I wondered if he'd stop in Barcelona to see Tristan.

I stopped myself before I could travel too far down that rabbit hole. Penny was right. I needed to get laid. Mostly, I needed to put myself out there, otherwise I'd keep obsessing over someone I was never going to have.

I could do this. I was a bloody grown-up who would like to have sex in this century. Everything else in my life was great. I had so many prospective clients calling I was turning down a lot of work. Word of us doing such a good job for Neela Wellbrook had spread, so now, the who's who of the islands—hell, of the international jet set—were calling us. And I had more job applicants than I could even sift through.

I just had to translate that success to my dating life. I snuck a quick glance at my phone, half expecting another call from Tristan. But nothing.

Penny leaned forward. "Oh my God, if you check your phone one more time I'm confiscating it."

I lifted a brow at her. "I'd like to see you try."

Jessa leaned forward. "Oh my God, Jinx, Bryna, who do you think would win the fight?"

The others seemed to actually ponder this. And Penny seemed to delight in it.

"Ooh, I bet they think it's you. Little do they know, I'm kind of a badass."

I grinned at her. "She is kind of a badass. She is also the queen. So if I so much as even look at her cross-eyed, in this club alone, there are ten armed guards who will put my head on a spike. Before, it would have been a good fight. But she's my bestie. We have never been in a fight. Not a real one with fists, and hair pulling, and elbows, and shouts of 'let me maim you.'"

Jinx giggled and took a sip of her drink. "Well, I for one am super excited that our queen is a total badass. I feel safer just being with you guys. Not that anything ever happens here on the Islands."

Penny and I exchanged a glance. Jinx was privy to some of the shenanigans that had happened in the last three years. She was Bryna's best friend, after all, and the soon-to-be-princess needed her confidant. *But* there was a lot more that Jinx wasn't privy to. Jinx had grown up just seeing a lot of the bright side of the island, not the shadowy politics beneath.

Out of the corner of my eye, I noticed someone watching me. The hairs on the back of my neck stood at attention, and I glanced around. Someone was watching us. I mean, technically, there were several guards watching.

No less than fifteen men combined. Sebastian was being reasonable these days. There was a time he had insisted Penny needed forty. Roone had tried to insist that Jessa needed more too. There had been some heated exchanges, something whispered, and lo and behold, they both got fewer men on their Guard teams.

Over the rim of her glass, Penny eyed me. "What's wrong?"

"I don't know. Just a feeling, like someone is watching us?"

"You realize we're being watched by no less than fifteen guards, right?"

"Yes, I know. I'm just saying." I shook my head to clear it, letting my artful curls fall over my shoulder. "You know what? You guys are right. I need to get out there."

Penny clapped. "Yes, oh my God, can we pick the guy?"

"Oh my God, no. I can pick *my* own guy."

"No, because I know you. You have to go on a date with the next guy who asks you out, okay?"

"Oh, come on. What if he's not good looking, or my

type, or—"

Penny held up a hand. "No. You just have to get some practice. It's like a muscle, so you need to flex your muscle."

"Oh my God, fine. If I agree to go out on a date, will you guys leave me alone?"

They all nodded enthusiastically, grinning at each other. Why were they smiling at each other like that? Oh God, they were plotting something, and I needed to know what the hell it was.

But before my brain could go down that rabbit hole, someone leaned over our booth and tapped my shoulder. My gaze flickered up. "Hi."

Okay, good looking guy, tall, dark hair, chiseled jaw. Insane shoulder width. Clearly, I had a type. I couldn't tell with the black lights in the club exactly what color his eyes were, but he was clearly fit. Yeah. Okay.

"Excuse me, I don't mean to break up your party or whatever, but I've been watching you from the bar."

Ah, so that's why my senses were going off. "Oh, have you?"

"Yes, I have. Look, obviously, you are busy with your friends, and I wouldn't want to break that up. Considering you guys are in a booth and no one is out on the dance floor, I figure this is a girls'-night thing, and I respect that. But I would very much like to ask you out, you know, just for a coffee. No pressure."

"Oh wow, that's really sweet, but I—" Penny kicked me under the table. "Ouch." I glared at her. Then she mouthed, *You promised.*

Damn it.

"You know what, I, um, my schedule looks a little crazy, but maybe on Monday?"

He flashed a grin. He had a great smile. And why did he

look so familiar? He pulled a business card out of his wallet and wrote on the back. "That's my cellphone. Just text me, and I'll be there. What's your name?"

I inhaled sharply. "It's Ariel."

"I'm Ian. It's nice to meet you. I look forward to hearing from you." And then he was gone, leaving me with his phone number.

"See, was it so hard to agree?"

"Yeah, but now what am I going to wear? Because I have a giant bruise from my last mission."

"You were about to say no."

"I was not." I turned and glanced back at him. I saw him on his way to the other end of the VIP area. I knew nothing about him, just that his name was Ian. I turned over the business card. It was all black. The phone number that was on it was in a glossier font. At the top left of the card, in the same sort of glossy embossed print, it read *Tellman's Sports Agency*. I frowned. "Holy fuck. Was that Ian Tellman?"

They all looked at me quizzically. Jinx and I were really into sports, though she preferred American basketball. No one else really followed football like I did. "Come on, you guys. Anyone? That's Ian Tellman. He was one of the youngest players to ever play premiere league football. He was becoming a legend until he got injured."

Still, they all shook their heads. Jessa shrugged. "I don't know who he is, but he is hot."

"Oh my God, you guys are the worst."

It looked like I had a date. The only thing was I hadn't gotten that rush, that excitement. He was cute, obviously, but I didn't feel *anything*.

But I had to start somewhere because it was beyond time for me to let go of the past and move on.

THREE

ARIEL...

It was good to be home.

Oh sure, I'd been at the palace plenty of times since I'd left the guard, but it hadn't felt the same. Entering that morning had a very prodigal-daughter feeling.

So far, my team was mostly keeping their cool about being invited into the palace. But Neela, Jax's fiancée, was the only one fully keeping her cool. She was mingling and chatting happily. Although every time she talked to Lucas, Jax narrowed his eyes.

I hid a smile. Lucas was a natural-born flirt. He was also a natural-born con man. So whenever he talked to anyone, they felt like the most important person in the room.

Jax needed to relax, because Lucas was completely and wholly in love with Bryna. And the two of them were finally getting their wedding plans together. So that meant I had to dig out a dress from somewhere, do something about my hair, and slap on more paint to make myself presentable for yet another royal wedding. I couldn't be happier. Although, given the way

Roone was looking at Jessa, it might be a double wedding. Neither one of them looked like they wanted to wait too long.

Jameson, as always, kind of kept to herself. But I knew her well enough to know she was happy. She still hadn't told me why she'd left the guard so suddenly, but given the time period when she'd left and who she was in charge of guarding, it was safe to assume that Prince Ashton had been responsible for her swift departure. Ethan had tried to keep her and put her on the queen's service, but she only lasted a couple of weeks. And then she was gone. She left and had gone to university. I was surprised she'd come back to the islands.

All around me, I watched my whole family. God, I was lucky.

My phone chimed, and I glanced down.

Ian: *I'm looking forward to our date.*

I couldn't help it. I grinned like an idiot.

"Oh, I know that look." *Busted.* I glanced up to find Penny in front of me looking like the cat who had just swallowed a canary. "What's got you smiling so much?"

I narrowed my gaze at her. "What are the chances you'll pretend you didn't see me smiling?"

"Slim to none."

"Any chance I'll be able to pretend it's nothing?"

She shook her head, sending her cascade of curls into riotous disarray. "What do you think?"

I rolled my eyes. "Fine. I got a text from Ian confirming our date."

Penny all but squealed, which brought Jessa over as she sipped from one of her classic mugs. It read, *This is what awesome looks like.* She liked that one best to psych everyone out during game nights.

"What's got Penny looking so excited? You have a plan to hack the game tonight?"

I rolled my eyes. "You can't hack Mafia. And even if I could, I wouldn't. I'm not the one who cheats. Look at your stepmother and Lucas for that."

Jessa nodded. "Good point. So why does Penny look so happy?"

"Ariel is texting Ian."

Jessa's grin was so wide, all I saw was teeth. "Oh, fantastic. I won the pool."

My brows snapped down. "Pool?"

Penny whacked her on the arm. "Jessa."

"What?" She shrugged. "Like Ariel wouldn't have taken bets on any of us."

She had a point there. "What was the bet?"

"Just that you'd cancel the date. I said you'd ovary up and go. Penny said you'd try to find a way to avoid it until we forced you. And Jinx and Bryna point-blank said you'd cancel."

I scowled at Penny. "Thanks for the vote of confidence."

She was completely unfazed. "How many times did you consider cancelling?"

"That's beside the point," I muttered.

Penny sighed. "See, but you didn't in the end."

What I didn't tell her was I'd started texting him to cancel. I was way too busy. *Scaredy cat.* But something had stopped me. And he'd been charming and funny. I could use some of that.

I forced myself to tap out a return message.

Ariel: *I'm looking forward to it too.*

God why was this so much harder than I expected? I held up my phone. "See, I'm going. Penny, pay the girl."

My bestie rolled her eyes. "Fine. But I know you. You were going to cancel or at least postpone."

I gave her a beatific smile. "Prove it."

Roone came over and started nuzzling Jessa's neck. We knew from experience that this was a moment to walk away. When she had me alone, Penny said, "You look happy."

Despite my niggling self-doubt, she wasn't wrong. "I am happy."

"Good. I'm glad this worked out."

"I don't know how you and Sebastian pulled this off and came up with this idea, but thank you."

"No, thank you. While Tristan may have insisted he doesn't need protection, I know it makes Sebastian feel better, knowing that he *can* send someone. He would have normally just sent Blake Security, obviously. But things are a little too tense to flout the rules right now."

I nodded. Blake Security was a very high-profile security firm in New York. They had assisted the royal family on more than one occasion. In the time of King Cassius and the early days of Sebastian, finding Lucas... hell, one of their agents had even helped me when I was looking for my father during the mission with Princess Jessa. But everything changed once the conspirators were all in jail. The Council had become a lot tighter about the rules. Rules like no civilians guarding royals. But hey, they'd found a loophole.

I swallowed hard. I just hoped that loophole wouldn't lead to me having to see Tristan. I had a whole capable team. Feelings aside, I knew my duty. The Regents Council was on a power trip. The prince should absolutely have an adequate number of guards.

Are you sure you don't want to do it yourself?

Nope. Swallowing that lie was getting easier. I had a whole team at my fingertips if need be. I could keep my feelings separate.

Sure you can.

The door opened, and Sebastian caught Penny's eye. His mouth was tight, and from where I was standing I could see the muscle ticking in his jaw.

"Shit. Something's happened," Penny muttered.

Something was definitely up. Sebastian made eye contact with the inner circle and one by one they all walked out.

Eventually, it was only myself, my team, Queen Mother Alexa, Jinx, Bex, Adam, and Neela left.

"Well, I guess we'll just—" The door opened again with Sebastian staring at me with his brows drawn down.

Shit. Was I supposed to have gone with the others? Zia deftly took over gamemaster duties as I followed after Sebastian.

"Sorry, I didn't think you meant me before. Been a minute since my last closed-door powwow."

His voice was low when he asked, "Do you command my knights?"

Well, when he put it like that. "I suppose I do."

"Then you're needed." I joined the others in Sebastian's office and I had to admit it felt like pulling on my favorite pair of worn, soft jeans that fit *just* right. How many Team Winston Isles meetings had we had in there?

Unfortunately, all the badasses in one room usually meant trouble.

Sebastian got straight to the point. "Prince Tristan was attacked two nights ago at a charity fundraiser. He's unharmed, But Frank Talbott was shot. He's currently at the hospital in critical condition."

Time screeched to a halt as I tried to process. Even though my brain couldn't grasp what was happening, my body knew. My skin had gone clammy and cold, my heartbeat boomed in my ears. Someone had shot at him again. He could have been killed, but instead, a friend of mine had been hurt.

Frank had been one of my trainers when I first joined the Royal Guard. To know that he was fighting for his life left an open hole at the center of my chest. What the hell was going on?

Somehow through the fog, I processed someone asking a question. "Is it personal? Or is the whole family under attack again?"

Lucas, maybe Roone. My brain couldn't filter accents to tell who'd spoken. It was too busy trying to process that Tristan was ok. But poor Frank. I blinked tears away as my brain finally decided to function. "You're bringing them both home, right?"

More threats to the royal family? I didn't know if I could take any more. Hadn't we had enough?

"Frank is already being airlifted home. I've sent a replacement guard," Sebastian said.

"Who?" Roone asked.

"Trevor."

My former partner nodded as if he approved. Then he pushed away from the wall. "When do I leave?"

Sebastian looked up, and his gaze slid to me and then back to Roone. "I need both of you."

I answered automatically. "Of course. I can have Trace and Jameson ready to go tonight. I'll need—"

Sebastian shook his head. "No, Ariel. I need my *best* team. The two of you have already proven that you get the job done."

No. No. No. That wasn't supposed to happen. That was not part of this bargain. What the fuck was I supposed to do?

Penny, though, was right there for the rescue. "Sebastian. Ariel does have a team to run. She just got Royal Elite started. She probably should send her team."

He stubbornly shook his head. "Ariel, you're a knight. And the best. It only makes sense that you and Roone go. Besides, it'll be a security assessment, and Ethan will support anything you need from here. I obviously prefer we keep this quiet until we assess the threat."

Sebastian was speaking words, like threat assessments, protection, team, but I couldn't process any of it. *Focus, damn it, your king needs you.* I dragged myself out of my reverie. Penny gave me an *I'm sorry* look, and I shook my head to let her know it was okay. No matter what, I was loyal to the Winston Isles, so whatever was needed, I'd do it. I just didn't prefer to personally guard the prince. I just couldn't.

Pussy.

Hell, yes.

I just had to figure out how to do this. I couldn't show any weakness. I'd just gotten back to where I was. "Your Majesty, of course, I'll defer to your wishes. But I'd be more useful here in front of my laptop. I'm good in the field, but I'm better with a laptop. You know that. I can run threat assessments from here and send them to the team in the field."

Sebastian looked like he still wanted to argue, but I needed him to just accept that there was no way I was going to Barcelona. Seeing Tristan again was not high on my to-do list this century.

I was being a coward, but so be it. This was about survival. If I saw him again, I'd only be dragged back into that abyss.

Ethan spoke then. He was Penny's father and head of Intelligence, but I'd forever think of him as my surrogate father. And right about then, I wanted him to tell me everything was going to be okay. He wasn't going to tell me that though. He was going to expect me to be up for the challenge.

"Prince Tristan and his fiancée were ambushed as they were leaving a charity benefit."

I choked back the wince of pain at the mention of his fiancée.

"Their exit was decided upon at the last moment from three possible routes of egress. It was a risky maneuver if someone wanted the job done. We need you to speak to the authorities and figure out what angle they are going with. We need a jumping off point. I'm inclined to think it might be related to his fiancée, but we need boots on the ground to assess."

I wanted to refuse. I *needed* to refuse. I had to refuse. There was no way. After ten years, I was going to see Tristan again. I couldn't be his personal guard. And well, he had a fiancée now, so me drooling after the prince wasn't going to work out that well.

I couldn't do it.

But you have to. If not you, then who? It didn't matter what had happened between us. I had sworn to protect him.

Beside me, Roone nodded. "You with me Ariel?"

"Royal Elite is at your command, Your Majesty. I'll send Trace and Jameson with Roone."

Sebastian frowned. He certainly wasn't used to being told no. I just hoped he'd eventually forgive me. There was no way I could see Tristan again. I just wasn't strong enough.

♕

TRISTAN...

Fear was like a cloying lover. No matter how many times I tried to shake it off, it just clung tighter, desperate to choke me.

Waiting to hear news about Frank was beyond nerve wracking. He wasn't just my guard. In the last two years, he'd been one of my few friends.

Ella and I had ridden with him in the ambulance, and I had to be honest... I had never known fear like that in my life, and two days later, I was still in fear for his life.

Sure, I'd been on edge after Vienna. But *this*, this was different. I could write the previous attempt off as a fluke. I could pretend that maybe someone hadn't been trying to kill me. But this situation was incontrovertible proof, and my friend was paying in my stead. I'd been unwilling to see it for what it was. Someone *was* trying to kill me. The real question was why. And more importantly, did I have enough time to still make arrangements for Max before something really bad happened?

"Is he going to be okay?" Ella asked as she stood close, but she wasn't touching me. Thankfully, she seemed to at least know that I needed *some* space. God, how the fuck did this happen? One second, I'd been with him. Following as always. The next, he'd been down, bleeding. Staring at me as if willing me to understand what I needed to do.

"I know he'll be okay."

"Do you? You haven't said a word. Not since we got here."

"I'm fine. I'm just thinking."

She audibly swallowed. "Tristan, maybe it's time we stop."

I turned to face her and leveled my gaze on her. "One thing has nothing to do with the other. You can't possibly think this is Max. He's a bully, yes. But do you think he has the brains and know-how and ability to stalk us? Just to take us down?"

"Or one thing has everything to do with the other. You don't know that. And to not even consider it is foolhardy."

I tried to gentle my voice. She was scared and worried, and it was currently my job to look after her. "Look, I made you a promise. I will keep it. What happened to Frank has nothing to do with what we're doing about Max, okay? This is something else entirely."

"You don't know that. Max has always been furious about our relationship. He didn't want me to do it. He didn't want this 'showmance,' romance, whatever. He said I should always appear available. He's been furious about it for three years. What if he decided to try and kill you? Worse, what if he knows what we're really doing?"

I placed my hands on her shoulders and gripped tightly enough for her to pay attention but not tightly enough to hurt her. "Stop. Stop it now. This isn't helping. Right now, I need to be strong for my friend. I understand that you're scared. I'm scared too. I know I don't seem like I am, and I know I make it seem like I'm coolly casual with everything. I'm not. I feel it *all*. I see it all. I'm just trying to keep my cool. In the end, we only have each other, and we cannot lose our shit. Do you understand?"

She nodded slowly. "I do. I just... I know what Frank meant to you."

"*Means*... what he means to me."

She flushed a deep shade of red. "Of course. No, that's not what I meant."

"I know. It's just that it's better if I think about how well he's doing, and not what could go wrong."

"Of course. I just want you to use some caution, Tristan. Maybe this is our punishment."

"I don't believe in punishment. Actually, that's a lie. I *do* believe in punishment. Just not for us, but for everyone who hurt us, for everyone who did us harm. They're going to pay. Every last one of them."

My phone rang, pausing our conversation. I didn't even check the screen. "Yeah?"

"Tristan?"

I cursed under my breath. I'd been anticipating Sebastian's call. I just thought I would have more time. "Hey, Sebastian."

"You want to tell me what the fuck is going on?"

As if it was my fault. "Well, someone shot at us. It was unpleasant. And, that's about all I have for you right now."

"What are they saying about Frank?"

"Not much. He's critical. It's what we know. I've already called his girlfriend. She'll be here tomorrow."

"Okay, I'll call and offer her the jet."

I ground my teeth. I didn't need him to swoop in and take care of it. I could handle my own affairs. Frank had been my guard. "I already did that, Sebastian."

He sighed. "Look, Tristan, I'm only trying to help."

I scrubbed my hand over my face. "I know. I'm sorry, I just... I know I'm out of the fold on a lot of things. I get it. There's a reason for it. But I could do that much. That one little thing. He's my friend. I can take care of his girlfriend."

"I hear you. And I didn't mean to overstep. I know it's important."

"Yeah. In the meantime, I'm staying close to the hospital. I'll probably grab a cab and go home soon."

"Stay at the hospital as long as you can. I'm sending you Trevor in the meantime. I think we can both agree someone is actually trying to kill you, so it's better to be prudent."

"Yeah. I won't argue that."

"Okay. I know that the Council had been difficult, but I'm sending you my personal knights."

"Excuse me?" What the fuck was he talking about? We didn't have knights in the Winston Isles.

"Yeah, look, it's a long story, but I found a loophole around the whole civilian thing. I have knights now. I'm sending a few to you."

Shit. He was sending knights, and it was going to be a big public deal. My deal in the works depended on discretion. And everything hinged on this deal. "Sebastian, I don't need knights."

"Yes, you do. Someone tried to kill you." He slowed down his speech as if speaking to a five-year-old. "And if you don't know enough to be worried about your own well-being, at least, I do."

"So, what? You're just going to take over my fucking life?" *Shit. Shit. Shit. Shit.*

I scrambled to come up with another alternative, another solution. This wasn't the way it was supposed to go. Sure, a guard, that made sense. *One.*

One couldn't possibly be looking over my shoulder all the time. The Royal Guards were usually two-man teams. The higher up on the royal food chain you were, the more guards you got. But if Sebastian was sending me knights, God only knew how many he was sending.

That meant people watching me, which meant my plans for Ashton and my plans for Max would be that much more difficult to carry out. "Look, I know what you're trying to do. You're trying to take care of me. You're my cousin. The king. I get it. I can get behind that. I appreciate it, but honestly, it's a little ridiculous. Someone shot Frank. Yes. But we were in an alley in not the best part of town. It could have been anything."

"Are you really going with this right now?"

"Anything is possible. I need my life to go back to normal. I have a lot going on. Sensitive deals."

"We're way the fuck beyond that right now, Tristan. Look, I get it. Penny is the same way. She doesn't want someone looking over her shoulder all the time and insists that she herself is a Guard."

If he wouldn't relent with his wife, he wasn't going to relent with me.

"Yeah sure. One guard. Makes a lot of sense. I need one to keep an eye on me, fair enough. I get it. But a whole team? Come on. I promise you that I can take the fuck care of myself."

"They're not there to watch you, Tristan. Fuck. I don't give a fuck what the fuck you're doing. Or should I?"

Bollocks. "No. I just... Goddamn it. I just want to live my life. I don't want to be under scrutiny all the time. That scrutiny may have well gotten my friend shot."

Sebastian sighed. "Look, I'm just trying to keep you alive. I never had any problem with your Dad. Even your Mom. You and Alix might as well be my siblings. I just want to take care of you. And right now, considering these two violent incidents... I can't just sit back and do nothing. Not only are you family, you're my subjects. Any citizen of the Winston Isles who I can do anything to assist, I need to. That is my duty."

I took a deep breath. Since I'd put the Max plan into play, I'd been laying it all out. If I was going to help Ella, I needed to do it in a way that never kicked back on her. And the way things were, I never coincidentally ran into Max. My team never played where he was. Ever. Not since Ella was traveling with me to the world cup two years ago, and then of course he'd been there. But blowback on Ella was the problem then.

I needed to be alone with him to make it all work.

He had a villa in Chile. And it just so happened that the Winston Isles home team played there twice a year. For over a year I'd been working on trade talks to play at home. It had been the biggest secret of my career, and Sebastian was about to ruin my carefully laid plans. The Argonauts had deliberately asked me to keep things mum. It was a big money deal, and they didn't want it leaking. A native son coming home potentially meant a fuck ton of money.

Maybe I could keep him from calling a whole team. "Look, send one more, okay? That way, it's a two-man team. Just like always."

"It's already done. They will be arriving with Trevor."

Fuck. "I didn't ask for this. I just want to live a quiet fucking life. I don't want to be in the crosshairs. Whatever loopholes you created to make this happen, you don't think the Council will punish me for it?" More like I needed this deal to happen, and I didn't want the council to block it.

"You know what? I weighed that against keeping you the fuck alive, and I opted for keeping you the fuck alive."

"You really should have asked me, Sebastian."

"Yeah, well, you don't get that luxury." He hung up.

Ella stared at me, her brow furrowed. "What's the matter?"

"Well, looks like we're about to have more company. My cousin is sending in knights."

"Maybe this is a good thing. If he sends in knights, there will be more people to make you rethink this plan. I don't care if I ever get my life back. Maybe that's not what's important. I'd rather have you alive than dead because you're doing stupid things."

I shook my head at her. "It doesn't matter. I'll figure out a way to get around it. The plans are already in motion. If everything goes right, sending me knights will be a moot point because I'll be home in the islands, anyway."

"And you didn't think it was a good idea to tell him?"

"No. I'll tell him when it's a done deal."

"I know you don't trust anyone, but you're going to have to trust someone eventually. Otherwise, we're both going to get dead."

"Nobody is dying. Not on my watch. I swear it to you."

I just hoped I wasn't lying to her.

FOUR

ARIEL...

My heart wasn't in this. But I said I'd go on this date, so date it was. Never mind that my brain was thinking about the assignment I claimed I didn't want, worrying about someone I couldn't have.

Stop it. Tristan was a grown up. And my team was excellent, he'd be fine. And I would be fine because I didn't have to see him.

There was a hot man *here*. A hot man who wanted me. Bird in the vagina and all that. Maybe that's not exactly how the saying went. But basically... same.

After a series of texts, Ian and I had gone from coffee to dinner and back to coffee again because our schedules were too hectic. He'd already flown to Miami and back. Apparently, he was working on a deal for some promising hot basketball player.

After another change, we'd finally carved out part of an evening and opted for a drink at the 'it' wine bar not far from the office, so I'd let Penny and the girls dress me up during video chat like I was some kind of a doll.

I stared down at my shoes and wondered how the hell I was going to walk all the way to the wine bar and back.

God, I just wanted to cancel. Why was I so scared of a simple date? It wasn't like I never dated. Okay, I barely dated, but still.

You're afraid of a lot of things lately.

I shoved down that wayward thought. I was *not* afraid. I could do this. It was just a date.

I took three steps out of the office and immediately decided to drive. My boots, as it turned out, were not made for walking. Trace was leaving at the same time and looked me up and down. "Uh, boss?"

"Yeah, Trace." I tried to remain casual as I sauntered over to one of the SUVs.

"Are you going somewhere? Do you have a... a meeting or something?"

The way he said meeting indicated that I did not look I was going to a meeting, which was accurate. Penny had made me wear a metallic top thing that was mostly backless. And then Jinx, the traitor, had suggested doing something with my hair that made it bigger. Not exactly curly but full of waves and more volume. Then, Jessa... well, Jessa was the worst. She'd had a makeup person come over and paint my face. Now I resembled some kind of social media starlet. Not overdone, but still beyond what normal me usually looked like.

"Yeah. I have a meeting." I refused to call this a date.

Trace grinned. "A meeting, huh? You know, I'm going to start doing our meetings in a backless top too, see how you like it."

"Word is, you have a hairy back, so I'm not interested in seeing that."

He frowned. "I do *not* have a hairy back. My back is awesome. Women love my back."

I rolled my eyes. "Goodnight, Trace. Tell your sister I said hi."

I caught a glimpse of his grin in my rearview mirror as I climbed into my seat. He stood next to his car and watched me as I slowly drove out. I felt dumb taking the car, but honestly, I could barely walk in these stupid shoes. What was Bryna doing suggesting them in the first place?"

She wants you to look hot so your date will think you look hot and will want to bone you senseless.

Ugh, I couldn't even think about boning. I was so nervous. My belly kept doing flips and flops back and forth, back and forth. My palms were sweaty, and I was watching my phone. My mind raced as it tried to think through all the logistics of sending the knights to Tristan.

Earlier, I'd briefed the team on what was happening with the prince. Trace's sister Emma had a college tour set up, so Trace couldn't go. I'd be sending Zia and Jameson in his place, and they would leave first thing in the morning.

Because you're too afraid to go yourself.

I wasn't afraid. I just knew better. For the time being though, I had it handled. My team was topnotch. If Jax hadn't just come off of the Neela assignment, I would have sent him. He'd become my right hand in the last couple of months, and I had grown to depend on him. When I pulled out and left Trace grinning like the idiot that he was, I drove the three blocks up to the wine bar.

It was still ridiculously early. I handed over the key to the kid wearing the valet jacket and confirmed that his outfit matched the other valet guys outside. And then I checked their footwear. They all matched too. Black sneakers. Serviceable, but not fancy.

The number of times I'd been called on to check for someone's wayward vehicle because they'd given it to someone who *looked* like they should be valet was kind of ridiculous.

When I stepped into the bar, an eager hostess approached. "Hi, I'm Ariel Scott. I'm supposed to be meeting Ian Tellman here. Is he here already?"

The hostess grinned. "Oh yeah, he's been here for twenty minutes."

I frowned. "Great." He was earlier than I was. I wouldn't get some time to settle my nerves. When I followed the hostess toward the table, he stood with a grin. "I guess, we're both anxious and excited."

"Yeah. Guess, so."

He slipped around the table and came over to give me a hug. "You look beautiful."

"Thank you."

"Yeah, I'm glad we finally get to do this, because I honestly didn't know when we were going to manage it."

"I know. The schedules are a little crazy."

I slipped into a seat and fired the opening question. "How was Miami?" It seemed like a safe enough topic. He would talk about his work. I would let him, revealing as little about me as possible. And then I would slowly back out of the room without having to really give much of myself away.

That's not how this works.

He leaned forward. "You look nervous."

"I am *really* nervous."

"That's fine. First dates are always nerve-wracking. But I

think you're beautiful, and I would love to get to know you. So, why don't we just see what happens? No pressure."

Was this guy even real? All my life, where had guys like him been?

"I think that's a fantastic idea."

The rest of the date went well. He regaled me with stories of some of his athletes. Some of his stories were like something out of the TV show *Entourage*. Crazy shenanigans, usually involving sports cars and women. Finally, I leaned forward. "I mean, okay, clearly, I know about your career. I followed it. And I love football, myself. But I have to ask, how did you become an agent?"

A shadow crossed over his gaze. "Well, I was injured. And my team, that I thought would essentially love me forever basically called in my best mate to replace me."

I winced. I didn't have all of his history. If I was being honest, I didn't really pay much attention until Tristan had joined Madrid's team. Then I'd found that I loved it. "It must have been so difficult."

"Yeah, you can't imagine. So there I was, young... told I wouldn't be able to play again. But I was determined to prove them wrong, so I worked my ass off. Physical therapy, all those things. And you know what? With the surgery, they were able to cobble me back together, but it was just never the same, and I needed to take a good hard look at what my future might look like. If I wasn't going to be able to play, I needed to figure out how to do something else, so I became an agent. You know, sort of my way to keep players from making bad deals, like I had. I was so young, when I started, you know? My agent didn't think we needed a guarantee in the income clause. It depends on the athlete and what they've got going on, but if I'd had one, then it wouldn't have been so devastating."

"God, I mean, teams must feel like family, right? And then all of a sudden, they're gone and you feel unworthy somehow, even though you had nothing to do with it."

He nodded solemnly. "Obviously, you understand."

I managed to school the automatic wince. "Understand?"

"Yeah. I mean, the story of you leaving the Royal Guard. Clearly, it wasn't voluntary. You were writing your own ticket. You returned the lost princess. No one leaves the Royal Guard after that. And I find it very interesting that not many news outlets reported that one of the conspirators was, in fact, your father."

My heart hammered against my ribs. How did he know so much? He couldn't have gotten that information easily. Not that it was inaccurate, because it was shockingly accurate. It's just that Sebastian had kept it quiet. Nobody knew my real reasons for leaving the Guard. All everyone knew was that I left and started my own thing. That's all I wanted anyone to know, anyway. I didn't want to leave room for judgment or condescension.

"Um, wow. You're shockingly well-informed."

He winced. "Sorry, that was too much. I have sources, and I was curious about you. I didn't mean to pry."

In truth, he hadn't done any more prying than I had. I'd taken Roone's advice and ran a background check on him. He was on the up and up. No debts, a partner at the agency, and he was up-and-coming in his industry. Hungry.

I liked hungry. It reminded me of myself. "It's fine. I won't say I didn't look you up either."

He grinned. "Did you like what you saw?"

"I mean, on paper, you look fantastic."

He cocked his head and studied me. "And in person?"

I laughed. "I'm just not used to anyone looking so closely."

He nodded. "No, I get it. But I want you to know that I—" He trailed off when his phone rang. He winced and shook his head. "I'm so sorry. I just have this deal going on, and I need to take this."

I shrugged. "You're fine. Go ahead."

When he excused himself I watched him, and I watched the way other women watched him. The other women watched him hungrily. Fully assessing, scanning for any physical abnormalities as if evaluating him for breeding capabilities. But he seemed completely unfazed. As if he didn't notice at all. I liked that. He'd taken a peek under the hood I'd rather he hadn't taken, but since I'd done the same thing, I couldn't really be that angry. Then again, I was also a world-class hacker. Who was he that he'd been able to dig, and who were his sources?

Stop being so suspicious.

I really did need to let that go if I was going to date.

I watched as he hung up the phone and strode over. "Ariel, I'm so sorry."

"Let me guess, you have to go?"

He gave me a sheepish smile. "Yes. Do you mind? Can we pick this up again at an actual proper dinner?"

I gave him a smile. "Sure. We can do dinner."

He leaned in, and the panic set in. I didn't know what it was, or why, but something cold and slithering wound around my spine and froze me. He brushed a kiss over my cheek, remarkably close to my lips, but he didn't quite go there. When he backed away, he gave me a smile as if he hadn't noticed I'd gone suddenly statue-like. "I'll talk to you as soon as this emergency is over, and then we'll pick a date for dinner, right?"

I forced my head to nod up and down. "Yup, works for me."

And then I watched as he walked out. His words had been exactly what I wanted to hear. But somehow, there was something about him I couldn't quite pinpoint. My body was rejecting him.

Because he's not Tristan.

Well, body, you don't get to have a say, because as far as you're concerned, Tristan isn't an option.

Ariel...

AS I WAS LEAVING the wine bar, I bumped into a familiar face.

Roone gave me a grin as he was coming up the stairs. "What's up, former boss lady?"

"Fancy seeing you here. Date night before you leave?"

He grinned. "Something like that." He looked around. "What about you. You're all kitted out. Hot date?"

"Something like that."

His gaze narrowed. The man knew me far too well. "You look tense. Why do you look tense? Was he a wanker? You want I should drag him out back for a lesson in manners?"

A smile tugged at my pursed lips, and I deliberately tried to force myself to relax. "I'm not tense. I'm fine. The date was fine. Just cut short."

He chuckled softly. "You forget I actually know you. I've

seen that look before. We worked so closely on the Jessa thing together that I know your moods now. What's up?"

I needed to lie. I needed something plausible and believable, and I needed to *lie well.* "I don't know. Something feels off with the assignment for the prince, I guess. You and the team can handle yourselves, of course. I just don't know. It feels off. We well and truly eradicated the conspiracy. I mean, they were dealt a heavy blow, so I'm just trying to figure out what the hell is going on now with Prince Tristan. It doesn't make any sense. There is no motivation. He's not in line for the throne. He gets a stipend, sure, but he has his own money. He doesn't need the crown, so I'm not really sure that this is a royal issue. You know what I mean?"

Roone nodded. "Yeah, you have a point, but royal issue or not, it's not like we can let the prince die. And for someone who adamantly didn't want the assignment, you seem awfully invested in the prince's welfare."

Shit.

"Right, but he is still a member of the royal family. I'm just trying to figure out exactly what we're dealing with, the mystery of it all."

Roone watched me. I wasn't sure if he was buying my bull-shit or not, but whatever.

He stuck his hands in his pockets. "So, are you going to tell me the real version or not?"

I squinted at him then looked around. "Jessa is late."

He shifted on his feet. "Yeah, uh..."

For fuck sake. "You followed me?"

He held up his hands. "Look—"

I didn't let him finish. Instead I stomped down the stairs and started down to the valet stand. "You called to find out where I was?"

"Ariel, wait."

"Bugger off as you like to say."

He sighed. "Shite. I'm sorry, okay? I didn't think you were going to hear me out. I need you on this mission. You know it. I know it. Shit, everyone in the war room knew it. So why did you say no?"

"You are unbelievable, Roone. You have my knights, which, by the way, is a ridiculous thing to say out loud."

"They're great, but Sebastian asked for this favor. He's worried he doesn't have you on board, and frankly, so am I."

I shook my head. "Roone, I just can't. Why does it matter?"

"It matters because we make a hell of a team. We always have. And if this threat is real, I need you by my side."

"There is no reason, no deep, dark secret. I just want some separation. I know me being involved with this could look bad for Sebastian." Partially true. The Council wouldn't forgive easily. But really, there was no way I was going to be able to do this. Not without giving myself away or losing my shit.

"Ariel, you've never backed away from a challenge before."

"Roone, let this go."

"I can't. You belong in the field. At least tell me *why* you don't want in. You don't want to work with me? I was too much of a pain in the ass? You're in love with me? I'm engaged to the princess, but—"

Despite myself I laughed. "You're such an idiot."

He shrugged. "Maybe. But you laughed. Tell me, Ariel. You're too good to hold yourself back."

I sighed. "Maybe I just want a bit of a life, Roone. If I do this, I'll get sucked back in." At least that was the truth. I would absolutely be sucked into Tristan's orbit.

He pursed his lips. "I hear you. I know you managed to do your own thing."

"And I'm grateful."

"But you, your career, everything was cut short. One last mission for the road. Sebastian cares too much to ask you again himself."

My phone buzzed. It was Ian.

Ian: *Sorry I had to cut the date short. But when I get back, I'm looking forward to seeing your smile.*

Despite myself, I smiled down. I was moving forward. If I really wanted to do that, I needed to sever my connection to Tristan. And to do that I'd need to see him again. I couldn't run and hide.

I stared at the text for a long moment, unsure of how to respond. He seemed like a great guy who was genuinely interested in getting to know me. What was my hesitation?

Tristan was getting married to someone else. There was no danger in seeing him again, no possibility of picking up where we left off. This would basically be aversion therapy.

I would go full cold turkey. No more Google alerts. I would go on a date, force my life to move on. Because left to my own devices, I would be stuck. Forever.

I lifted my gaze and said the scary, bat-shit crazy thing. "I'll go with you. You can tell Sebastian his plan worked."

Roone widened his eyes as if confused and surprised. "I have no idea what you're talking about."

"Shut it. Just so you know, I'm not taking orders from you."

He grinned. "It'll be just like old times. The team is back together again."

My phone buzzed again pulling my attention away from Roone.

Ian: *In case I didn't say it before. You looked absolutely breathtaking tonight. I'm looking forward to seeing you again.*

I stared at the text for a second longer and then hit reply.

Ariel: *I can't wait.*

Ian: *That's perfect. I'm really excited to see you.*

That was sweet, and I was interested to see him. Excited was maybe the wrong word.

What the hell is wrong with you?

I had no idea. The man was perfectly shaggable. He seemed nice, and he seemed wholeheartedly into me. What could be better?

I lifted my head to find Roone watching me still. "What?"

"You're smiling to yourself. Why are you smiling? One second you're tense; the next second you're smiling. What's up?"

I held up my phone. "I have a date."

"A date?" He waggled his brows. "Pray tell, who's the lucky bloke?"

"Just this guy. I met him when I was out with the girls a few days ago."

He grinned. "That's fantastic. You should be dating. Hell, I don't think I've ever even seen you dating someone."

I rolled my eyes. "Why do you guys keep saying that? I get it, but it's not like I'm some virgin."

Although pretty damn close, considering how long it has been.

He chuckled. "Look, I think we all just want to see you happy."

"I am happy."

"Uh-huh. I see guys ask you out all the time. And you always deflect or scowl. I figured you weren't into them."

"Well, why should I settle?"

He chuckled. "You know what? That's a good point."

"I mean, just because Jessa settled for you..." I let my voice trail even as I started to laugh.

Roone just rolled his eyes. "Hardy-har. I happen to know I'm the best she's ever had."

I rolled my eyes. "Please, don't talk to me about your sex life. It's not something I need to know."

"Don't worry, I'm not going to expound on my skill set, though it is extensive."

I laughed. "Men. You always think your skill set is extensive. And then you find out you're basically average."

He laughed. "Sweetheart, there is nothing average about me."

I rolled my eyes.

"Who is the guy, anyway?"

I shook my head. "It's this sports agent guy, Ian. He seems nice enough."

"You realize Ian is due a full background check, right?"

I stared at him, waiting for him to break into a laugh, but he was dead serious.

"You can't be serious."

"Why not? If you're going to start dating someone, you need to check him."

I said a silent prayer. "I don't know who appointed you my big brother, but I don't need one. Stop."

"Well, at least let Lucas and I meet him."

"You are the last two I'm letting meet him. Besides, it's just dinner. Why are you interested in my dating life in the first place?"

He chuckled. "Well, because it's so fun seeing you riled up. And now you don't look so tense anymore."

I scowled at him. "Jackass."

"God, I missed this."

My lips twitched, but no way was I admitting that I had missed it too. Roone and I had come up with a shorthand while we were watching Jessa. And despite his annoyance, I learned to love and respect him. But no way in hell was I relying on him for dating advice. It didn't matter how much of a disaster my daily life was.

I just had to hope I could keep the real reason I needed to stay away from Tristan a secret from him.

FIVE

TRISTAN...

When I got the call that I had visitors downstairs, my gut twisted.

Don't be an idiot. This is necessary.

I'd made it clear to Sebastian I didn't want a visible presence. So maybe he'd listened and kept shit low key.

But I still understood what this meant. *Babysitters.* The police were on what happened to Frank. They would figure it out. I didn't need minders. If I was the kind of guy who needed babysitters, the Argonauts weren't going to take me. I needed to look as perfect to them as possible. The prodigal son returned.

Brother of a traitor.

I had a few things going for me. I was injury free. But at nearly thirty, I didn't have that many playing years left.

I was low stress.

Bullshit. Some asshole is trying to kill you.

Okay, it didn't look great. And it was going to look worse if they thought I was the prima donna who needed an armed guard.

A part of me knew Ella had a point. Maybe Sebastian's

interference was the universe's way of saying 'hey, don't get dead.' But the ball was already rolling. The plan just had to play out.

Maybe she sees that the revenge is eating at you.

At that point I didn't care what happened to me. But men like Max who preyed on people who were less powerful than them deserved what they got. Besides, it wasn't like I was going to kill him. I was just going to make him *wish* he were dead.

I'd made it clear that she didn't have to repay the favor. But she said if I was going through with it then she was too, which was dumb. This might have started as a *quid pro quo*, but that was then. Now I knew her. Now I cared about her, even if it wasn't in the way she wanted me to. I'd never ask her to do something dangerous.

Ella came out of her bedroom, dressed to the nines in a brilliant white, off-the-shoulder sweater that hugged her curves. She looked beautiful.

But she did nothing to arouse me. Beautiful blonde hair flowing down her back, bright blue eyes, just a hint of freckles that I knew for a fact weren't real. Ella was so pale, and she avoided the sun like the plague. Even when she deemed to come to one of my matches, she had to be in the owner's box where not a ray of sunshine would touch her.

The few times she did do an outdoor event, it was something like Wimbledon, and she was always under a massive hat and a gallon of sunscreen.

This was the one you chose.

I *had* chosen her. I was presented with a list of choices. All beautiful, all stunning, all with careers that could use a boost. There had been something vulnerable about her.

And Ella had done her job. We had helped each other. But

now, now I didn't want this anymore. I didn't want to pretend. I lived in a 4,000 square foot penthouse with a woman I barely knew and who I didn't want. All so I could have a chance to go home where the people didn't want me.

Or maybe they did. I had no way of knowing.

I pressed the buzzer. "Yup, send them on up."

Ella placed her hands on her hips. "You think this is the best idea?"

"Nope. But it's not like I have much choice in the matter."

"They'll find out about our arrangement, and I'll be a laughing stock."

"I promised I wouldn't say anything. No one will know. And you can relax, these are my cousin's men. They won't say a word and you will not be a laughing stock."

She pursed her lips. "Okay, if you think so. But I don't understand why I just can't hire guards. If we're always together, my guards are your guards."

"I know. It's just complicated. With my family, everything is complicated, okay? It's not you. It's legitimately the Regents Council. Right now, I can't be guarded by someone who isn't a member of the Royal Guard or are royal themselves. I have a very narrow window. They can't be commoners."

"You know, when they said I was going to be a prince's fiancée, I thought this would be some amazing trip. And you know, it has been amazing. I just thought you'd be... I don't know, more royal."

"What, a fabulous penthouse and living the lifestyles of the rich and famous isn't enough?"

"It's enough. And I don't need your money, you know that."

I swallowed. "Yeah, I know. I know this is an intrusion and you're worried about how this will all affect you."

She shook her head. "I'm worried about you, that's all. This has all gotten out of hand. But hey, there's no going back now."

"I keep telling you that you don't need to worry."

She lifted a brow. "How about I worry for the both of us?"

The doorbell rang, and I strode into the foyer to open it. When I did, a familiar face greeted me with a smile. "Your Highness. If it's not too much trouble, I'd like to request you stop trying to get yourself killed."

I grinned. "Roone, mate, how long has it been?"

He strode in and we clasped each other tightly, clapping each other's backs. When we were kids, Roone had often come home with Sebastian on breaks. He'd also served in the military with Sebastian. I had been two years behind them, so just as they were getting out, I was going in. But I'd gotten to spend some time with Roone, and I really liked him. "Sebastian didn't tell me he was sending *you*." I might not have fought so hard.

"Well, technically, this is just an assessment to see what you need. And you know—"

Even before he started to speak, my skin prickled. The hairs on the nape of my neck stood at attention, and every cell in my body received a signal from my brain to detonate in *five, four, three, two...*

She rounded the corner, and it was her hair I saw first. Fire engine red, cut in layers that framed her face. When her bright green eyes met mine, I couldn't fucking swallow. I couldn't breathe. I couldn't think. I knew Roone was uttering words, probably important ones and something very vital, but all I could see was her, looking every bit as beautiful as I remembered.

There wasn't a picture I had taken from that time that had

done her any justice, because in person, Ariel was nothing short of stunning.

And what was worse was she had no idea.

Her wide green eyes met mine, and she slanted her head. "Your Highness."

Her voice, that fucking voice. I'd called her just to hear it again and take myself back to that time. It was low, soft. I remembered the time when she used to whisper my name over and over and over again. *Tristan. Tristan. Tristan.*

Like a magnet, I was drawn to her. It didn't matter how much I fought the pull, I wanted to hold her tight. I wanted to press my nose into the hollow of her neck and inhale deeply. The memory of her scent made me want to slide into her deep and lose myself.

It was too hot. Far too hot. My skin was too fucking tight. My heart beat at race-horse pace. I wanted to pull her to me and press her against me and never let her go.

Instead, what I said was, "What the fuck are you doing here?"

Ariel...

HOLY HELL. I could be cool. I *had* to be cool.

It wasn't like I hadn't seen a million pictures of him. It wasn't like I didn't *know* what he looked like. Oh, I knew exactly what he looked like. Sandy blonde hair, lean, tall frame, muscles for days, lips I knew the exact texture of, shape of, ability of, and those eyes.

Hazel. The clear kind of hazel that could be many colors.

His eye color was entirely dependent on what he was wearing. You could definitely see flecks of blue and green in his gaze. If he wore blue, you would swear his eyes were navy. Or if he wore something forest green, everyone would swear that his eye color was emerald. I just knew that his eyes were the color of aged whiskey and that one look from him could strip me to the soul.

Even though my hands were shaking and my throat was dry, even though the fight-or-flight response screamed in my skull and my body was cold and I was completely terrified, I stepped forward and tipped up my chin. "Your Highness."

When I met his gaze, I could see it. He made a sharp intake of breath, and we were locked in that moment. It felt like eons. We could have been there for a minute, an hour, a day, a week. I certainly wouldn't have noticed. Maybe he would have. Maybe this pleasure-pain of thinking of that God-awful wiggly tooth was only affecting me. After all, I'd been the only one in love.

"What the fuck are you doing here?"

Roone frowned, confused. "Your Highness, the king sent us. He wants us to do an assessment of your security needs. I assure you, Ariel is the best there is with digital security, and you and I are well acquainted. We're the best at what we do. We'll give him an assessment, and then he'll provide you adequate coverage until the police and Interpol can discern what is going on."

It didn't matter that Roone was speaking, Tristan just kept his eyes glued on me. Finally, it was his fiancée, Ella, that came forward. "For the love of Christ, Tristan, let them in."

On sight, I didn't like her. She was everything I hated. Perfect, rich, and she had Tristan. But she had a point. The door *was* open. And even though this was a penthouse flat, there was no good reason to be asking for trouble with our target in the doorway. He backed away, still glaring at me. Roone entered, and I followed behind. "Miss Banks," Roone said.

For him, she had a wide smile. "Oh, well then. Tell me, are you going to guard my body as well?"

Ugh, the gag reflex was strong. A little vomit snuck up my esophagus. Wasn't she engaged to the prince? Why was she openly flirting with Roone? I just adapted my guard stance and then looked straight ahead while getting the lay of the land in my peripheral vision.

This place was terrible. Nothing but goddamned windows. I at least hoped that Frank had been wise and had them change everything to bulletproof glass.

Little Miss Sunshine turned her attention on me. "You're a guard too?"

"I'm a knight, miss. I *was* a guard."

Her brows furrowed as she inspected me. "They made a woman a knight? Oh, I get it now. You're one of those girls chasing after the boys and wanting to play in the mud with them." Her gaze slid over me with full disdain. "I have never understood women like you."

I gritted my teeth. God, this was his fiancée? She was a bitch. But I gave her a cool smile. "Well, I didn't have the luxury of a choice. But yes, I'm a knight, as is everyone on my team. Our concern is Prince Tristan." Just saying his name after a complete moratorium on those words was like a lance to my throat, making it burn hot and dry and rendering me unable to swallow.

Miss tall and leggy continued to examine me. "I mean, you're tiny."

I was five foot six. "I assure you, I'm quite capable." Just because she was a leggy giraffe with ridiculous fake tits, that did not mean I should feel inadequate.

Then why do *you feel inadequate?* Jealousy was a bitch.

"We will make sure His Royal Highness is all set. As for you, I think it's in your best interest to hire a security team."

She rolled her eyes. "You're going to tell me what to do too? I'm Hollywood's A-lister. I already have my own security."

A-lister? Come on, that was a stretch. Only since hooking up with Tristan had her profile gone up. It was like a meteoric rise. I'd felt bad for her when I'd seen the tabloid reports of her refusing to sleep with a director and then him blackballing her. Her profile rose, though, when she and the prince had started dating. Then, she was everywhere, and she'd started raising her credits again.

Having her on his arm had done something for the prince as well. He remained mostly unscathed by the whole scandal surrounding the islands. His popularity was still up, and people still loved him. Also, it helped that he was an international soccer star. Football fans all around the world knew his name.

Not that I paid super close attention, but I knew his contract was almost up. And he was weighing his options for teams. A couple of them were offering him stupid money, which, of course, he didn't really need, but there it was. He had landed on his feet, and I was pissed off about it.

Just do your job and you can go back.

I inhaled a deep breath. "Of course, ma'am."

She wrinkled her nose. "Ma'am? I'm barely twenty-five."

"How would you prefer I refer to you?"

I cocked my head, and from my peripheral vision, I noticed Tristan's lips twitch. He could see it. I was pissed and about to volley a flame of destructive fire. Unfortunately, Roone knew me well too, and he stepped in. "Miss Banks, I assure you, we're well-versed in whatever your needs might be. But our priority is the prince. What Miss Scott was saying is true. You should engage your own security. And you need to give us thorough information so we can coordinate with them."

For him, she smiled. "I mean, do you think I need more? And can I hire one of your knights? Particularly, you?"

Tristan's voice was low as he glowered at her. "Give it a rest Ella."

"What? I'm just having some fun." She slid her gaze back over Roone. "Yes, of course. You can have full access to my team. They're the best money can buy."

Tristan rolled his shoulder. "Don't I know it?"

Ella turned to me then. "Look, Tristan, I won't tell you how to do your princely thing, but when it comes to knights, I would skip over the tiny mermaid. I don't think she has the skill set. Him, on the other hand, I think he's just what you need. Darling, you know how important this is. We have a lot of events lined up. It's pre-Oscar season. You're in the midst of negotiations. We have to be out and about. Whoever is trying to hurt us, they need to be stopped. So if your cousin sent you some Knights, I'd take it."

He sighed. "Fine. You're here now."

Roone gave him a smile. "See, that was easy. Ariel has a whole team, so we will only make the assessment, then she'll send her people here."

I could feel his gaze on me, even though I wasn't looking at him. I felt like the blade of a heated sword hit me everywhere his gaze touched.

"Ariel has a team?"

Roone chuckled. "Been a long time since you've been home.

She's in charge of the most badass security agency on the islands."

I turned to face him, and I saw his lifted brows. "I thought you were a guard."

I swallowed that ball of pain. "Not anymore."

"I guess things have changed."

I inclined my head. "Indeed, they have, Your Highness. I'm a completely different person now, as I'm sure you are."

Roone's gaze ping-ponged between us, and he frowned. "You two have met?"

I nodded. "Of course. Prince Tristan and I used to hangout as kids. But that was a whole world ago."

"Might as well be strangers now," Tristan muttered tightly.

Wasn't that the truth?

SIX

ARIEL...

WE WERE SHOWN TO THE FLAT AT THE END OF THE HALL. Considering it was meant for the Royal Guard, it was still huge, spacious, and contained three bedrooms. As if it was meant to house a full security team. *Fantastic.*

Once in, I closed the door behind us, finally able to breathe. Roone studied me. "Are you okay?"

"Yep, I'm perfect. Fine. Why do you ask?"

"Well, you forget I know you. You're tense. And you're busy saying things like 'fine', and 'perfect', and 'uh-huh.' You think I don't know when you're lying?"

"I'm not lying. I'm just tired."

He lifted a brow. "Uh-huh. Why does the prince seem like he hates you?"

"I don't know. Maybe he does hate me."

"Did you do something to him?"

I sighed and met his gaze directly. "Look at me, Roone. I'm a Royal Guard. Well, not really. I'm actually a Knight, but whatever I am, you think I have at all entered into the Royal Highness's sphere?"

He frowned. "Something is up with him."

"Nothing is up. He clearly isn't thrilled about having us here. You two are friends, so if you have questions about what his problem is, you can ask him."

"Okay, I might. I just have never seen you so... I don't know, unsure of yourself."

"I'm perfectly sure of myself. I'm fucking awesome."

A smirk broke out over his lips. "Ah, there she is. I know that face."

"Yeah, whatever."

He grinned then. "You seem upset. Is everything okay with Royal Elite?"

"Yeah. Except, I'm here and my whole team has jobs they're on, so I don't exactly have people available to look after the prince in a week."

"Yeah, it's going to get tricky. Sebastian needs me back. There is going to be a vote for new Council Members."

I nodded with a smile. "And the new Earl is up for a position. That's pretty badass."

He shrugged as he eased onto the couch. "It's... whatever. It's just a title."

It was my turn to study him. He seemed calmer somehow. Before, he was always a little brash. "Jessa is good for you, isn't she?"

His smile was broad and easy then. "Yeah, she is."

"I'm really happy for you, in case I never said that before. I know I was kind of on your ass about falling in love with her and stuff, but you look happy."

The smile only broadened into a grin. "I am happy. I could have no title and nothing to my name, but I would still be happy with her."

"Good. Then enjoy it. Including your new Earldom or whatever the hell they call it."

"Yeah, I guess. It's just all so complicated and tied in with my dad, you know?"

I nodded. I remembered that for most of his life, Roone had thought his father hadn't loved him. But it turned out the old man had, and it was his stepmother who tried to keep him from his inheritance. I bet she was a lot to deal with when you were falling in love and getting shot at and shit. "You and your brother, you're closer now?"

He nodded. "Yeah. That part at least is actually really good."

"Well, then everything is coming up roses."

"For you too. You've got a team. Your business is thriving. I mean, what more could you want?"

"That's right, I have everything I could ever need."

He cocked his head then. "So, do you like, get out and stuff? I know you went on that date. Hopefully the first of many."

I raised a brow and then turned my back to him as I marched into the kitchen. I was going to need alcohol for this. "What? You worry that I work too much now?"

"I don't know. Maybe you wouldn't be so tense if you, uh, got out more."

I grabbed a beer and rummaged for the opener as I glanced up at him. "Roone, are you suggesting I get laid?"

He coughed a laugh. "Well, it couldn't hurt. Because you're tense, mate. Like, on edge. Even more so than you were when we were in London."

"I'm not tense." Even as I said that, I forced my shoulders to drift down to where they belonged instead of up around my ears. "Okay, it's been a lot. I'm just beyond grateful that I even have a business, considering how everything ended up."

He nodded slowly. "Have you been to see him?"

I choked on my beer. "My Dad?"

He nodded.

"No. I haven't been to see him. They informed me when he was out of medical care and transferred to the prison, but that's the last interaction I've had with him."

He shrugged. "I mean, maybe you should see him?"

"What for? He betrayed me. He betrayed the Crown. Because of him, I'm not with my family anymore. So that pisses me off."

"But you're right back in the family. You're a Knight now."

"Only because my best friend pressured the king to bring back an ancient group of protectors. I mean, how crazy is that?"

"You know full well Sebastian would have done it without any pressure from Penny. He wanted to send you before you were knighted. Ethan talked him out of it though. The way things are with the Council right now, rocking the boat is a bad idea, so he found an alternative method. He wasn't allowed to send civilians, so it couldn't happen. But knights, he can send King's Knights."

"It's a hell of a loophole."

"I know, right? Okay, I'm going to go grab a shower and call Jessa. I'll check with Sebastian too. Do you need me to tell him anything?"

"Yeah, tell him we're going to need a lot more knights, because I don't have enough team to cover the prince. So we need to start looking at resumes, military, private security, everyone. From what I've seen on the file, and what the police sent over, that was too damn close of a call with Frank. Tristan could have been killed."

"I know that you mean His Highness."

I blinked at him, careful to keep my face impassive. What did he know? "Well, right now, he's a client, so all that royal shit... It's out the window."

He nodded slowly. "Okay, whatever you say."

When he went to his room, I finally sagged against the counter. Shit. Why had this happened? Why did I think I could just turn up here and everything would be fine?

There was a knock at the door, and I frowned. It could be the police. Hell, it could be anyone. I had my gun out of my holster as I approached the door and peered at the security panel.

Tristan.

I didn't holster my gun though. When I opened the door, I glared up at him. "Your Highness, is there something I can help you with?" I ground my teeth, fighting the response to him, the dropping of my belly, the rush of blood in my veins, the shortened breath, I tried to ease it all with nice deep, even— Oh, fuck it, my body went haywire.

"You never did answer my question. Why you? What are *you* doing here?"

"I'm so sorry my presence here is irritating you, Your Highness, but I didn't really have a choice. When my king requests something, I have to do it."

"Ariel, you look—"

I shook my head. "Please don't. Let's not pretend to say things we don't mean, shall we?"

He shut the door behind him. "Where is Roone?"

I inclined my head toward the closed bedroom door. "In there."

He nodded. "Ariel, you just—"

He stepped forward. I didn't move back.

We were within inches of each other. And when he finally touched me, I recoiled, not because his touch was so awful, but because I wanted it *too* much.

It was too hot, too electrified.

"I said, we're not going to talk about this." I turned to put some distance between us, because God knew, I needed it. But his hand reached out and snagged me around the upper arm.

I whirled back, pissed, ready to force him out, but he was right there, smelling like ocean breezes and something fresh and green.

"Tristan..."

"Why are you here. I can't have you *here*."

"You think I want this? This was the last assignment on earth I wanted. But duty calls."

His gaze roved over mine, and his voice was whisper soft. "Your face is exactly how I've pictured it all this time. Your fucking eyes. I have never forgotten them."

Shit. I was gonna lose it and start bawling. *Distance. Get Distance.* I blinked rapidly and tried to move back, but his hand reached out and wrapped around my wrist tugging me forward.

"Just what the hell do you think—"

I didn't get to finish because his lips slammed down on mine.

Firm.

Unyielding.

Unforgiving.

At first, it was a complete, utter shock to my body. All systems shut down. The alarm bells rang, sirens wailing, warning me of imminent disaster. And then something long dead that I'd buried, flared into life, like a single green leaf in a barren desert, pulling low in my belly, growing roots and taking hold. It smelled, looked, and tasted like hope.

I didn't mean to respond. I didn't. And maybe it was shock, but I gasped, and my lips parted, and then his tongue was on mine. His fingers were in my hair and he was gripping me and angling my head. I had no choice but to respond. My tongue slid against his and I could hear the low rumbling growl.

Somewhere in the distance, someone whimpered, and I looped my arm around his neck and God, yes. That felt amazing. Incredible. God, he could still kiss like every move was calculated to melt bones. As his hands slid down my face, around my back, pressing me into him. I could feel every, single, inch of him. The thick length of him twitched against my belly, hot and pulsing and promising many orgasms.

Then finally, one of the sirens broke through, wailing, warning me.

I shoved against his chest, but I barely moved him. He eased the kiss, but he didn't stop. And God, I did not want him to stop. His tongue turned coaxing, his lips going softer. And then suddenly we were rocking into each other in micro movements designed to get us even closer.

I was ruined.

I *couldn't* stop.

No matter how much I needed to. *You need to stop. He will leave you again.*

With that harsh splash of cold water, self-preservation won out. I slid my arm between us, raising it up, creating an arm bar across his trachea as I applied gentle pressure.

He choked as he tore his lips from mine. "Jesus Christ, Ariel."

"Back the fuck up," I muttered through gritted teeth.

He stared at me. His gaze hot and burning on mine and then dipping to my lips. At first, it was anger. Red hot, then white. And then he shook his head, and I could see it. Confusion. Was that contriteness?

You know better. Don't believe that.

"Shit. Fuck. I shouldn't be here. Why do you still do this to me? After everything—"

I swiped my fingers across my lips. "Don't touch me again."

"Last fucking thing I want. Trust me."

My hands shook. "Your Highness, I'm here to do a job. That's it."

"We can't work together. I'm having you pulled."

I marched past him to the door, opened it, and stepped aside. I glared at some spot over his shoulder. "Unless this is about your security, please leave."

He paused at the door. "Go home."

"Go home? Believe me, I don't want to be here. This... is never happening again."

He said nothing as he closed the door behind him. When he was gone, I sagged against the door and slid down until my ass hit the cold tile. Holy fuck. I was in so much trouble.

I was still fucking in love with the prince.

Tristan...

WHAT THE FUCK was wrong with me?

As I marched down the hall back to my flat, I tried to breathe deep.

It was supposed to be easy. Walk in there, ask her why the

hell she'd shown up, why she hadn't sent someone else. But instead, she'd looked just like I remembered. Wide eyes full of wonder, those lips shaped in a perfect bow, begging me to kiss them. And all of a sudden it was ten years ago, and she was the girl I couldn't resist no matter what I did.

We had been kids, and in essence, it was a summer romance, but it had been so much more than that.

We had intended to leave together. Get her away from her old man, start something new. And then I'd gotten the chance to play for Madrid. It had been an overnight thing.

Don't forget the other reason.

I shoved that down. I didn't want to think about it. I knew she wouldn't want me. It was fine. I had a whole new life now. My brother couldn't torture me anymore. But he'd spent a good amount of time torturing Sebastian and the queen and also conspiring against Sebastian. So it was an exile behind prison bars for him. It was probably a very nice prison. But still, not being able to do what he wanted, when he wanted, was probably driving him bat shit crazy. Which was good. I wondered if I should go and see him just to rub it in his face.

Or, to burn that fucking house to the ground.

No, I wasn't going to think about my brother. I wasn't going to think about Ariel anymore either. That was dangerous. Kissing her had been—

Amazing. Hot. My dick was still hard enough to cut diamonds and fuck me if I didn't need her so much.

I had to get rid of the tension coursing through me. I needed to put it somewhere.

Well, you do have a fiancée for these purposes.

Absolutely not. I wouldn't use her like that. Not ever. Trying to use her once to forget had been an unmitigated disaster. I'd never forgiven myself for giving in that night. And I hadn't forgiven myself for calling out Ariel's name that night. I honestly didn't think Ella had ever forgiven me for that either.

It would have been one thing if I'd told her it wasn't going to work out. But to know I'd been actively thinking about someone else... I knew that had hurt her.

Afterward, she looked at me and said, "If I thought that was me you'd been shagging like that, we'd give this a real go. But I was just the replacement body."

The kind of shame that had washed over me, I'd never been able to shake. And now she knew exactly who I'd been calling for.

When I walked back into the flat, Ella was on the couch. "Did you have a nice time with your girlfriend?"

Of course she knew what I'd done. "Ella, give it a rest."

"Absolutely, Your Highness."

The way she said it, with a hint of hurt, cut me to the quick. "Those big green eyes blinking up at you. Her and her bottle-red hair, I can see the appeal. There's something strong and vulnerable about her all at once."

I swallowed around the sawdust. "It's natural, actually."

Ella's brows rose. "Oh, I was kidding about the girlfriend bit. But if you know the carpet and drapes match, then I guess, she is."

Fuck. "She's not."

Her brows furrowed. "Why not? What happened?"

"Didn't I just tell you to give it a rest?"

She studied me for a moment. I could tell that hurt inside her wanted to flair and protect herself, because I wanted Ariel and I didn't really want her, even though she didn't really want me either. But she fought it and then said something kind. "That's love, isn't it? What I saw between you."

I swallowed hard, my palms going clammy. I stopped at the fridge and opened it up, pulling out a beer. "I don't know what you're talking about."

"Oh, yes, you do. You love her."

#*Truefacts*. "No, I don't."

"Sure, you don't. And even if that's true, you *did* love her once. What happened?"

"Doesn't matter now. She's not staying. And as much as I like Roone, he's not staying either. They'll do an assessment and then they'll leave. I'm going to make damn sure of it."

She sighed. "God, you are so measured. Why are you doing this?"

"You'll never understand."

"You can try me. We're actually friends when you decide you want to tell me things."

I winced. "I'm sorry. It's just safer."

"So," she said quietly. "She's the one you were thinking about that time. That name..." Her voice trailed.

Cue the guilt and shame. "Ella, there's no point in rehashing this. You know I'm sorry about that."

She shook her head and blinked away tears. "That was my fault. I should have seen you were emotionally unavailable. I'm just trying to understand who she is to you. You have never looked at me like that. And if you love her so much, then why aren't you with her?"

I ran my hands through my hair. "Let's not okay. I don't want to hurt you."

"I'm a big girl, Tristan. Is that her?" She pressed the question again.

"Fuck. Yes. Happy?" Frustration was taking hold and setting its nasty roots. "I told you you'd regret that night."

"That's the problem. I didn't regret it. I wanted to shag you. You just wanted to shag someone else."

I sighed. "Ella." I scrubbed my hands on my face. "I don't know what I'm supposed to say here."

She waved her hand. "No, you're right. Just that night, I don't know, I thought, what if we gave it a real try? And then I realized your heart would always belong to someone else. But, at least I know now who I was replacing. And she is beautiful. I was just being catty about the hair."

"Thanks," I muttered.

She swiped away at a tear. "So, how do you want to play this?"

"I need to talk to my cousin. I can't have her here."

Her gaze searched mine. "Okay, do you want to hire some other people?"

"Well, I want us to figure out what the hell we're dealing with. If we can get some word from the police, something definitive, some stalker, more royal conspiracy, someone after you, whatever the situation is. I don't know, and that's the worst. Right when I'm in the middle of these fucking negotiations."

"You really want to go home?"

"Yeah. I do. For a long time, I couldn't. Now that I can, I still *can't*."

She frowned and studied me. "I know you, and I would never, you know, talk about why you couldn't go home before —" Her nearly clear blue eyes met my gaze. My skin chilled, the cold sweat starting at the nape of my neck, sliding down.

Nope, I'm not going to talk about this.

"I don't know what you mean."

"Look, I know the Winston Isles is important to you."

"Yes, it is."

"Like I said, I will do everything to help you get to play there. But you and I are going to have to figure out what we want to do with *this* situation. Now that you have seen her, how long do you think our arrangement is going to work for you?"

"Our arrangement works perfectly. I can't have her. I never could."

"I wish you'd tell me why."

"She wouldn't want me." The admission was like a lance through my heart.

"You can't be the protector for everyone, Tristan. Sooner or later you'll need someone to protect you."

"I love that you want to try. But I've got this entire situation under control. I'm going to grab a shower."

As I went to go take the coldest shower on the planet, I knew I could never touch Ariel again. Not if I wanted to keep my plan on course. Too much was riding on me having a clear head.

SEVEN

TRISTAN...

I COULD DO THIS. IT WAS FINE. ALL I HAD TO DO WAS survive Ariel.

The good news was, Ella was kinder when Ariel came to the door looking like every dirty-librarian fantasy I'd ever had.

Her red hair was pulled back into a bun, and she had sunglasses shielding her eyes. Her pencil skirt showed off her slender curves, and the tight blouse underneath her tailored jacket accentuated her fuller curves on top. Christ, had she been so full before?

Stop. That won't help.

My gaze swept over her again, and I honestly couldn't tell where in the hell she would have hidden her weapon. She wore heels, bringing her height closer to five foot nine.

"Wow, you certainly look the part of security."

Her voice was soft when she mumbled, "Your Highness."

The way she said that sent molten heat straight to my dick.

Fuck. This isn't going to work.

When she walked past me, her fragrance was something slightly sweet, making me want to lean in and lick her.

Jesus. Get yourself under control.

"If Your Highness is ready, we'll get going on your day. I understand that you have an agent meeting and then a meeting with Brixbrack shoes?"

I nodded. "Yes, um, and then Ella and I are supposed to have lunch at Kowa."

Ariel's eyes went wide. "Kowa? That paparazzi trap? It's completely open air."

"I know."

Ella came out of her bedroom then. Her smile was warm for Ariel, which I didn't trust. "I know, probably not the greatest idea, but we booked it ages ago. I have a film shooting in the area and it's a good photo opportunity."

Ariel's gaze rocketed between me and Ella. "I understand a photo opportunity, but we have to think about safety here."

"I'm sure you and your team will figure something out."

I leveled a gaze on Ella. "Okay, let me help her out. Maybe it's not the best idea."

Ella pouted. "Well, it's really important. We need to be seen enjoying ourselves. This is important for you too, not just for me."

I sighed. "Kowa has that back patio. Full-on hedges everywhere, harder for a sniper to get a shot, right?"

Ariel sighed and pulled open a tablet. "I'm checking now."

She tapped her ear and then spoke quietly, presumably to Roone. "Hey, I need to check Kowa, back patio. How are the sightlines?"

There was a bit of silence and then she was talking again. "Yeah, that's where they're having lunch today."

She smirked and then said. "I know. I already told them." She listened again and then apparently hung up.

"We can make the back patio work."

Ella frowned. "But then no one is going to *see* us eating together."

Ariel shook her head. "My job is his *safety*. Considering he almost lost a Royal Guard and someone almost took your head off, I think safety is tantamount. It's going to be risky getting you in and out of there, but we can make it work. If you really must have a paparazzi moment, you can walk into the front and that's it. You'll exit through a side exit. There's an awning there. Roone is already arranging it. That's the best I can do. Take it or leave it."

Ella pouted but nodded. "Fine. As long as I can Instagram it."

Ariel rolled her eyes. "Ugh, whatever. Is there anything else?"

I nodded. "I'm supposed to deal with a charity thing tonight."

She frowned. "I don't have anything on your schedule."

"It's not a big charity event. There is just this kid I visit in the hospital sometimes."

Ariel lifted a brow. "Oh yeah?"

"It's in a hospital. No one ever knows I go. But the kid gets pictures to show his friends. Sometimes they show up online. I never announce it. I just turn up." I'd met Alejandro through one of the other charities I ran. He was a good kid. When he fell sick his parents reached out again.

Jesus. "Okay, fine. I'll have Roone on it. Anything else?"

I shook my head.

"Fair enough, let's go."

Ella strode over then and wrapped her arms around my

neck, and I frowned. She placed a kiss on my lips. I couldn't help it, I darted back. "Um, what?"

Ella darted her gaze over my shoulder and I scowled down at her even as she said sweetly, "See you later, darling."

When I turned around, Ariel wasn't even watching us. She was already at the door, back to me, shoulders stiff. *Oh yeah, she'd seen that.*

"Have a great day, baby." Ella's voice was light and fun, and she grinned at me.

I just shook my head. "Yeah, I'll see you at lunch." I rolled my eyes and followed Ariel out. I wanted to say something to tell Ariel that what she saw just then hadn't meant anything. But I couldn't let her know this was a whole fake arrangement. First, because it would ruin my plans. Second, well, it's probably better if she didn't know. I wouldn't want to disappoint her again.

You more than disappointed her. You broke her heart. You think she's going to go anywhere near you again?

No, I did not. And that was for the best.

When we got to the car, I opened the door for her and she scowled. "How this is supposed to work is that *I'm* supposed to open the door."

"Remember, you're supposed to be undercover. I'm a prince. I'm a gentleman."

"You might be a prince, but you are no gentleman."

She had a point. I wasn't very gentlemanly the previous night when I'd resorted to trying to get rid of my erection with several showers.

"How long have you been dying to say that one?" I asked her.

Her lips twitched. "I use that one on Lucas all the time."

I frowned. "How is he? He was here a few weeks ago, but it was only a quick visit."

"You know Lucas, glib and entertaining. He's happiest when you're telling him he's not a gentleman. But despite that, he has learned how to settle in and find his niche."

"Good. I really like him."

I slid in the seat next to her and the driver headed us south toward my agent meeting.

"Ariel, about last night—"

She shook her head. "Don't. None of it matters."

I couldn't just say nothing, "Look, in the last few years when I have been home, I've wanted to talk to you."

"I knew when you were home. I could have talked to you then too. But I didn't. It's just a lot of water under the bridge, Your Highness."

"Would you stop with that 'Your Highness' bullshit?"

She put up her hand. "How about we agree to something. Neither one of us is going to bring up the past. It doesn't exist. You and I on that plane, don't exist."

I swallowed hard. "Last night existed." Her eyes flared wide and I could see my misstep. "Okay, if that's the way you want it."

"Yup, that's the way I want it."

There were a million things I wanted to say to her. A million things I wanted to do. But it wasn't going to happen.

By the time we reached my agent's office, I was tense and on edge and so fucking keyed up, my dick could probably have cut through steel. Mark Klein had been my agent for over a decade, and I owed everything to him. His office in the city was light and airy and full of windows.

Ariel preceded me in and then scowled when she saw all the windows. "Jesus, You guys can't meet in a darkened hovel?"

Mark laughed. "Where did you find her? She's hilarious."

I smiled at him. "This is Ariel. She's my new PR person."

Mark frowned. "You fired Amy and her team?"

I shook my head. "Ariel works for Amy's team."

"Fantastic. Okay, here's where we're at, since I assume she has signed an NDA, everything is good?"

Oh, hell yes, she'd signed the ultimate of NDAs. "Yeah, she's fine."

Ariel took up post at the back of the office with a notebook on her lap. It took me a double take to notice that she had a gun under that notebook.

He nodded. "All right, so the Argonauts, they're not coming up on money."

Shit. I hadn't thought we'd be discussing the Argonauts deal, but Ariel gave zero indication that she'd even heard him. Dragging my attention back to him, I said, "Money doesn't matter."

He stared at me. "Well, it might not matter for you, but it sure as shit matters for me. They're low-balling you."

"It doesn't matter. As long as I get to go home, it doesn't matter at all."

He sighed. "What is with you and going home?"

"Just that, it's my home. I want to be there."

If Ariel was shocked, she said nothing. Her gaze stayed trained on her notebook like she was taking notes. Was she planning on stabbing me later? It was difficult to tell.

"I want this deal. I want it done. So, whatever it takes, just do it."

"Okay, let's see if we can sell them on the cachet you'll bring to the Argonauts. I mean, after all, you're the prodigal son returned. That would bring them a lot of money, put asses in seats. Having the Prince play on home turf, crowds will eat that shit up."

Ariel lifted her head. All of a sudden, it was like she caught on. "The Argonauts, as in the *Winston Isles* Argonauts?"

I nodded slowly, waiting for it to sink in. Her eyes went wide, but she didn't say anything else. The rest of the meeting went by quickly with Ariel in complete silence. It wasn't until we were back in the car that she turned to face me. "You're trying to come home?"

"Yeah. You're pretty much the only one who knows."

"Jesus Christ. Why?"

"Hah, like I already told Mark, it's my home. I've been gone too long."

She shook her head. "This is not part of the deal."

"What, you think we can't coexist in the same place?"

"No, I just—I never expected to see you again. That's all."

"Yeah, me neither. So, this is just as uncomfortable for me as—"

The car shook, and the crashing sound drowned everything else out.

The driver, Leo, swerved and tried to maintain the car on the two-lane road.

"Fuck."

We were hit again from the side, and Ariel cursed under her breath.

Before I knew what was happening, Ariel had her hand on the back of my neck and was pressing me down, right into her... lap.

"Well, that's one way of asking for what you want. I'm happy to oblige."

"Don't get cute. I'm just trying to keep you from getting shot in the head when I open the goddamn window."

"Why would you open the window?"

"So I can shoot at them." She said it wryly as if I were an idiot.

My eyes went wide, but I did as she told me. However, I figured maybe the best place to put my face wasn't on her lap. I would just be asking for temptation.

I hit the deck and she rolled down the window. She pulled out the gun from the small of her back, and God help me if that wasn't the sexiest thing I've ever seen in my entire life.

When she fired though, there was no loud banging. There was just a succession of three muffled sounds, like *pfft, pfft, pfft.*

Then I heard the screeching of tires and a loud crash.

Horns honked and blared. And then there was chaos. But we went whizzing by. To Leo, she shouted, "Drive. And don't you dare stop until we are under cover."

Leo resisted for a moment. "But Miss—"

"Shut up and drive. Head straight for the penthouse. I'll have Roone meet us there with the police."

Then she was on the phone. "This is Lady Ariel Scott of Royal Elite Security and a King's Knight. I need a clean-up on the story of Prince Tristan being run off the road in Barcelona. There was gunfire. Unsure of casualties."

She was silent for a beat, and then she gave a clearance number and hung up.

I stared at her. That girl I'd once wanted to protect didn't exist anymore. The woman who replaced her was all but unrecognizable. "Just what the fuck is going on here?"

She studied me closely. "I don't know. But someone really, really wants you dead."

"The only person I pissed off enough to want to kill me is sitting in the car with me."

"Yeah, well, at least you admit that you pissed me off."

"And I'm sorry about that."

"Don't bother. I don't believe you. And right now, all we need to focus on is who the hell is trying to kill you. The sooner I figure that out, the sooner I get to go home and never have to see you again."

"Probably for the best. What are we going to do about the other meetings today?"

"You're canceling those. Someone tried to run you off the road. Maybe that will sink in. You're never going to have a moment's rest until we figure out who the hell is trying to hurt you."

I knew she was right. I hated it, but I knew she was right. Until I figured that out, I had a feeling I would be stuck with her.

Ariel...

SIDE BY SIDE, Tristan and I walked from the car to the elevator. He was silent as a tomb, and I was ever so careful not to touch him. Even though I wanted to make sure he was okay.

Why do you care?

"Your Highness, I have a text from Roone. The police will be here shortly to speak with you."

He nodded his head. "Fine."

"I—" Shit what was I supposed to say? I was within my rights to be angry with him. I also didn't want to see him dead. And I'd had a narrow escape myself.

But what the hell was I going to say? 'Sorry, some asshole has tried to kill us. Do you need a hug or something?' And if he did need a hug, I would volunteer somebody else for that duty. The less I touched him, the better.

His voice was hollow when he said, "I need to call the publicity department."

I nodded. "As you heard, I already have the team at home working on suppressing the story. I texted your publicist already that you would be reaching out and there was an incident today. I obviously don't think it's a good idea for you to go to your endorsement meeting today, or any other meetings right now."

He scowled. "Are you enjoying this?"

I stared at him and shook my head. "You know what? It's fine. Everything is fine. Let's just carry on, get through the rest of the day, okay?" Clearly a civilized conversation was not in the cards for us.

"My life is spiraling, and you're getting a kick out of it, aren't you?"

"Is that what you think is happening? True, I'm not a fan of yours. But I serve the crown, and I'm a decent human being. So while I believe in karma, even I'm going to side-eye her for trying to kill you."

His gaze searched mine. "I look at you and a flood of questions is all I get. Why can't I get you the hell out of my head?"

Fuck. This was not the conversation we should have. "I apologize, Your Highness. Obviously, we shouldn't be having this conversation."

He glared down at me and asked through gritted teeth, "Why did you come?"

I tilted my chin up and kept my gaze pinned over his shoulder. "Sebastian asked me to."

He shook his head. "No. Why did you *really* come?"

I considered lying. "I—I came to forget you. Are you happy now?"

He frowned. "Forget me?"

"God, you're such an asshole. For ten years you've been this looming presence in my life. And I just wanted a fucking reprieve. Every time I see something about you or hear something, I'm locked up and unable to function. And then you fucking *call* and you don't *say* anything. Who does that? I just want it to stop. I thought if I took the assignment, that I'd stop feeling how I feel."

His frown deepened. "Why do you care? I haven't heard a word from you all this time. Not a single word. Not a letter, not a note, nothing."

I frowned at him. "What the hell are you talking about?"

A blaring ringing filled the elevator. Tristan covered his ears, and I was on him. I covered him and had my gun out from the holster.

He shook his head. "Jesus Christ woman, it's just the fucking alarm because we stopped."

I frowned. "I knew that."

He pulled the stop button, and we were moving again almost instantly.

"You're not going to answer me?"

"Why on earth do you think I would chase somebody who was clear he didn't want me?"

He frowned at me. "What in the—" The elevator doors opened, and Roone was waiting on the landing.

"Your Highness, Ariel. I have notified Sebastian. The Royal

Press Corp is already on it. They'll handle it if anyone got wind of anything. Like I said, the police will be here in thirty minutes. You two are okay?"

I nodded, still staring at the prince. What, he thought he could leave me and I'd just chase him, asking him why he didn't love me anymore? That was some extra-special asshole right there.

"It's fine. Thanks, Roone."

He nodded. "Ariel, if you can see to His Highness for a bit, I'm still making some calls. Sebastian has a couple of other knights he might be able to send. There's a question on how they'll be managed. I'm looking into some decoy cars too."

I nodded absently, not realizing that this was going to put me still in Tristan's company.

When we walked into the apartment, it was empty. No obvious sign of Ella anywhere. "Your fiancée, Ella, seems... nice."

He chuckled. "Oh, *nice*. Tell me how you really feel."

"I don't feel anything."

"Yeah. Wasn't that always the problem?"

Damn. If that wasn't ever shots fired. "What the fuck do you mean?"

"I can't—" His phone rang. He yanked it out of his pocket. "What?"

He was immediately contrite. "Sorry, Mark. No, we... there was an accident of some sort, so um, I'll need you to move that."

There was silence. Mark must have been talking.

"Yeah, I know. Oh, okay. Yeah, put him on speaker... Coach Simmons, I'm thrilled to speak to you."

Coach Simmons, was that his coach? I really didn't need to learn more about soccer. I was already a football fan.

Whatever it was they were saying, though, it was the first

time since I'd picked him up this morning that Tristan looked happy.

His Royal Highness.

I really needed to remember that. He was saying something. "Oh, I'm so thrilled that we could come to an agreement. You have no idea how long I have waited to hear those words."

I was missing something. Something important was happening. I listened more closely.

"Yes. I can't wait. Believe me when I say, I haven't looked forward to anything more."

What was happening?

"Yes. I will notify the team. I look forward to working with you."

He hung up the phone. He was smiling. It was the kind of smile that I used to love. Like he had a secret and he was going to share it with just me. But then his gaze met mine and away went that secret. Away went that smile. Who the hell was he to be pissed off at me? He was the one who'd abandoned me.

"I take it you have good news?"

He smiled, but it wasn't that same sweet smile. This one had a harder edge to it. "Yeah. Looks like you're getting your wish. I'm going home. I've just been signed with the Argonauts."

EIGHT

ARIEL...

I COULDN'T RELAX. AFTER WHAT HAD HAPPENED THAT afternoon and the news about the prince, I was a ball of nerves. Yes, I was worried about his safety, but I was more worried about him coming home. But before I could even process that, I wanted to know why the fuck the police weren't doing anything.

Inspectors Santiago and Morales stalked around the penthouse. They were slicker than most police detectives I knew. More polished. These guys weren't Interpol, but they were used to international cases.

Roone watched them carefully. Tristan and Ella sat side by side on the couch, not touching, but also not moving. "Inspector Morales, what do you have so far? Can you give us anything?" I asked.

His gaze slid over me and he spoke directly to Roone. "So far, the evidence we've seen points at a potential stalker for Miss Banks."

Oh, so he was just going to pretend he didn't hear me? I tried again. "So, there has been evidence of Ella being stalked?"

When he spoke this time, he did pay attention to me, but his tone was derisive. "Yes. She's a famous actress. These things happen. Someone becomes obsessed, you know, that sort of thing. That's what we're dealing with here."

I tilted my chin up and met his gaze directly. "With all *due respect*, you'll need to be clearer than that. We need specific evidence, something that's not circumstantial that points to Ella having a stalker."

He frowned. "And you are again?"

"You were introduced to us when you came in. I'm Lady Ariel Scott. King Sebastian's personal King's Knight. That is Sir Roone Ainsley. King's Knight and Royal Guard to the Winston Isles. I'm the ranking officer here. So, when you speak, I'd like you to address *me*. And you will actually have to provide specifics. While I am not in charge of Miss Banks's security, I am in charge of Prince Tristan's, so I'd like some specificity about what evidence you have. Thank you."

Roone's lips twitched. He was enjoying this. He liked to see me throw my weight around. Which was irritating, but I also kind of liked it. I felt strong. And God knew I needed to feel strong right then.

Inspector Santiago was less openly hostile than his partner. "Forgive my partner. What we have is evidence in the form of anonymous emails written to Miss Banks. According to her team she had been receiving email threats prior to the previous incident in Vienna."

"And have you called Interpol? Since that incident happened in Vienna and the most recent one happened here, they would likely be able to help. Has there been anything else?"

I slid my gaze to Ella. "Anything you can think of? Someone who seemed off? Anyone from your past? We need something to go on, otherwise, the two of you are sitting ducks and we don't have enough security for this. At least not for the prince."

She slid her gaze over to Tristan, but she shook her head. "No. Nothing. I've already called my security company to ask for more men."

"I think that's a good idea, especially if these detectives are correct. They can't be assigned to Prince Tristan, but for your safety and well-being, please allow Roone and I to vet the new hires."

I almost felt bad for her. The guilt was still riding me hard. Because of what I'd done yesterday, I could afford to be charitable today. Besides, I didn't want to see anyone hurt. Not when it was avoidable.

"Yes, I think that's fine."

She was nicer today. Much nicer. What had changed? Or maybe that was my guilt talking.

You didn't do anything wrong... except enjoy it.

"You know, if you're in the market for a team, I might know some people. They're based in New York and have a busy case-load, but you never know." Blake Security was a long shot, but at least if she hired them, we'd have some friendly faces to assist if need be. When I turned to Roone, he winked at me. He knew what I was up to.

Tristan spoke then. "Inspector Santiago, when we spoke after Vienna, Ella said that she felt she'd been followed from the airport. Your men said they would look into it, but you never found a suspect?"

Inspector Santiago shook his head. "No. Without a specific target to go after, we're shooting in the dark. We can put some men on her, but even that is limited for the time being."

I shook my head. "The problem is, Ella wasn't with us today.

If she's the intended target, then why the hell did someone side-swipe our car?"

Morales shrugged. "Perhaps whoever was stalking her wants the prince out of the way. These things are very common."

I locked my jaw and suppressed the urge to go all Wolverine on his ass. "You don't have to explain stalker mentality to me. I understand that. But has anyone considered that maybe Miss Banks is *not* the intended target?"

Inspector Santiago sat forward. "We have seen no evidence that suggests the prince is the target, but some of the emails Miss Banks has received are concerning. There is currently nothing to suggest someone would have a grudge against the prince. We've had our men go through his fan mail already."

Didn't he know that shit was sanitized? "I understand, but the prince is also an international football athlete. I just want to make sure all bases are covered and that you are taking the threat seriously."

His gaze narrowed. "We do know how to do our jobs. And we would normally have identified a suspect already, but considering Miss Banks's celebrity profile, these types of attacks are more sophisticated. Hackers running relays in different countries, and they're impossible to track unless you can catch them in the act. Still, you are here as a courtesy to His Majesty, but we shall run point in the investigation."

Roone coughed and slid a glance toward me.

I ignored him. If I so much as looked at him, I'd start laughing my ass off and call for my laptop to show them how dumb they were. "So you're asking me to put the prince's safety in your hands, but you're telling me you can't do anything until someone is caught in the act?"

"Well yes, it's very difficult unless you can point to someone specific."

"I'm going to need you to provide me all the information you have on the investigation and access to your servers."

Morales didn't seem keen on that idea at all. "And what are you going to do?"

"Well, I'm going to look at the investigation from the very beginning. From the time Tristan and Ella called the police. You should have made it an Interpol case. There is nothing you can do about what happened in Vienna because you have no jurisdiction there. If there's a pattern of behavior, we can at least attempt to try to compile that data and figure something out What's happening here is not working. And I have a prince to protect. Not to mention that this is no longer a local problem."

Morales glowered at me. "Sure, you have a prince to protect, but we have a job to do. If you think we're going to let you impede our investigation--"

"What investigation? So far, you're telling me that Ella has a stalker. Okay, I can buy that. But you're telling me you don't know anything, and you can't get anything, until he, God forbid, actually gets his hands on her? And then, what if she's *not* actually the target and someone gets their hands on the prince?"

"Isn't that what you're here for?" He snickered.

"Yes, but apparently, it seems you can't do your job. So that's fine. I'll just go over your head. This case should have been transferred to Interpol anyway. After this afternoon's incident, I called in a favor. We just wanted to see if you had anything actionable."

The two detectives blinked at each other. "Wait, just a minute—"

"Look, I don't care about your investigation. Run your own

local investigation, if that's what you want to call it. And you can report your findings to Interpol who will loop us in."

I didn't wait for a response. I didn't wait for compliance. I just walked out. The prince was safe for the moment, and I need to get the hell away from the Barcelona detectives. I kept my gait easy until I was within the confines of the suite, and then I sagged.

Jesus Christ. I had called in every favor I ever had. In the past, I had worked with a few different Interpol agents. Miguel Ruiz was located in Barcelona, and he'd been one of the agents I'd worked with when I was chasing my father. I was perfectly willing to believe that Ella might have a stalker, but someone had tried to run us off the road today. I wasn't convinced the Barcelona Police Department knew what the hell they were doing.

Roone followed me into the suite. He didn't say anything when I closed the door behind him and just went to the fridge. He pulled out the wine, grabbed a glass, poured it three-quarters of the way full, and then handed it over to me. "Did that feel good?"

"No. Because I still don't have any answers."

He nodded slowly. "Morales was an asshole. I'm pretty sure Santiago knows it. He's going to give us a call with all the data and information we asked for, so you'll be able to do your thing. See if there's any connection."

"Thank you."

He shrugged. "You got this look on your face. I knew you were likely going to shoot him."

"You're right. I *was* going to shoot him. How can they just be so lackadaisical? Tristan's life is in danger, and they don't care?"

"I don't think it's that they don't care. I just think, especially guys like Morales, unless they have something tangible or real, they don't buy it themselves. He's not really a thinker. He's more of a doer."

"Jesus, that kind of attitude is going to get someone killed."

"Yeah, but not the prince. You're far too smart to let anything like that happen. So, let's control what we can. We'll get the data, analyze it, and we'll go from there. Don't let these guys stand in your way. You know how to do this."

"Yeah, I do know how to do this. It's just that the proper way to do this is irritating and also requires that you not shoot people."

He grinned. "I'm very, very happy that you're on my side."

"You should be, every single day."

He grinned. "I am. So, are you getting the update to Interpol, or am I?"

I laughed. "Already done. I have an old friend at Interpol, Agent Ruiz. I'm going to see if he can make sense of the information we have. If it is a stalker, then it might be wise to have Tristan separated from Ella for a bit."

Roone studied me. "Yeah, if you think it's best. You're the boss."

There was something about the way he said that, as if he knew that I had something to be guilty about. I knew that was just my paranoia talking, but still, I couldn't share it. I forced myself to grab my laptop and calm down. This, I knew how to do. I could solve problems like this. Never mind my own problems with Tristan. I was going to control what I could, because everything else, if I focused on it, was going to drive me to complete chaos.

Tristan...

SOMEHOW I'D MANAGED to pull it off. I'd managed to get exactly what I wanted. Except... why did that make me feel hollow?

Oh, I don't know. Because someone is trying to kill you?

I had known all along how serious gunshots were. I knew if I went home, the Council couldn't stop me from having any guards. It would be a PR nightmare. Or at least the optics would be shitty. But I hadn't counted on Sebastian actually sending someone.

So now, that was all up in the air. It didn't matter though. I was finally going home.

Is it still your home?

Regardless of how much physical time I had spent in the Winston Isles when I was a kid, it was the only place I ever felt comfortable.

Unless he was around.

But Ashton wouldn't be there anymore. I had gotten exactly the contract I wanted. No increase in salary, but I was basically going to be an endorsement cash cow for everything Winston Isles. Not that I needed the money. I'd been playing at the highest levels for over five years. Even if my monthly stipend as the prince decreased, I probably would have more money than I would ever need. It wasn't about the money, anyway. It was about the ability to play. To be me, to do what I loved. And I would finally get to do it at home. The only unanswered questions were related to dealing with Ariel.

Back in the islands, she had a job. Would she even still be running my security team? I suppose that was a question for my cousin.

Or you could ask her.

No. I would not be doing that. To see her standing there in the elevator acting like she was mad at me when she was the one who never wrote back infuriated me. Yes, I'd screwed up. I'd messed up and disappeared without saying goodbye, but I had to get out of there. If I hadn't left, Ashton would have told her everything. But I had written to her. I had written to her every single day for a year and not a single letter came back. But that was okay, I'd gotten over it.

Liar.

Just having her in my space was messing me up. It was making me remember all the things I didn't want to remember. Like her smell. It wasn't overly girly and not overly citrusy, but there was something alluring about it. It had a spicy scent to it. Slightly intoxicating. She wore it all the time. Just a hint of that scent was enough to take me home, and suddenly, I was eighteen again with the chance of a lifetime to both escape and pursue a dream. But now I was going home on my own terms.

"You're sure this is a good idea?"

I glanced up from my laptop where I'd been checking the final contract to find Ella directing three people with her luggage.

"Yeah, it is. You don't have to come."

Her brows drew down. "Are you kidding me right now? My future is tied to your future. So, if you're going back to the Winston Isles, so am I. I can easily catch a flight from there to LA, or London, or wherever I have a job."

I sat back and studied her. "So you want to continue then?"

"What choice do we have? This is it. We made a deal."

I nodded. "Of course. The terms of that deal can change though. It's not like we signed in blood."

Her completely unlined face seemed to pucker. Her lips pursed, her brow furrowed, and she narrowed her gaze. "Are you trying to back out?"

"I thought that's what you wanted. This was my deal, my end game. So, if you don't want to do it, I would understand."

She lowered her voice. "It's just the most dangerous aspects I wanted you to stop. Look, I have my own reasons for still doing this."

"Ouch."

"Oh, really? You're developing feelings now?"

"I always had feelings, Ella."

"Sure. You just keep them so close to the vest."

I sighed. "Okay. If you're coming, that's great. But you probably won't need that entire wardrobe. You're going to the islands. Do you realize how hot it is 99 percent of the time? You can leave the winter wardrobe and have someone send it later."

She lifted a brow. "This *is* the summer wardrobe."

"Of course, it is."

The driver was already at the door. Roone would be with us. Ariel would be in the follow car. I had specifically requested it that way. Once I double-checked everything, I closed my laptop and packed it away. I glanced back at the Penthouse that had been my home, but not really a home.

"Well, it's been nice."

Downstairs I frowned when I found Ariel waiting for us instead of Roone. "Where is Roone?"

"He'll meet us at the airport. He wanted to double check the security protocol."

Oh, fantastic. Now, I'll be stuck in the car with her. And that scent. "Fine."

"Yeah. You seem really happy about it." She rolled her eyes, opened the door for Ella, and then watched as I climbed in.

As I passed her, I caught another whiff of her, and my whole body went tight. I kept trying to reassure myself that once we were back, I would never have to be in close proximity with her again.

Or so you hope.

I was full of hope now. I was going home. The prodigal prince returned.

Ariel...

I WAS TOTALLY EXHAUSTED. I hadn't even realized how tightly wound I was until we were finally off the plane and I could feel my muscles uncoiling. I'd done it. I had seen him again. I had exorcized that demon out of its deep dark hole and let it go.

You really think you let it go?

Yeah, I'd let him go. I had seen him, and I didn't die. He'd kissed me, and I still didn't die. Now I was home and would be free.

Liar.

As if to prove the strength of my own self-deceit, my mind played back that brutal kiss. The harsh press of his lips on mine, the angry swipe of his tongue, the desperation that seeped into my bones. The way my mind had nearly bent to his will. Just like that.

It was fine. I could survive that. It *was* just a kiss. I barely thought about it all.

There were lies and there were full on blatant attempts at whoppers. Okay, so I had felt the kiss. And it had been just as I remembered. Worse, because now he had the experience of manhood behind it. Clearly, he'd been kissing a lot of people, and he'd only gotten better. But I couldn't focus on that.

I was back, and I could go back to my job, and pretend. Pretend that none of it had ever happened. It was over. A quick stop to see Penny and I'd be out of here.

Or do you want to check to see if the prince has settled okay?

No. Not even I was that dumb. Not even my level of delusion went that deep. I knew the sooner I got away from him the better.

After all, I'd barely survived. But, that was the point. I *had* survived, and I was going to keep surviving. I had a job to do. And while he may be back, there was no need for me to see him. I'd have to negotiate with Penny on game nights.

But I could make this work. He sounded like he wanted to be home, but upfront and present for all the royal intrigue? I didn't think so.

I headed to the private quarters of Sebastian and Penny, and when I knocked on their door, it was Penny who greeted me. "Bestie."

I gave her a nod. "'sup?"

She rolled her eyes. "Seb, one of your Knights is present."

I had to smirk at that. "Why do you look disappointed that I'm not actually wearing armor?"

"Because it sucks that you're not wearing armor."

I laughed. "Next time, I'll wear armor."

Sebastian called out from the back. He must have been in his office with the doors open. His office was technically further away down the hall, but the rooms were joined by one of the palace's many tunnels. She glanced back to make sure he wasn't on his way. "How did it go?"

I shrugged. "Fine. You know... fine. Totally fine."

Her brows lifted. "So *not* fine."

"No, it was okay. He is safe, and, um, he's home, apparently, so that was a surprise."

Penny's gaze darted over my face. "You're freaking out."

I shook my head. "No, I am not freaking out. I do not freak out. I am Ariel Scott. I never freak out. It's fine that I had to see him again because I survived. The name of the game is survival. And it's totally fine that it felt like I was getting kicked in the gut. It was also totally okay when he kissed me and all of a sudden it felt like he'd forcibly erased the last ten years. But you know what, it was fine."

Penny. "You guys talk about it?"

I shook my head. "Yeah. That's the thing. We can't have a single conversation without a fight. And well he has a fiancée, and we hate each other, and um..."

She pulled me into their quarters and closed the door behind me and took my hand. "Get yourself together. Sebastian is going to be here in a second."

"Oh, I'm together. I'm a professional."

"You look like you're freaking the fuck out."

"Thanks."

"Hey, that's the truth. Deep breath."

I forced myself to inhale deeply, and then I forced myself to release it slowly.

"Another one."

I did it again three times, and what do you know, I did feel calmer.

"Right. Okay, thank you. I just, you know, once we got here and I got off the plane, I started to spin out."

"Yeah. Um, we're going to have to discuss that kiss over a drink."

"Yeah, definitely. I mean, what was he doing? He has a fiancée. And what right does he have to be mad at me?"

"He doesn't. I—" She abruptly stopped talking at the sound of footsteps down the hall.

Sebastian came out of the tunnel and through the expansive living room. "Ariel. I didn't expect you first. I was waiting for Roone in my office."

"I figured as much. I think he's with the prince, getting him settled or whatever. I just wanted to let you know that we're back and everything for extraction worked fine."

He nodded. "Thank you. I know I disrupted your business by rolling in with the request."

I shook my head. "What are King's Knights for? I've been briefed out by my team. Everything is on schedule and working out the way it's supposed to for the most part, so it's okay."

He nodded. "Are you okay? You look... I don't know. Tired?"

I gave him my best smile. It probably looked more like a grimace, but whatever. "Yeah well, it was a long flight. I need to get back and make sure Jax and Trace didn't wreck the house and then get ready for my date."

Penny grinned then. "Oh my God, I forgot about your date."

"Well, I'm leaning in. Ian will be a good distraction."

She studied me closely. "You actually like him, right?"

"Of course I like him." She knew I had to move on. What was she doing?

She held up her hands. "Okay, then, great. I'm sure he's great."

But then I realized she was just doing it for Sebastian's benefit. "Oh, you know... we'll see. I know now not to get too excited about these things."

She rolled her eyes. Sebastian shook his head. "Ariel, want me to give you love advice?"

"Your Majesty, as much as I respect you, the last thing on earth you should be doing is giving *anyone* love advice."

He shrugged with a grin. "Yeah, you might have a point there. But maybe try and have fun. Who is this guy? Should I have Roone do a background—"

"Oh my God, no. No background checks. Besides, I've already done one."

He frowned. "I just wanted to help."

"I know. Besides, Penny already offered."

Penny grinned. "I did. After all, there's got to be some perks to working in Intelligence."

"You guys seem to forget that I'm a hacker. I can do it myself."

"Yeah," Penny nodded. "But you want a buffer. Get someone else to find out all the bad things and then give them to you in a manner that won't make you crazy."

I couldn't help but laugh. "Okay, I'm going to head back. Your Majesty, I'm at your service. Call if you need anything else." I didn't mean that. What I really wanted to say was, 'Please don't fucking call. If it has to do with your cousin, I don't want to hear from you.'

But that was not what I said and certainly not what I'd ever say. It was one thing to weave Penny in on my past disasters, it was another thing entirely to sit in front of my King and tell him all my heart's woes.

"Sure. I will. But I think with Tristan home now, we'll be

okay. Within the palace walls, he's safe. We've got Trevor guarding him. I did requisition one of your knights for when he's off palace grounds."

"Yeah, I saw the email come through. I saw that Trace handled it?"

He nodded. "Jameson has been assigned."

"Yep, Jameson is great. She's smart. Measured. Nothing rattles her. She'll be good."

He nodded. "Well, in that case, thank you for everything."

"Yeah, no big deal. You know, just fly to Barcelona on a whim, save a prince, come home. It happens every day."

He shrugged. "Actually, with us it sort of does."

"That's a good point."

With quick hugs and goodbyes, I was headed back to the relative normalcy of my life. But even as I marched along the halls, I just prayed that I would not see Tristan.

NINE

TRISTAN...

"When you said you were a prince, you left out the part about the ridiculous castle." Ella's head tipped up like every tourist I'd ever seen as she took in the ceiling work of one of the masters.

"Well, I mean, I'm pretty sure *prince* indicates castle. Or in this case, palace really."

"Yeah, but this is another *kind* of palace. And I have seen the palace in Monaco. The prince had an event I attended there a couple of years ago. But this—this is next level. This is a fairytale kind of palace."

"Oh, it's not like you haven't seen a palace before. Our British cousins have them."

"Yeah, sure. But come on, even you have to admit this is cool."

I shrugged. "Yeah, it's not bad, but it's not mine."

Her gaze flickered to mine. "So, are we going to meet your cousin, or what?"

"Yeah, Roone scheduled a meeting with him in a little bit, and then we'll all have dinner tonight. You'll love Penny."

Ella frowned. "Penny?"

I kept forgetting that part of our arrangement was that she ignore any of the royal drama. I didn't know if she was faking it or if this was real. "She's the queen."

She blinked twice. "I don't think I have anything to wear fit for a queen."

I rolled my eyes. "Penny isn't your typical queen. There is a good chance she's going to have paint on her face, or her hair, or even her clothes when you meet her."

Ella's brows snapped down. "Paint?"

"Yeah, she's actually a really good artist. It's one of the things that bonded her and Sebastian."

"Wow, okay. So like, in-a-loft, paint-under-the-fingernails kind of artist?"

"Minus the loft. I think Sebastian gave her a room to paint in or something. I don't know all the details. And I don't know if she's painting as much anymore. When she returned to the Winston Isles with Sebastian, she took on more Royal Guard duties, so probably not."

"Royal Guard?"

That was a closely guarded secret. Well okay, not exactly a secret. It was common knowledge that Penny had been a Guard, but no one knew that she was *still* in the Guard. Hell, I didn't even know how that worked. As queen, she needed to have a guard herself, and I knew for a fact Sebastian wasn't going to take any chances with his wife. Especially after what Ashton had tried to do to her.

That brother of mine, he really was the devil within.

"Yeah, long story short, she was a Royal Guard. She guarded Sebastian, then they fell in love."

Ella grinned. "So you mean she guarded his body?"

I rolled my eyes. "Funny. Yes, basically. But she's still a Guard now."

"So she's a total badass."

I nodded. "And really sweet too. You'll like her. Everyone likes Penny."

"Okay, noted. Make friends with Penny."

It was my turn to grin. "You might want to start by being super nice to Ariel too. The two of them are best friends."

Her mouth dropped open. "What? You could have mentioned that before."

"Well, it didn't seem important before. But now that you mentioned it, yeah, kind of important."

"Great. So basically, I've already made an enemy."

"Well, Ariel doesn't need to be an enemy."

"Right. So, I should make friends with your ex?"

Ex didn't seem like the right word for what Ariel and I were. But for all intents and purposes, it worked. "Look, the match in Chile isn't for another few weeks. You'll be free after that. But until then, you probably should make a friend or two."

"Right. Sorry, I'm not used to having friends and stuff. In Barcelona, I was just trying to keep to myself, you know?"

"No, I get it. Trust me. Me, of all people, I get it. But here, you're safe. More so than you were in Barcelona. So make friends and try to stay out of trouble."

"Right, got it. You're so sure about this plan."

"Well, as sure as I'm ever going to get. When everything works right, you'll be free to do anything you want."

"What if I want to stay here?"

My brows lifted. "Oh, I didn't even consider you'd want to stay here. Of course, you can. We can find you a really nice flat."

"I suppose I wouldn't stay in the palace anymore, would I?"

Why would she want to? "Um, no. It wouldn't really make sense. Anyone with a residence inside the palace generally needs a Royal Guard. I'm not sure if we could get away with you staying. Especially after the news comes out."

"No, I get it. I'm just—I don't know. I think I could get used to living in the palace."

"Right. Well, at least one of us will be enjoying it."

"Sorry, I forgot. For you, this was basically hell on earth."

"Not always. I had Sebastian. We're not staying though. Don't get caught up in this. Things are different now, so don't buy into it. You will only end up disappointed."

"So what, when we're done, you'll just get out of here?"

I shook my head. "No, I'm staying. This is my home. I have no reason to avoid it anymore. But I probably won't stay in the palace. Too many bad memories."

"I understand. So it's just a little longer, and we'll both be free?"

"Yeah. Freedom." It wasn't what I'd often thought about. To the outside world, of course, I was free. I was a prince and an athlete. I could have anything that I wanted in the world. Except peace. But soon, I'd be able to have that. And then I wouldn't have to be afraid anymore.

"Once Chile is over you'll be able to do whatever it is you want in the world."

"Right, just as soon as I help you with Ashton."

I frowned. I didn't want to think about it, *her,* anywhere near Ashton. But that was our bargain. We were both making sure that the skeletons of our past didn't haunt our future.

"I've already told you. You don't have to do that anymore. We're way past that."

She searched my gaze. "I always pay my debts. And after

everything we've been through, we're friends. I don't want you to have to carry around pain either."

I wasn't used to letting anyone take care of me, and I wasn't starting now. Just as soon as I had Max under control, I'd find another plan for Ashton. Because no way was I going to put Ella at risk for my own benefit.

TEN

TRISTAN...

CONSIDERING HOW THINGS HAD TURNED OUT, SEBASTIAN was remarkably calm. I expected more yelling. But no, he just leaned back in his chair and stared at me under a hooded gaze that was hard to read.

"So, you were just never going to tell me your big plan about coming home?"

Here went nothing. From now on, navigating through the truth and the lies was going to get trickier. "The deal was sensitive, and I had no control over the situation. I'm sorry about that." Not to mention there were members on the Regents Council that would have actively tried to stop the deal from going through. And I couldn't take that risk.

"I was working for your safety, Tristan."

"I know, and I appreciate it, but I told you I had it under control. I didn't need you riding in to the rescue."

"Riding in to the rescue? Some idiot shot at you. Some idiot *shot* Frank."

Yeah, that one burned. Some idiot had shot Frank. All because of me.

"Do you even care?"

My brows snapped down. "Are you fucking kidding me? Of course, I care. I just—"

"Why the secrecy?"

"It was a tough deal. The Argonauts had been burned before, so they didn't want to announce the trade."

His gaze narrowed, and he watched me warily. "Are you sure that's all it is?"

"Yeah, what else could it be? I'm just happy to be back again. I honestly don't want anything to do with the politics, I swear. I'm just here to play." And that was the truth. I wanted to stay off the Council's radar as much as possible.

"It's good to have you home. But I want you to be careful. The Regents Council isn't going to be particularly thrilled."

"I'm anticipating that. But it's not like they can forcibly remove me or kill me, so I think I should be okay."

"Don't joke. I'm not sure how many of them took part in this whole conspiracy. Obviously, Lucas, my mother, Penny, Ethan, Jessa, and Roone are all safe. But I wouldn't trust anyone else. Not with your life."

"I hear you. I'm not planning on giving you any trouble. I'm just here for football." *Liar.*

"Who knows? Maybe it'll bring cachet for them. After all, my cousin is a famous football star."

"Well, I don't know about being a star, but I do know what to do with my ball."

Sebastian snorted. "Despite what it sounds like, I'm happy to have you home. It's been too long."

"I'm happy to be home. It feels good."

"Okay, let's talk about the elephant in the room. What are

we going to do about your security? Obviously, there was a plan before, but now you're home."

This was the question I'd been anticipating. "Well, it only makes sense to have Trevor continue guarding me since he's been doing that already. I'd still love to have Frank, but he's going to be recuperating for a while."

Sebastian nodded at this. "Yeah, he's taking a much-deserved break. So, all right, Trevor it will be. And then I have a couple of King's Knights that will be assigned to you as well."

My ears perked up at this. "Knights?"

"Ariel has a team, so I have asked her for two of them to watch your back."

"I get it. There were a couple of troubling incidents, but no one is going to touch me here. This is my home."

"It's your home, but in some ways, it's a lot more dangerous. You have to be careful."

"I think it was isolated to Barcelona."

"I doubt that. Are you forgetting the attempt in Vienna? And what are the chances that I can get you to keep a low profile?"

I laughed. "Are you kidding me right now?"

"I'm saying you need to keep a low profile."

"And I'm telling you that's not possible. It's just not. I'm here to be the returned son... the return of the prince. It's what the media is saying. I do need to make appearances. Give me *one* of Ariel's Knights. And fine, I'll take Trevor, but you can't give me any more Royal Guards. Ariel, I'm sure, has a business to run, and I need to do my job."

"You're a prince."

"Maybe, but *that* is not my job. I was cast out of the palace, not by your doing, but still, the same result. So you can't hamstring me. You can't tie my hands behind my back and expect me to be able to function, to perform."

"I'm just trying to keep you alive."

"And I hear you, I do. I get it. But just assign me another Knight and my Guard, and I will be out of your way. As it is, Ella will have her own personal security. I can't technically hire them, but they're not going to let me die. So ban access to anyone you need to, but I'm not going to be a prisoner inside these walls. Not again. Not anymore."

Sebastian frowned at that. "You were never a prisoner here. This was your home."

"I know you didn't always see it, but living under this roof with my brother, I might as well have been in prison. I'm not going back to that. I plan on being free."

"Fine, I can live with that, but I also plan on you staying alive."

I sighed. "Fine, I hear you. I'll take extra precautions. I won't take any unnecessary risks."

That was a lie. In a few short weeks, I'd be taking one hell of a risk. But while I might not have any more of the cachet of being a prince, I did at least still have diplomatic status. And I had full intentions of using it to the extent of my ability.

"That's all I ask. In the meantime, we're interviewing the police in Barcelona. We'll get things rolling on this, and then I want the Royal Guard looking into it."

"What the hell? No. That's not necessary."

"Yes, it is. Someone is trying to kill my cousin. It's absolutely necessary."

Fuck. That is not what I wanted. Anyone looking will tie the attempt on my life back to Max. He was the only real, conceivable threat from Ella's past. If people were starting to watch him more closely, I wouldn't be able to execute the plan. And for her sake, I needed to execute this plan.

"Nothing is going to happen here."

"So, you prefer me to wait until something happens?"

"Well, maybe it was just a random hit-and-run driver in Barcelona."

"You want to believe that? Three times you've had near misses. In Vienna, you were shot at, and in Barcelona you were nearly run off the road *and* shot at, and you really want to believe those were just random coincidences?"

"There is still no evidence to suggest the first incident was targeting me. The second could have been targeting Ella, and Frank got caught in the crosshairs. It's entirely possible."

"And that nasty bit of business with that car trying to run you off the road. You still want to tell me someone isn't after you?"

He stared at me. I was wondering if he could tell that I was lying or if he could see the cracks in my armor. I certainly hoped not, because I needed that facade to hold.

"Someone might be after me, Sebastian. But I'm home now. You said it yourself; I'm safer here than anywhere else."

Now if only either of us believed that.

Tristan...

ALL IN ALL, it could have gone worse with Sebastian. At least he supported me being home. If he hadn't, I'd be dead in the water.

I took the hallway leading to the Rose Tower, my bearings

going on autopilot, my memory taking over. Belatedly, I realized some of the paintings had been swapped out along the familiar hallways. I recognized some of Penny's work from the bold colors and island landscape.

When this was all over, and I was finally free to go where I wanted and live how I wanted, maybe I'd buy one of her paintings for my place. I had to laugh at that. A real place of my own. Somewhere to belong with total freedom and no fear. I'd kill for that.

You just might have to.

And as close as my cousin and I were, he wasn't the only support I'd need. The Council's support would come later. For the moment, I'd settle for them not exiling me outright. They had no cause to, so I should be safe.

My gut twisted. Gilroy might become a problem, but I'd deal with that when it came up. But no doubt news would travel to Ashton that I was home, so I was working on borrowed time.

I rounded the corner, opting to take the garden path to my suite, when I nearly ran headlong into Lucas by the pool. He was just how I remembered him. Proud smile, tanned skin, glowing, he looked happy as he approached. "Tristan, man, what's up? Sebastian said you were back."

While most everyone on the island had an American or British accent, or slipped between a patois and the two, Lucas's accent always surprised me. He'd been raised in the States, so clearly it was American, but somehow it flowed easier.

He didn't sound much different from Sebastian, but there was something that said he'd grown up abroad in the States. When someone from the Winston Isles traveled, people always wondered if we were possibly Canadian, or maybe grew up on a military base somewhere.

I grinned back at him and accepted his easy hug. "Hey Lucas, what's up, mate?"

He clapped me on the shoulder then stepped back with a grin as he looked me over. "I kept hearing stories about you dying and shit. I'm glad to see you're in one piece."

I shrugged. "Well, it looks like the news has been greatly exaggerated. It would seem I'm indestructible."

"I can see that. It's good to have you home. I know you've been trying to come back for a while. Now maybe we'll actually get to spend some time together."

"Yeah, well, I finally got the deal, so here I am." I'd first met him when Penny and Sebastian got married. I'd been allowed home for the festivities, and I'd liked him immediately. I'd only seen him on his brief visits abroad after that.

He nodded slowly and casually glanced around. I realized then that it was his casual nature that made people dismiss him. Especially the elite on the Regents Council who were none too pleased about having my uncle's bastard children legitimized.

But underestimating Lucas would be a mistake. Because even though he was easygoing and generally playful, he was shrewd. Ever watchful. He paid close attention to every single person and conversation near him. He masked the shrewd calculation with easy charm, but he was whip sharp. And that was exactly why I needed his help.

"Well, I, for one, can't wait to get front row seats to your matches. I don't want the royal box and shit. That's boring. I want to be right on the pitch."

I laughed. "I think that can be arranged. Do you want to sit with the team?"

His eyes lit up as his brows rose. "Can I?"

"You realize you look like a kid now, right?"

"You don't understand. I grew up with soccer. We moved around a lot, and I lived in a lot of places where soccer was the only thing considered football, and basically the only sport. And my fucking cousin is an international soccer star. It's basically Christmas morning as far as I'm concerned."

"Star is hardly the word."

"You were number one in Barcelona for the last three years."

"Well, a lot has changed. Let's hope I can keep the same record for the Argonauts."

He waved a hand. "This is modesty nonsense. Be like me. You should accept how awesome you are."

I laughed. "Okay, fine. I'm bloody fantastic."

He grinned. "Nah, you've been spending too much time with Roone."

I grinned. "Why do you say that?"

"He's been trying to get me to use all his Britishisms. I'm just waiting for him to say 'dude' one day."

I shook my head. "You lot are hilarious. You're forgetting I went to Eton. British slang is ingrained."

Lucas inclined his head toward the pool and I followed him. When he took a seat on a lounger, I did the same.

I could almost feel his dark, penetrating gaze behind his sunglasses. "Okay, real deal? Sebastian wants me to keep an eye on you. Keep you out of trouble."

I grinned. "Of course, he does."

"He asked Roone to keep you from getting killed too. At least, you know, from basic poisoning and stabbing here on the palace grounds."

"Well, Roone is a Royal Guard and a Knight, so that makes sense."

"My question is why."

I tipped my head. "What do you mean why?"

"If the incidents in Barcelona were as isolated as you tried to make us believe, then no one would follow you here. I looked at the reports from the police in Barcelona, and they think that it's some kind of stalker Ella has. So, if it's a stalker of Ella's, you're not on manifests coming into the country. Private jet, black flight, nothing. Until your first day in the Argonauts, no one knows you're here. So why does my brother think you needed watching?"

I shrugged. "I have no idea. I don't think I should have any problem here."

LUCAS PULLED his shades down then and met my gaze with his. "I think it's a mistake to discount anyone on the Council wanting to do you harm. You need to watch your back here. Seriously."

"All right. I hear you. But no one on the Council wants me *dead*. I'm the second son of a forgotten king. I'm unimportant."

"You'd be amazed. I thought a den of thieves was bad. The Council can be... difficult, so trusting them is a bad idea. I guarantee there are those who supported the sons of Angelus who are still on the Council. And those who didn't will worry that if *you* supported the sons of Angelus and are getting close to Sebastian, you could be trouble. Especially now that you're home, so be careful."

"I hear you." I considered for a moment. "Maybe it's not the best idea I stay here?"

Lucas shook his head. "No one is dumb enough to try anything in the palace, but it's a good idea to be careful. Ariel's team, of course, can be trusted. And Trevor is solid. He was with us through the shit in London, so he's good. But anyone else... just keep your eyes open."

I watched him for a moment. He was dead serious. I don't think I had ever seen Lucas communicating so seriously before. "Actually, since we're discussing real shit, cousin, I wonder if I can ask you a favor."

"Anything. What do you need?"

"I want you to teach me to be you."

He blinked and slid his glasses back down his nose. "What?"

"Well, you *before* you became a prince. The prince part, I have, believe it or not."

Lucas's grin was quick, bright white teeth against bronze skin. "Yeah, I think you do. Besides, I am hardly a prince."

"I think you'd be surprised. You're probably one of the best princes we've ever had. But yeah, show me your ways. I know you were a con man. I know before all this, you were a thief. Not that I think you still are, but I'd like you to show me how you did it, if you don't mind."

He frowned. "I get the feeling this isn't something Sebastian would want to know about?"

I nodded. "Exactly. What your big brother doesn't know, is probably not going to hurt him."

He lifted a brow. "Should I ask why?"

I shrugged. "Mostly, I'm curious. Clearly Sebastian and Roone don't do this, but I think a lot of other people overlook you. And while they're overlooking you, you're taking a full assessment of them. You know what to say, how to make them feel, how to distract them. I want to learn that."

Lucas angled his head as he studied me. "But you already know that. You grew up with the lords of leisure your whole life. You know who's genuine and who's not."

I grinned. "Spoiler alert. None of them were genuine. But I'd like to learn how you do it in an unfamiliar situation."

"And there's no particular reason you want to learn this skill?"

"Maybe it's not in your best interest to know that. I also think learning some sleight of hand would be fucking fantastic."

Lucas laughed then. "Awesome, because I already stole your watch."

I frowned and glanced down. And sure enough, my Tag Hauer was off my wrist. "Shit. When did that happen?"

Lucas held it up. "I was going to put it back in your room later."

"Why? That was bloody fantastic."

"Well, it's sort of a habit. I like to keep the skill fresh. Never know when they'll all get wise to me and send me back. Gotta take care of my lady love somehow."

Did he really worry about that? "I'm sure you make an excellent thief, but maybe a better prince."

He shrugged. "The jury is still out. I know Sebastian would lose his shit if I did that to anyone else. I just like to make sure I *can* still do it. Don't want to go all soft."

"I want to learn that."

He leaned forward. "I think you're right. This is not something Sebastian needs to know about."

"So we have a deal?"

Lucas nodded. "Yeah, we have a deal. But whatever you *don't* need these skills for, whenever it's going down, I suggest you get back up. Because most people won't take too kindly to being manipulated."

"I promise you," I lied through my teeth, "I don't intend any practical application. I'm just curious."

His signature grin was back. "Great. So about how long is this curiosity going to take?"

I had to laugh. "About four weeks."

"In that case," Lucas stood and gave me back my watch, "we'd better get to work."

Tristan...

AFTER TRAINING WITH LUCAS, my hands felt numb. He had practiced for years with nimble fingers, years of making it work, forcing his fingers to work the right way. I, on the other hand, was clumsy as fuck.

You can't afford to be clumsy.

I had a month to get my act together, or my whole plan was toast. One month to figure out a sleight of hand so good it would make a magician jealous. But I could do it. I had to do it. Ella was counting on me.

Tired and weary, I followed the familiar path to the Rose Garden. The scent of roses, mixing with gardenias and hibiscus, smelled like home. In the distance I could hear the waves crashing on the shore below. I had always loved this garden. I'd almost always found Queen Alexa walking through it, working on something, thinking about something. I'd always been closer to her than my own mother.

I still hadn't seen her. Sebastian told me she was on some kind of diplomatic mission, so I wouldn't see her for another few days. Maybe that was best. She always knew when I was up to something. Hell, she always knew when *any* of us were up to something, so it really worked better for my plans if I didn't see her.

But I was home now. I refused to hide. When I opened one of the massive gold-embossed French doors, I stopped short. Ariel was striding down the hallway. That was Ariel. No nonsense. Fast clip. Direct.

I spoke without thinking. "Considering you never wanted to see me again, you spend a lot of time trying to see me."

She stopped short. "Jesus. I swore I got rid of you." And then she rolled her shoulders. "Sorry, was that rude? I didn't mean to be rude. It's just your face does that to me." She shook her head. "I had a meeting with Sebastian."

I worked my jaw. Fighting with her wasn't going to take away the gnawing, clawing hunger. "You don't have to explain it to me. I'm hard to forget."

She frowned at me, but I couldn't make heads or tails of her expression. Yeah, sure. I got it. She was unhappy with me for some reason, but I didn't know what the reason was this time. "All due respect, Your Highness, go fuck yourself."

I grinned. "In the palace? So dirty. I'm shocked you would suggest such a thing." I was being a twat, but fuck if I gave a damn. She was on my turf.

"I don't have time for this. I have a date."

Her aim was sure, and it hit me center mass. "With who?"

She narrowed her gaze at me. "I'm not sure that's any of your business."

"I'm not that interested anyway."

"God, you are such a prick. Stay away from me."

"Happy to. You're in my family's palace, remember?"

"While we're at it, keep your lips to yourself. Your fiancée doesn't deserve that. She's a pill, but she doesn't deserve it."

My gut twisted. "Don't worry, I'm not touching you again. Burned once."

Lies. My hand itched to touch her again. I wanted another damn fix. I wasn't sure why I couldn't get it right with her. There were questions I wanted to ask. Like how is your life? Are you okay? Why didn't you reply to my letters? But instead, every word that came out was wrong. I was antagonistic.

You want her.

I didn't want to fight with her.

Oh yeah, like you can be friends? When you still remember vividly exactly how she tastes?

"You know what, we don't even need to have this conversation. None of this matters. It's fine."

"Fuck. Why are you like this?"

Her green eyes flashed. "We don't have to do this anymore, okay? I have completed my mission. I kept you safe for the one week I was designated to guard you. Don't get dead on your own from now on, okay?"

I don't know what made me ask, but I did want to know. "Why did you come?"

Her eyes went wide. "Why did you call me that night?"

I cursed under my breath. "Would you believe me if I said I didn't know?" I opened my mouth. Shut it. Opened it again, trying to think fast, to make up some explanation.

Finally, something akin to the truth tumbled out. "I'd felt the heat of that bullet. It whizzed right by my goddamn ear. And when all was said and done, the one person I could think of to call was you."

It was her turn to do the gapey thing. Her mouth opened. Closed. Her eyes shimmered. "I don't even know what that means."

"Fuck. Neither do I."

"You barely said a word."

"There are a million words to say and a million not to. You were the only one I could think of to call. Every part of me was delusional and thought you would give a damn."

Her russet brows frowned and then lifted. "I don't understand—"

I shook my head. "You're not supposed to understand. I shouldn't have called."

"You know, at some point, you should probably explain all this to me. You called me, didn't say anything, and then you were pissed off that I showed up to save your ass. Then, you kissed me. Do you know what an invasion that was? You're fucking engaged. I'm done. Have a nice life, Your Royal Highness."

And then she marched out the door.

I reached for her automatically, but she was faster than I was. The girl I had known would never have slipped my grasp. But she wasn't that girl. She was a grown woman, and she'd had enough. Rightfully so. She wasn't *my Ariel* anymore. She was somebody entirely different, and I needed to remember that.

ELEVEN

ARIEL…

My hands weren't clammy.

As a matter of fact, I felt mostly nothing. No flood of adrenaline-fueled anticipation. No jitters. No nothing. And it wasn't because I'd wasted it all on the first date with Ian. It was because I was *pissed*.

The stupid prince and his stupid kiss. He'd dominated my thought space for more than enough time. I'd been almost scot-free today too. I wasn't supposed to see him. So what if I'd tapped into the palace feeds to make sure I didn't see him? And still, I'd run right into him. It was as if he had a homing beacon on me.

As I marched up the Spanish stairs of Faustino Restaurant, I tried to cool my temper. For the last two hours, I'd tried everything to get my mind on my future and not my irritating past. I'd had a quick run earlier, then a shower, but that hadn't helped. I'd made it a point to take extra time with my makeup and my hair, to try to get in the right frame of mind. I'd worn a gray sheath dress that dipped dangerously low that Penny had made me buy last year.

I looked pretty. I felt pretty. But my irritation hadn't worn off. God, what the hell was his problem? I just wanted to be left alone. I hadn't even wanted to go to stupid Barcelona, but Sebastian had called. So honor and duty and all that. And then I'd gotten the kiss of my life for all my efforts.

If I'd never gone, my life wouldn't be like this. I would be sitting in my office, minding my own business, happy to date Ian.

But oh no, now I was thinking about Tristan and what he could possibly be up to and why he was trying to torment me. Decidedly, *not* focusing on my date.

You'd better get it together.

Barring our previous date when I'd listened to stupid Roone, this was my first real date in over a year. One that wasn't a hookup scenario with someone who couldn't possibly be a viable option. Ian was a grown up. He had his own business just like me. And he was cute. Very cute. And he had a totally hot bod. Hello, former athlete.

A soccer player just like your ex.

No. I would not compare them because I didn't need to compare them. I was on a date with Ian. Tristan, I wanted to kill. So, best not to think about murder on my date because that is something I *would* think about. And that would ruin everything.

I walked up to the hostess and she gave me a broad smile. "Lady Scott, your date is waiting for you."

I blinked at her. "I beg your pardon?"

She merely grinned at me. "Bright red hair and no-nonsense march. Ian Tellman very clearly described you. He said you'd be walking through with bright, flaming-red hair just past your shoulders with a no-nonsense attitude and the greenest eyes he'd ever seen. He also said if I could coax a smile out of you, it would light up the room."

I nervously smiled at that. "Oh, I, um. Okay, I guess. That's fine."

She grinned. "He was right about the smile. Lucky girl. He is completely smitten." She wore a Marc Jacobs wrap around dress, somehow draped in all the right places, that made her tits look amazing. She also looked comfortable in her own skin.

I was double-sided taped into my dress, with the most uncomfortable corset bra I'd ever worn in my life holding everything in position. But somehow, I didn't look nearly as elegant as she did, and I was distinctly uncomfortable. I'd feel a hell of a lot better with all my weapons strapped to me, but I was pretty sure it was frowned upon to bring weapons on a date.

The inkling of self-doubt tried to flare into life, a little bud of a flower. I cut out the light and cut off its water supply. No. Ian had asked *me* out. He was the one who was lucky, so I was going to go on this date and I was going to enjoy myself and forget all about the person I didn't even want.

Tristan. His name is Tristan. His Royal Highness.

Otherwise known as fucktard.

As I approached the corner table by the window, Ian stood with a smile. The charcoal gray suit he wore was impeccable and complimented my heather grey dress. His smile was wide, and that suit hugged his shoulders in an absolutely tailored fit. He was handsome. Every woman in the restaurant turned to stare, whether it was to see who he was meeting or to watch the man himself I wasn't sure, but they were definitely looking. "Ian, this is beautiful. You didn't have to do all this."

He shook his head. "Of course, I did. When you want a beautiful woman, you need to impress her first."

"Thank you." Luckily that was the word that came out and not, 'Hey, you could basically impress me if you showed me your handgun skills.' Because what guy wants to hear that?

"Oh, I see you already ordered wine."

"Yes, a delightful Rosé."

I forced a smile on my lips and bit my tongue to not tell him I didn't like Rosé, or wine at all, really. Instead, I smiled and nodded my head. "Oh, thank you so much. That was so thoughtful."

You mean presumptuous.

I was out of practice. That was all. This was just me being out of practice. He was being sweet.

Or you're still thinking about Tristan.

Nope, out of practice.

"So sorry it has taken so long for us to get back together. Work just sort of spiraled."

"Of course, I mean you're a King's Knight after all. I can't expect you to be at my beck and call. Even though I'd very much like that."

I frowned. I hadn't told him I was a knight. "How did you even know? It's not like Sebastian had some kind of public announcement made."

His brows lifted. "Um, you didn't know?"

"Didn't know what?"

He chuckled softly. "You should probably ask your employer, but you're on the website. All of the Knights are named. There was a press release."

I groaned. "Christ. That would probably explain the rush of calls. Everyone was asking for appointments."

He grinned. "Well, everyone wants the best. And if Royal

Elite is good enough for the royal household, obviously it's good enough for Joe Smith."

I sighed. "I wish someone had given me a heads-up."

"Well, like you said, you've been working on assignment. So maybe you missed it."

"Yeah, but Penny— Uh, you know what, Penny probably didn't even know. Sometimes she has her head in the clouds if she's painting, so—" I made a mental note to kill her later.

"And by Penny, you mean the queen?"

I grinned. "Sorry, we've been friends since we were kids."

"Well, that's a good friend to have."

I shook my head. "I don't want to talk about the palace or my friends. Thank you for taking me out today. I'm glad we're getting to do this. Tell me more about you."

At least that much was true. He *was* interesting. He'd led a fantastic life. He had been an athlete all his life, playing first professionally for Manchester United, then being traded to Barcelona until he was injured so early in his career. Then came the surgeries and physical therapy, and he did try to go back to the game. First with Chelsea, and then Arsenal, but he had never been the same. Eventually, he'd been forced to retire. Not that I'd stalked him or anything. It was probably best not to mention I knew all that.

"I'm boring. But, Lady Ariel, you are endlessly fascinating. Last time we didn't really get to talk much before I was called away, so why don't you tell me why you're in—"

The hairs on the back of my neck stood up, just as I started talking. Ian's gaze flickered away from mine. From behind me I heard, "Ian? Is that you?"

I knew that voice. It had been grating on me for the last several days.

Liar.

Okay fine, it had been weaving into my dreams, taunting me, coaxing me, willing me to fall again, like an idiot.

My back stiffened. Ian's gaze flickered right back to me, and he smiled broadly. "Ariel, I'm sorry, we'll have to continue that part of the conversation in a moment. I'd like you to meet a friend of mine."

Ian stood, and with my stomach tying into knots, I turned. Sure enough, there was the bane of my existence, and Ella was with him. She wore vermillion red that skimmed her body like satiny milk and cut off right at her knees and made her look spectacular. Granted she was also five foot ten, so most things looked spectacular on her. She smiled wanly at me. "Oh, Ariel. Funny seeing you again."

"Oh yeah, funny," I muttered.

His Royal Highness, Prince Tristan, turned to me. "Ariel, you didn't mention your date was with my good friend Ian."

Good friend? Oh yes, Ian had just said that. But then I hadn't been really paying attention to what Ian said. Why hadn't he mentioned he knew the royal family though?

Because you just said you didn't want to talk about the royals.

I shook my head. "Ian, I didn't realize you were acquainted with the royal family."

"Of course, I am. Tristan here is an old mate. We trained together in the under-18s. A couple of years later, he replaced me."

Tristan winced at that. "That's not how it was exactly."

Ian waved a hand. "I know. I'm the one who jacked up my own knee. Come on, would you and Ella like to join us for a drink?"

My head snapped to Ian, and I scowled at him. "What? I'm sure His Royal Highness and Ella want to have a quiet romantic date. They've had an eventful couple of weeks."

Tristan met my gaze, mischief lighting up his eyes. I'd seen that look a million times, usually before he'd chase me and I'd let myself be caught. And then he'd kiss me deeply, and I would lose all train of thought and only think about his touch.

Steady on.

Tristan's voice was smoky when he said, "Actually, yeah. Why don't Ella and I join you for a drink?"

I gawked at him. "Excuse me?"

Ian smiled. "Yes, I'd love to catch up. Ariel and I will continue our date later."

This wasn't happening. Had Ian really invited Tristan on our date? Why would he do that?

Time to go.

But I couldn't go. I had to stick this charade out. I didn't want Tristan thinking he could make me run. Two fresh plate settings were brought to the table. While Ian asked Ella something, Tristan leaned closer and dropped his voice so only I could hear it. "Gosh, imagine running into you here."

"You knew."

He grinned. "Well, it's the best restaurant on the island. And well, you're the kind of woman who deserves the best. *And* I asked Penny."

I scowled at him. First, I was going to kill my best friend. Second, I was going to kill him. I just want to slaughter the whole family. Never mind that I'd been sworn to serve and protect them. "Why are you doing this?"

His gaze met mine. "Because I don't like the idea of you going on a date."

"Even with your old *mate*?"

"Especially with my old mate, or with anyone else."

"You should probably tell your fiancée that."

He frowned and snapped back to attention.

I deliberately turned my gaze to Ian, and then I did the thing. The thing where I leaned over, placed my hand on his knee, and slid it up his thigh. Oh yeah, I had his attention now. His gaze stayed on me the rest of the night. With every bump of Tristan's knee, Ian squeezed my hand and smiled, deliberately pulling me into every conversation. Before I knew it, drinks turned into dinner which turned into desert, and my date was thoroughly hijacked.

At one point during the desert course, Ella excused herself go to the bathroom. When she came back, she whispered something to Tristan. And then she gave us both that chilly smile. "I'm so sorry. I have to catch an early flight first thing. There has been an emergency I need to deal with."

It was on the tip of my tongue to ask her, 'What, a modeling emergency?' But I kept that to myself. I was the one in the wrong. I had kissed her fiancé. I didn't get to have any sort of feelings about her other than guilt. I was not the heroine of our triangle.

Tristan gave her a kiss on the cheek, and then she floated away with her gazelle-like gait. How did she do that? And then it was just Tristan, Ian and I at the table. I could have sworn Tristan deliberately knocked his knee into mine again, then brushed the back of his fingers along my thigh. The shock of contact sent a shiver up my spine, and I jerked, gritting my teeth.

"Well, isn't this cozy? Just the three of us." Ian laughed and turned to Tristan. "Just so you know, I'm the one taking her home."

Tristan laughed. "Oh, I'm not here to interfere."

Asshole.

But if I was being truthful, I wasn't too fond of Ian at the moment either. He'd invited those two on our date. All I'd wanted to do was move on, and he'd invited my past to have dinner with us.

Cut him some slack. He didn't know.

When the evening wound to a close, Ian walked me to my car, leaving Tristan inside with his Royal Guard, Trevor. He took my hand. "I'm sorry about that."

I shrugged. "No, it's fine." I wanted to pull my hand back, but then I figured it might be rude.

"Look, I'll make it up to you, okay? I just hadn't seen him in a while, and there he was just walking right up to us. I didn't think I could say no."

"I get it, but maybe this isn't a good idea."

He didn't let go of my hand. "No, wait. Come on." He tugged my hand, pulled me closer, and looped his hands loosely on my waist. "Look, I'm sorry, okay? One more chance? I think the third time's a charm. We can really make it work the third time."

I frowned. "I don't know, Ian. Maybe this is too much work. You seem cool and interesting, but—"

"If you want to run, make sure it's because you really don't want to get to know me better, not because you're afraid."

Busted.

I chewed my bottom lip. "I'm not afraid." Seriously, I needed to get better at lying.

"Please, I'm not taking no for an answer, because technically, this wasn't our second date. We were just some friends having dinner. So, second date. You already agreed to it."

A smile tugged at my lips. "Fast talker."

He shrugged. "I'm a sports agent. Of course, I'm a fast talker."

I just really wanted to say no, but the fact that it annoyed Tristan made it that much more appealing. "Fine, but honestly, maybe we just keep it low key."

"I can do low key. I just really want this to work. The night was stolen, and that was my fault. One more chance. Please."

"Yeah, okay," I nodded.

He leaned forward, and I couldn't explain the flare of panic as I thought he was going to kiss me. I held myself perfectly still, like an animal that knows it's about to be eaten, or the prey lying in wait.

But he diverted his head just in time to kiss me on the cheek. His gaze locked on mine when he whispered, "I'm going to earn that kiss."

I tilted my chin up. "You're welcome to try."

Tristan...

I'LL ADMIT, that was a twat move.

Penny had been oh so helpful in telling me exactly where Ariel was going to be, and I had moved quickly, changing our dinner plans to make sure that we were able to crash.

Ella hadn't been too pleased when we walked in and I pointed out Ariel and Ian. She'd given me that grim, deter-

mined, flat line of her lips that told me she was all the way
pissed off. But she'd gone along.

You are a dick.

I knew it. Still though, my normal sense of rationality was
completely gone when it came to Ariel and the possibility of her
dating. Let alone *who* she was dating. Ian Tellman. He was a
mate. We'd played together in the under-18s in the UK. He'd
come from a different background than I did for sure. He didn't
go to Eton or to any of those other fancy prep schools. He lived a
hardscrabble life. And the guy was pure talent. Then he'd been
injured.

And you took over his life.

It wasn't like it was my fault. It wasn't like I could control it.
I'd had no say. I'd gotten a call that I had an opportunity to play.
What was I supposed to do? Turn it down?

I'd taken his spot. I'd always felt a bit bad about it, but that's
the way these things went. Injuries were common. How was I to
know that Madrid would trade him?

After the trade, we'd talked a little. I had tried to apologize
because I didn't know what else to do. But last time we talked
about it, he'd said it was all right. He understood. Not like it was
my fault. Not like I'd deliberately gone out for his spot. And I
hadn't.

But I certainly hadn't said no to the position either. It wasn't
even my only way off the island. I could have gone back to
school at Eton. Carried on with the original plan with Ariel. But
eventually I would have had to go home. Taking that spot meant
I'd never have to go back. I'd never have to answer to anyone. I'd
never have to see my brother. My career became my ready
excuse.

And then, well, Ariel had never joined me. Everything back

on the island had gone to hell, and suddenly the feeling of not wanting to go home became a scenario where I *couldn't* go home. Not without express permission from my cousin. Or at his behest like for his wedding.

The last time I had been home, Lord Gilroy had told me in no uncertain terms that I wasn't welcome, and that he would personally see to it that I would never return. He blamed me for his daughter going missing.

I tried to explain to him that she was a friend of mine. I knew nothing. But still, a worried father was not to be ignored. And I had been worried about his daughter too. Amelia. We'd been friends and part of the same circles. Good friends actually. But never anything more.

She was the only other person who'd really known about my plans with Ariel, and she'd been supportive. Why her father thought I would have anything to do with her vanishing was beyond me. But Amelia had said it herself. She'd always wanted to go see the world, run away, strike out on her own. So I hadn't really thought anything about it at the time. But Gilroy had seemed convinced, *more* than convinced, that I'd had something to do with his daughter's disappearance. And given everything else on my plate, it was the least of my worries. But it did mean that I would eventually have to deal with him one way or the other. But currently he was the least of my problems. Luckily, Ashton hadn't made good on his promise to ruin me if I ever tried to come back. I'd still bought myself some time. He might not know that I was home. So priority number one was Max. Nothing else mattered until I had dealt with him.

"And what are you doing in your old spot?"

With Ella on a plane, there'd had been nothing, really, to stop me from revisiting old skeletons and memories and dreams.

I had peeled my shoes off at the start of the walk, socks too, and I reveled in the feeling of sand between my toes. God, it felt good to be home.

It was my first time actually putting my feet in the sand since stepping off the plane. It was also my first time back to that particular spot.

The spot had significant memories for me. Ariel and I had gone there all the time. It had been *our* spot. I made the quarter-mile trek down to the old bungalow. It had been kept up of course. It was still on the royal grounds. It looked exactly the same. Cheery on the outside. The doors had been replaced though. Probably due to weather during the last several hurricanes or so.

I heard her voice before I saw her, and it gave me pause. Maybe this had been a bad idea after all.

"Of course you would be down here."

I turned slowly and found her sitting on the flat rock we'd spent countless hours on watching the waves come in. "Well, I wanted to think. It sort of felt natural." When I looked closer, the moonlight glistened on her face, and there was something shimmery on her cheeks. Was that glitter?

No, you wanker, she's been crying.

White-hot pain lanced through me. "Fuck? Those because of me?"

"Fuck off, Tristan."

I approached her slowly. "How was the rest of your date?"

She gave me a harsh laugh. "You mean the one that you did everything you could to ruin?"

"Hey, I'm sorry about that. I just wanted to say hi."

"You knew I was going on a date. I had specifically told you I was going to be on a date."

"Yes, I know. I just hadn't seen Ian in a long time. I replaced him you know."

She sighed. "Yeah, I know."

I could see on her face that her shield was going back up, and I scrambled. "Okay, you know what, we both came down here for a reason. So maybe we just don't talk about anything in the past. You know, call a truce for a minute."

Wide, moss-green eyes blinked up at me, and she gave me a curt nod. I indicated the seat next to her. "Do you mind?"

She looked like she might refuse me for a moment but then shook her head. "It's your beach, right?"

"Actually, it's my cousin's beach."

"Yeah, well, if your father had never abdicated it would be yours wouldn't it?"

"You know, I've never really given it any thought. I led exactly the life I was supposed to lead. Sebastian doesn't get to be a world-famous photographer. I wouldn't have been able to be a soccer player. Better he made that sacrifice than I."

I could tell she wanted to say something. Ask something, but she watched the water. "Why did you come down here?"

That was a damn good question. After spending dinner with her, I had been eager to recapture something of the person I'd been. But, I'd also needed clarity on the person I was going to become in just a couple of weeks. I needed calm. And this was the place I used to get it. "I'm just thinking through some things. You know the whole reason I came back. So I guess it was habit."

She nodded slowly. "Yeah I guess so."

I didn't dare look at her. I might be tempted to hold her, comfort her, and ask her why she was crying. "What about you? What are you doing down here in our old place?"

"I don't know, I guess habit and letting some things go."

That burned but I didn't say so. She was allowed to be honest. I also wanted her to let me go. If she didn't want to let me go, then she'd be paying a whole hell of a lot of attention to what I was up to. And I couldn't have that. "You like Ian? He's a solid guy."

"Yeah. He's completely solid," she clipped back.

I chuckled low. "That sounds like a glowing endorsement."

"Oh, what right do you—"

I held up my hands. "Sorry, I was being facetious. I didn't mean anything by it."

She winced. "Sorry. I guess even in truce we can't help but have a fight."

"I really wish it wasn't that way."

She opened her mouth to say something, and then closed it again. "Yeah, me too." We sat there in companionable silence for ages. Finally, I turned to her. "Your company, where is it located?"

She pointed in the opposite direction from where I'd come. "See that glass building over there on the rocks?"

I nodded.

"Yeah, that's me. I took the path down. It's about a half mile down here."

I frowned. "You walked by yourself?"

She raised a delicate russet brow. "You recognize that I carry a gun, right?"

I chuckled low. "Yeah. Sorry. I went into full protector mode, and it turns out you don't need anyone to protect you, do you?"

She met my gaze then. The tears were gone from her eyes, and suddenly I was faced with the girl I once knew. "No. Not anymore."

I nodded. "Good. I'm glad. Despite everything, I like that."

She inhaled deep. "Is it everything you wanted?"

I frowned, getting her meaning and then trying to think through my answer. "I think so. I think it will be. Maybe not right away. But I needed to be home."

"I remember when you would have done anything to be here. And then anything to *not* have to be here."

"Yes, well the whole reason for leaving is no longer a reason, and the moment it was no longer a reason, all I wanted to do was come home."

"Well," she gave me a small smile, "for what's it worth, I'm glad you were able to come home. It's a terrible thing to not be able to, to think that you can't."

I nodded slowly. "I was really sorry to hear about your dad."

She shook her head. "Let's just file that one under past things we're not going to talk about." She checked her watch and then stood. "I have to get back. It was nice having this momentary truce, Your Highness."

"Can you do me a favor and, just once, use my name?"

Why the hell was my voice deeper? The intimacy wrapped around us as the waves lapped onto the beach and the ocean called to us. I could almost hear Sebastian the crab and his little chorus of underwater creatures singing "Kiss the Girl."

Her lips parted and trembled slightly. "Tristan."

I couldn't explain the warmth that jettisoned through me. Like all of a sudden someone had turned on a bonfire in the stark cold of winter. But hearing her say my name was like the balm that I needed to push me forward and keep me going. "Good night, Ariel."

"Good night. You realize that the truce is over now?"

I nodded. "I'd expect nothing less."

"And your Guard?"

I chuckled softly. "I was wondering when you were going to ask about that." I waved my hand. And the Guard they'd given me for the night, the sharpshooter, what was his name? Jonathan? He turned on his laser and it pointed directly at her heart. She looked down and chuckled. "Well, at least he can shoot."

And then, about twenty feet away, around the corner and just down the stairs from the palace, was one of her knights. Trace waved and called out, "Hey, boss lady."

She grinned and waved. "Hey, Trace." She nodded at me. "Good, at least you're following protocol."

"Yes. There's a redhead with a short temper I don't want to piss off."

"Yeah, best you don't do that."

Then she turned and was gone, and my heart went with her.

TWELVE

TRISTAN...

THIS WAS HOME.

The rapid clamor of footsteps behind me. The sticky, muggy air clinging tight to my skin. The salt in the air. The breath heaving in and out of my lungs, causing them to constrict and contract. The sweat pouring down my face. The tussle of bodies, grappling, fighting, trying to get the upper leg, the tripping, the shoving, holding my own. I was as close to euphoria as I had ever felt. Christ, it was good to be home.

During the contract negotiations of the last month and then the attempt on my life, I hadn't practiced properly in a while. Just basic conditioning. One thing was apparent; I was out of practice. My muscles felt lethargic, stiff. But hopefully, in a week or so as I got used to moving them in the right way again, I'd start to feel like myself.

The whistle blew, and Coach called us all in. I felt a couple of claps on my back. Billford, a guy I'd played with before in Madrid years ago, grinned at me. "You're a little rusty, Your Highness."

I rolled my eyes. "Shove it, mate." I'd already instructed them that none of them were to call me 'Your Highness,' which would honestly only apply to five men on the team and the coach, since they were the only subjects of the monarchy. Everyone else was an import. But sure enough, that little announcement had made *all* the guys start referring to me as HRH to give me shit.

He chuckled. "Whatever you say, *Your Royal Highness.*"

"Wanker."

He chuckled as he ran ahead of me. "You're still rusty though."

"Yeah, I know it."

The coach had us gather around as he gave instructions on what he wanted to fix. When his gaze turned to me, he lifted his brows. "You're kind of slow today, aren't you?"

I used my shirt to wipe my face even as the kids who were acting as towel boys ran over to us with fresh towels. "Yeah. I'll get used to it."

"Billford, listen, you're supposed to give the ball *to* Tristan. I don't know what you're doing out there with all the show boating, but it wasn't working."

Billford just smiled. "Well, I wanted to make him work. Let's see what he's made of. The guy I knew would have knocked me to the ground and taken it."

The coach was not having that though. "Wait, do you double duty as a coach for the Argonauts? Do you? I had no idea. Please tell me, what salary did they pay you to be in charge of me?"

Billford stuttered. We all knew Coach Simmons wasn't screwing around. He put up with no shit from anyone. As a brand-new coach two years ago, he had taken the team all the way to a third-place finish in the World Cup. And in all honesty, they'd had no business at the World Cup. The team had been young and cobbled together, but still, he managed to lead them to pulling off a miracle. So as the team grew now, we could probably do anything.

He pulled me aside as I grabbed a towel and wiped my face again while I waited for him to give me the verbal ass kicking I was expecting. Bottles of water were passed around. I grabbed the one with my name and sprayed it on my hair and my face. Just as I was about to take a drink, Coach leveled his gaze on me. "You're rusty."

I sighed. "I know. I'll get it together."

"See that you do. Are you distracted by all the royal nonsense?"

I frowned. *A little.* "No. I'm ready to play. I just want to get to work."

"Good. Because I think you're good for this team. A son of Winston Isles come to carry his boys into glory."

"Well, I don't know about glory, but we're certainly going to have a blast getting there."

He clapped me on the back, and before I knew what happened, Billford sent the ball directly for me. He thought I was going to miss it. He thought I hadn't anticipated it. But while my legs might not be moving as quickly as I was used to, my brain still functioned. Plus, I'd been working with Lucas to hone other skills.

I headed it back in, and my teammates cheered. "Are we done with this little pep talk?"

He nodded. "Seriously, pick up your feet. I want you

working on drills tonight and tomorrow morning. Footwork. Just to get the lead out. I also want you to see a masseuse. You look stiff."

I nodded. "I am. Constant travel. I'll get it together."

"Good. Now, go lead them. They are your team. They will follow you."

I didn't want to lead anyone. What right did I have to that? But I nodded. "Yeah, I'm working on it."

I ran back in. After a few practices, I should be tighter than hell. And I was pretty sure my hamstrings were going to be burning later, but I started to loosen up. I just felt better. When I managed to wrestle the ball away from my teammates, I worked on the fancy footwork on my arch behind my foot, the dance of my feet around each other, *tap, tap, tap, tip, tap, tip. Pant. Pant.* It was almost as if I felt like myself again. And out here, no one cared what I'd done or what had been done to me. No one cared who I was. They just wanted to play.

For the remainder of the practice, the guys stopped coddling me. They started to make me work for the ball. Started to push me, test me. Cornering me, coming for me, tested my mettle. But God, I felt fucking fantastic. Especially when I was able to easily outmaneuver someone. At one point, I put Billford on his back.

He just grinned at me. "Look who started to play."

"On your feet, you wanker."

He jumped up easily and chased after me. Yeah, it was good to be home.

After practice, Coach had a few more words for us, and we all grabbed our water bottles. I headed back for the locker room. Trevor watched me from the stands. The moment I was moving though, he was down the stairs in a flash.

I took a sip of my water and swallowed it, the cool nectar icing me from the inside, cooling off the steaming heat inside my body. I sucked down some more and relaxed. Everyone else had their sports drinks, but I preferred water right away. Once I got inside, I'd change out for whatever sports drink had been packed for me.

I'd managed it though. One full practice and I hadn't died, despite what my lungs thought at first. We were only a couple of feet into the tunnel when I heard the commotion.

"Billford. Fuck. Billford."

Several of the guys ran past me. It felt like slow motion. I couldn't move my body around quickly enough. And when I did, everything sped up too much, too fast. Billford was on the ground, seizing.

Trevor was on me, hand on my collar, shoving me to the side and trying to push me toward the door, but I held my ground. The team medics rushed past us down the tunnel. I heard the sound of the ambulance rolling up. Someone had already called them.

Then I saw my friend on the ground. I knew it wasn't the safest course of action, but I shook Trevor off and rushed to his side with my teammates. I kneeled beside them with no clue what to do or how to stop it. "Jesus Christ, Billford."

In all the commotion, we rolled him to his side and tried to brace his head, trying to keep his limbs from seizing too much. The trained nurse shoved us off, and we all backed up, gritting our teeth while hoping and praying our teammate would be okay.

Things were happening simultaneously too fast and too slow as we were forced to watch in this awful limbo, completely helpless to do anything to help.

It was after the paramedics had him loaded onto the gurney with some kind of IV running into his system that I saw his towel and water on the ground where he'd fallen.

Then I noticed it. His water bottle said *HRH* on it. I glanced down at the one in my hand and saw it said, *Big Money*. I had grabbed his by mistake. Billford had the same habit that I did; water first, sports drink later. We'd learned that in our early days.

Shit. Bugger. Fuck.

Trevor ran to me. "Your highness, the medics have him now. We need to get you out of the open."

"At least grab the water bottle."

He frowned at me. "You have your bottle."

I growled at him. "Yeah, but I'm pretty sure *that* one, which was supposed to be mine, was poisoned. We'll want to have it tested."

The delusion I'd been under shattered. No one had been after Ella in Barcelona. It was me. I'd been the target all along.

ARIEL...

As I addressed my team, I shifted my weight around, still smarting from my conversation with the prince the night before. He was such an asshole. But I couldn't even dwell on it properly because I had to work. "Okay, so these are the potential client files. We've got three newbies looking for event bodyguards. And then two long-term job prospects looking for security team build-outs and then handing off their operation."

"So, my top pic is probably the billionaire, Logan Right, with the last name, get this, Royal," Tamsin said as she laughed.

I chuckled too. I couldn't help it. Come on, who had that name?

Zia snorted. "Oh great, one of those assholes who changes his name to give the world the impression that he is somehow important?"

"Right?" God, I'd missed my team. It was good to be back in the swing of it. Not that Jax hadn't managed just fine in my absence. With me being in and out, he'd been my right-hand guy. And to think, when we first met not so long ago, he thought I was annoying. *Shocking*.

Jax shrugged. "Honestly, I think we only take one long-term job at a time. The team isn't big enough yet, and anything could come up at any time. It's obviously up to you, but I think we'll be stretched."

Jameson was quieter. She was the analytical one. Focused on the numbers. She didn't like stepping out of bounds. "Actually, I have to agree with Jax. The numbers don't make sense. Not for now, especially since you may or may not be done with the royal family."

"Oh, I'm done. The assignment is over. I'm back in the pool. But that said, the king does want us to train additional knights and manage them. I'm as yet unsure if they'd be prospective hires as well. I need to look at our budget. It would nice to have another tech expert on hand."

Trace moaned. "No offence, but we don't need another geek. Another weapons expert would be ideal."

"Okay, I hear you. I'll see what Sebastian has planned. Obviously, any new hires will be knighted. I just don't think that works vice versa."

Jax shook his head. "Even if you're back in the pool and the king doesn't need you all the time, you need to keep running this place. I don't need to be running it. I need to be in the field, so new hires make sense. Not to mention the slew of calls we received after the announcement was made about us being knighted."

He had a point there. "Okay, fair enough. Let me examine the applicant pools again. Trace and Jax, I might need you guys to vet them. We might be able to do a trainee program if they show potential as a way to try them before we've got them in the field—"

There was a knock at the door, and the hairs at the back of my neck stood at attention. Before I even checked the monitors, I knew. We all knew just by looking outside the glass wall. There were two SUVs and two hulking men in plain clothes doing their very best to look natural as they walked dogs along the street. I sighed. "Fuck."

Trace chuckled. "What was that you were saying about being done working for the royal family?"

I slid him a gaze. "Shut up."

"Don't be mad. It seems like they can't live without you."

"Well, you guys can't live without me either."

Trace shrugged. "You are kind of annoying and really bossy. You're like an irksome big sister."

I rolled my eyes. "One that happens to write your checks."

Jax guffawed. "Oh, burn."

But Trace was poking me all in good fun. We had all become a family. These guys were my team. I had recruited each of them on recommendations from my friends in the palace that they were solid. We hadn't worked together long, but these were the people I trusted... literally with my life, should it come down to it.

In the past, I'd only ever trusted someone in the Royal Guard like that, so to be able to trust these guys was everything.

I sauntered over to the door and called behind me. "Jax, keep running the meeting and put the two long-term jobs on the back burner, then take care of the smaller ones. Give me a minute."

When I pulled open the door, the king stood on the other side with a sheepish smile. "Should I have sent Penny instead? Would you be more likely to help her?"

I sighed and stepped aside to let him in. "You know, you could actually use the phone. Would that kill you? Give me some warning. You have a habit of showing up unannounced."

"Yes, but I also made your team into gentry, so doesn't that count for something?"

I rolled my eyes. "You didn't even ask them if they wanted to be King's Knights. I think they all hate it."

From inside, Jameson and Trace shouted back. "No, we don't."

I sighed. "Traitors."

Sebastian grinned. "Can we talk privately?"

I studied his face. I knew exactly why Penny had fallen in love with him. Yes, of course, he was handsome in the kind of way that made little girls dream of princes. His stupid jawline and a literal panty-melting smile were irresistible. But there was also something earnest in his gaze. At the core of it, Sebastian truly cared about his people, and he had the heart of an artist.

It had been a while since I'd seen him with his camera, but I remembered the way he'd loved it. He'd even given me a couple of photos for the office, and he had been determined that I not lose my position at the palace, no matter what my father had done. He might be King of the Winston Isles, but he was also my friend, and he was about to ask me for a huge favor. One I might not want to give him. "If you need us, you might as well talk to the whole team."

He gave me a brisk nod, and I showed him in. Everyone paused and turned their attention to him.

Once we were in the big conference area that doubled as our dining table for monthly team dinners, I leaned back against the banquet, my nerves feeling every current of electricity acutely. Something bad had happened. I could feel it.

When he spoke, his voice was grave. "There was an attempt made on Tristan's life this afternoon at practice."

The floor of my stomach fell, and dizziness swirled around me. Was he okay? Was he hurt? I'd been so cavalier about his safety. Well, he'd been cavalier. I'd just been anxious to get back to my team. And God, I'd been desperate to get away from him. Was I to blame?

Sebastian was still speaking, and I forced my attention to him. "At practice today, one of Prince Tristan's teammates was poisoned. He's at Royal Crest Hospital in critical condition, but he will pull through."

I shook my head. "You said the attempt was directed at Tristan. I don't understand."

He sighed. "After practice when they were grabbing water bottles, Tristan grabbed his teammate's bottle by mistake. Billford drank out of Tristan's bottle."

My heart squeezed. "Shit."

It sounded like I had an echo as Jax and Tamsin swore under their breaths. Zia's brows knit together, and Trace scrubbed his hands down his face. Jameson's jaw worked, but she was cool, analyzing. Her gaze was on me.

I turned to Sebastian then. "Where is the prince?"

"He's back at the palace. He wanted to move off palace grounds, but I think in light of this problem, it's probably not the best idea."

"I agree. And the Council still won't give him any additional guards?"

"I have called an emergency meeting. I will see what I can do to get him more coverage. In the meantime, I need my Knights."

I nodded briskly. "Of course." Then I turned to my team. "Put those long-term projects on the back burner. Jax, level out the short-term requests and get them done. We will work out an assessment profile."

The team nodded, and they all immediately made themselves scarce to the kitchen.

Sebastian watched me carefully. "Look, I know when I made you a Knight, you had just started Royal Elite and you need your team, and you need to run a business."

"It's fine, Sebastian. We've been talking about this. A way to train more knights. To bring more into the fold and how best to do that. I didn't anticipate this, but it pushes us in the right direction."

"It was more about giving you the status you deserved at first, but now, I actually need your help."

I didn't want this. Didn't want to be tied to Tristan. But I wasn't going to stand by and let him die either. There was that rebellious part of me that didn't want to help, that didn't want to be pulled in or have to deal with this. But the dutiful part of me squashed that. Sebastian was my king, and he was asking me to protect one of his princes, so I would. "We're at your service, Your Majesty."

"Thank you."

I cleared my throat before any embarrassing emotional display could escape. "What do we know? Who the fuck is trying to hurt him? The profile in Barcelona pointed at a stalker of Ella's."

Sebastian pursed his lips. "Clearly, that profile was wrong. But I have a couple of guesses."

I could guess where he was going. "You really think it's someone from the Council? They have nothing to gain."

"Since Tristan is back, I could attempt to put him on the other vacated seat. Roone is a sure one, preliminary numbers show he has the votes. But there's another seat vacant. I could put Tristan in there. And then, just like that, I'll have the majority with or without my extra votes. I imagine there is more than one Council member that doesn't want to see that happen."

I whistled low. "Christ. Just what we need. More royal intrigue."

"Yeah, it's fucking brilliant. So I need a team I can trust. One that doesn't have their own agenda."

"I still have no idea why anyone would ever want to become a prince."

"That's only because you see the bullshit. Most people only see the fantasy."

"All right, try and keep the prince out of sight, at least until I can get a plan formulated."

Sebastian gave me a lopsided smile. "How easy do you think that's going to be? He's already at the hospital with his team."

I cursed under my breath. "Fucking fantastic. I'll pull the team together. We'll meet him there."

Sebastian nodded. "Thank you, Ariel. I want you to know

that you're family to me, and I appreciate you stepping up for mine."

I did the only thing I could; I bowed low. He was my king, and I was going to have to swallow my personal feelings to put this right.

THIRTEEN

ARIEL...

ONCE SEBASTIAN WAS GONE, WE WASTED NO TIME. TEAM assignments were shuffled around, and it was all hands on deck.

I had wanted to believe Tristan and the Barcelona police when they suggested that the previous attempts were isolated incidents and not that someone was actually trying to kill *him*. I'd wanted to believe that because it would have been the simpler assumption. Occam's Razor.

It was easier and more convenient to believe it was a stalker of Ella's; that it was a crazed fan in Barcelona; or that a jealous fan of Ella's had run him off the road. But none of those things were the truth. We might well have another royal conspiracy on our hands. Jameson, Tamsin, and Jax would handle the current jobs we had going, which left me, Trace, and Zia to cover Tristan on a daily basis. If there were larger events that Tristan needed to attend, I'd pull in more of the team for those.

I was tense. I needed to calm down. The prince was fine. Whatever was going on, so far, he'd survived. And he would live to tell the tale. No thanks to me.

Right. So, why is your heart beating too fast and your skin clammy?

I tried to tell myself I didn't care and that whatever happened to him was none of my business. Total bullshit.

This situation was my fault. I hadn't used my bullshit meter with the police back in Barcelona. Interpol had been chasing down leads of potential stalkers, but nothing had led anywhere so far. I'd been so eager to leave his presence that I'd put his life at risk.

I'd failed him. Just like I'd almost failed Sebastian and Penny because I couldn't see what my father was up to for so long. But what I felt wasn't just because I'd failed to do my job. It wasn't just because this had happened on my watch. No, it was for another reason entirely. I was scared for him.

The anger coursing through me that had been my constant companion for ten years only masked my real emotions. I still cared about him. That part of me that couldn't let go was horrified and sick with worry. That part that still loved him wanted to kick my own ass. He'd almost been killed because I hadn't been doing my best job.

God, I was sick.

That was the only explanation. After all these years, I was insane and had lost my marbles. I was still pining after someone I could not have who had already shown me that he would not choose me.

Now, when I had the chance for a real relationship, I was hedging on that one. Still pining. And now, I was racing into the fire to protect him like a crazy person.

It took me several moments to realize that Trace was talking to me.

"Boss?"

I shook my head. "Yeah?"

He frowned at me quizzically. "Did you hear me?"

Shit. "Sorry, what did you say?"

"King Sebastian said that he wanted one of us to check with the investigators. Do you want me to do that?"

I wasn't sure which would be better. But honestly, I wanted to see Tristan for myself just to confirm that he was okay.

"Yeah. Um, you talk to the investigators, and I'll go with Zia to the palace. We'll need to work out protocol with Trevor. I want no less than three people on him at all times."

Trace nodded his understanding as we maneuvered the streets up to the palace. Our offices were close, just down the hill. But to actually get up to the palace, we had to take the most secure route. Trace dropped us off and then headed back out again. We arranged for a time to meet back up, and then Zia and I headed into the palace.

Next to me, Zia glanced around, and I realized she'd never been here before.

"I know, it's kind of daunting, right?"

"I've only been where the Guard goes. When we were all knighted, we met the Guards because we'd be working with them, but I've never been *in* the palace proper where the residences are. And ballrooms, and wow."

I couldn't help but smile. Since I'd become a Guard and started working more closely with the royal family, I suppose I'd just gotten used to it. But that was sad. I should never get used to it. All around us was marble and polished gold. Priceless artifacts and paintings that could make the soul cry.

In the Rose Tower alone, there was a Rembrandt and a Picasso. I knew that Penny and Sebastian's private quarters had a Pollock on display. I didn't even think about it anymore, which probably meant I should take some time to smell the roses, be-cause I was getting far too used to the opulence. When I finally headed down the corridor to the king's office, Zia hesitated. "Maybe I should... I don't know, wait in the garden or something?"

I grabbed her arm and tugged her along behind me. "You're being ridiculous."

"Okay, I've met him several times, and he's lovely. I mean, so nice and stupidly good looking, like stupid hot. How does your friend even deal?"

"You've met Penny. She knows he's hot, but she didn't even see that."

"How do you not see that when that's the guy who wakes up next to you? Like you're either counting your lucky stars and squealing every day like, 'Jesus Christ, you're my husband' you know, or eyeballing every woman who comes in his vicinity."

It was good to laugh about something. "I mean, Penny is no slouch."

Zia's eyes went wide. "No, she's gorgeous. And really sweet."

"Yeah, well, you don't want to see her mad. She's kinda badass with a gun. Honestly, I think that's the appeal."

"So, she really was undercover to protect him?"

"In a nutshell, we had posted up right next door, well, across the hall actually, and he was none the wiser."

"You recognize that you guys are basically legends, right?"

I shrugged. "You know, it's been so long, so many gunshots and firefights ago, that it's all a blur. You get used to it."

"How do you get used to something like that?"

"I haven't really had any downtime to think it through. I'm sure if I do, I will freak the hell out. But until then, onward. We have work to do."

Outside Sebastian's office, Zia squared her shoulders. She had been recommended by Ethan, so she was sort of familiar with this. But she'd been military, not Royal Guard, so there was an extra level that she would have to get used to. I hoped she was a quick study. I knocked on the door, and Sebastian called us in. And what do you know, the gang was all there.

Ethan, Lucas, Tristan, whose gaze I avoided, Roone, and Penny. "Aww, the gang is all here. You guys know Zia. Most of you have met her. If you haven't, make friends."

I turned my gaze to Ethan automatically. He'd been my boss and father figure for so long. "Where are we?"

He gave me a warm smile, the kind a father gives a daughter when he's proud of her, and he continued talking. "Now that you're here, we'll get everyone all caught up. Yesterday, at some point during the practice, Prince Tristan's water bottle was laced with Ricin. We don't know who did it. Cameras show a lot of people in and out of the team areas with plenty of opportunity for access. Ariel, since you have the tech chops, if you have a better way to sift through the data, I'd love to hear it. Luckily, there are only a few access points, so it should be fairly easy to narrow down. We have investigators on the scene, and there are some at the hospital just in case Billford *was* the intended target.

Tristan shook his head. When he spoke, his voice was gravelly. My heart pinched, but I resolutely did not look at him. "No. The son of a bitch was just unlucky. Hell, I was damn lucky I didn't actually drink out of that water bottle. I used it to spray my face. I could have been the one in the hospital. But I didn't even think about any of that until later. There was a water fountain right next to the pitch. I just drank out of that. I didn't even bother coming in."

"When did you spray it on your face?" I asked.

Tristan's gaze drifted to me and then away. "I don't know exactly. Coach called us in. He talked to us and gave us pointers, and he yelled at me for being slow."

Lucas snickered. "He ain't the only one."

Tristan continued. "I think I sprayed my face then to wash the salt out of my eyes. I remember the water boy. He was just a kid, probably not even sixteen. We take local kids as part of the youth program to come and watch practice and stuff. They help us out by working there, I guess."

I nodded. "Zia, see if we can get a full roster. See if anyone's parents are under financial hardship."

Ethan nodded at me. "Okay, you get that roster and you can do your hacker thing."

I grinned. "My hacker thing, Ethan?"

Ethan then purposely bent himself at the waist, acting like he was leaning on a cane, and said, "Well, you know, whatever you young kids do with the computer fizzle. I don't know."

I rolled my eyes. "Yeah, you act like you have no idea what you're doing, but you're not half bad."

He shrugged. "Yes, but you're the expert, so you can dig into backgrounds a lot faster than any of us."

I slid my gaze to Sebastian. "Um, do we want this done *legally*, or you know, *back access*?"

Sebastian lifted his brow. "What do you think?"

I risked a glance to my best friend, whose gaze was ping-ponging between me and Tristan. When she met my gaze, she gave me a wide beaming smile. "We always want you to use back access. There's no point in asking *you* if that's not what we want."

I shrugged. "Good point."

Tristan frowned. "What are we talking about? What's back access?"

Lucas laughed. "No one told you? Ariel is pretty much a white-hat hacker."

"I'm not a *hacker*. I just happen to know *how* to hack. So occasionally I have a peek under people's boots and things, you know, without their permission."

Roone's voice was low and amused. "And exactly how is that not hacking?"

Penny was quick to jump to my defense. "That's not hacking. That is investigative research."

Ethan calmed us all down quickly. "Anyway, Zia, get that list for Ariel. Ariel, do your thing. Your Royal Highness, in the meantime, you're not to go anywhere without Trevor and two of the King's Knights."

His brows lifted, and his gaze pinned on me. "Two Knights?"

I nodded but deliberately didn't meet his eyes. "Yes, a three-person team should be able to cover you properly. For the rest of today, Zia and I will handle it, but the rest of my team will rotate in and out. Obviously, you have Trevor. Ethan, is there any way we can spare another Guard? Trevor will need to be off rotation at some point. Unless the prince and he can work out a way where he actually gets a break, he will need some days off."

Roone pushed away from the bookshelf. "When Trevor needs a day off, I'll step in. Then the Council can't balk."

Sebastian was shaking his head, but Roone held up a hand. "I know you need me on the Council, and I'll make sure to do that. I'll work out with Trevor when those dates are, but we should have coverage."

Penny hopped up off the desk. "And don't forget, I make a darn good Royal Guard too."

Sebastian, Ethan, and Roone all answered at the same time. "No."

She grumbled and frowned. "I swear to God."

I shrugged and gave her a smile. "What? Seriously, you want to stay in front of the target of an assassin?"

"I'm a Guard, goddamn it," she mumbled.

I decided to appeal to her rational sense of spirit. "You are also extremely conspicuous."

She pursed her lips and then muttered. "Fair point."

Tristan shook his head. "Right. Okay, I guess I'll just have to get used to you guys talking about me like I'm not here."

Sebastian tried to ease his cousin's worries. "Sorry, we're just used to jumping in and dealing with the problem."

"Right, but is a full team of three absolutely necessary?"

I stared at him. "So, you mean someone is *not* trying to kill you? Someone *didn't* just poison your teammate?" I glowered at him, and he glowered back. The tension between us was thick enough to skewer with a katana.

Or maybe it was just me who was feeling it, because Ethan started talking, handing out assignments, and making plans. When everyone was excused, Penny gave my arm a squeeze and told me she'd call me later. Then she led Zia down to where our palace headquarters would be.

I stayed back to speak to Sebastian, but he gave me a shrug. "Sorry, I have another meeting. Can we catch up later? I know we need to review those resumes and narrow down the candidates."

"Ugh, fine. But with the additional load, it's becoming urgent."

He nodded. "Yeah, I know. Remember, we have the Royal

Arts Gala at the end of the week too. With Tristan being home, he's expected to attend."

Shit. I'd forgotten all about it. "Fuck me. I'll rearrange and make sure the whole team is here. Which also makes more team members pertinent."

"I don't anticipate any problems in the palace, but obviously, it's concerning."

"Yup. Understood." Sebastian excused himself and I thought I was alone. But when I turned, Tristan was there, looking all kinds of pissed off.

"What's the problem now?"

"What is my problem? Why do you have to be the one riding in on a fucking white horse?"

I gave him a harsh chuckle. "Oh my God, I am *literally* a Knight. So, if anyone should ride in on a white horse, it's me."

"You know what I mean. If someone is trying to kill me, then the last place you should be is in the crossfire."

"I'm sorry you think I'm the little woman you need to protect. But I'm not Penny, I'm not married to the King, and I don't need a forty-person guard. No one knows me. And I promise you, I'm pretty deadly."

"Are you insane? I've only been back a few days, and already, everyone is telling me all the legends of Ariel Scott. You and Penny are iconic in the Guard. And you and Roone, Jesus. When did you become this person?"

"I have always been this person."

He shook his head. "No, you're completely different. The girl I knew was unsure and wanted to leave here. She didn't want any part of this. But you... you are someone different."

"Well, I'll tell you what I am. I'm a survivor. I managed to make a home and carved one out of stone for myself."

He softened his gaze. "Are the other rumors true?"

"I don't know what rumors you're talking about."

"The ones about why you left the guard?"

I swallowed hard, my throat drier than the desert sands of the Mohave. "I don't see how that's relevant."

"Well, it's relevant because maybe you're already a target. I don't want anyone coming after me *and* coming after you."

"Look, I'm doubtful that this is royal conspiracy. Besides, people who are coming after me are completely different people than those who would be coming after you. We dismantled the Sons of Angelus faction. There might still be some sympathizers on the Council, but we're going to clean house. If Sebastian gets his way, he'll have the full majority vote, and he won't need them. So, it's fine. I'm not in danger, you are."

"I don't want you any closer to this."

Why? "That's awesome. Good thing it's not up to you."

"When I talk to Sebastian, it *will* be up to me."

"I hate to be the one to point this out to you, but you're not in charge here. Sebastian is. And for some reason, he seems to want to save your ass. I mean, for me, I could go either way really. But that's the job. That's the assignment. Guard *you*."

He licked his lips, and it was more than I could do not to focus on his tongue. It had been a long-ass dry spell, and he was looking like what I needed to quench the thirst.

Stop it.

"I just want you safe," he ground out.

"What does it matter? My job is to guard *you*. Keep *you* safe. That's why Sebastian pays us the big bucks."

"Can I fire you then?"

I grinned. "Again, it's Sebastian's call. But when the king of your country turns up on your doorstep and asks you to get your team together and come protect his cousin, you do as you're told. So I'm sorry if I cramp your style, or whatever. You're stuck with me at least part of the time."

"Can't you send someone awesome from your team?"

"Well, that's the thing. We have other jobs, you see. And because this is so sensitive to the crown, you get me. Sorry to disappoint."

He stepped into my space. "Stop it. This isn't some macho, alpha nonsense. We have too much history."

"Well, in that case, we'll need to figure out how to get around it because my job right now is to watch you. So we'll both have to figure out how the hell to work together. The first rule of Keep You Alive Club is no one talks about the past. *Ever*. Second rule is you don't ever kiss me again."

His voice dropped to barely above growl level. "Even when you like it?"

Something pulled low in my belly, and my stomach flipped. *Asshole.* "Who said I liked it?"

His brow lifted, and the smile was slow to spread over his lips. "You think you're safe. It's admirable. But rest assured, I'm going to get Sebastian to change his mind."

"You're welcome to try." And then I sauntered out, leaving him alone in the office.

FOURTEEN

TRISTAN...

I HAD FUCKED UP AND MADE A DISTINCT MISCALCULATION. I had wanted to believe the police when they said the incidents in Barcelona were very likely a stalker of Ella's. It had been the easier thing to believe. It had fed into my plans anyway. My goal. For Max. It made it easy to know I was on the right path.

I didn't think my path needed to diverge. I was still on track, but goddamn it, I had put Ella in danger. This was about me. For someone to have the kind of access to nearly get me during practice, on my own home turf, made it clear this was about me.

And now I had fucking Ariel in the crosshairs too.

So much for protecting everyone. I'd just made everyone a target.

Goddamn it.

Sebastian looked like he was going to be on the phone a while, so there was no point in waiting for him. But I did need to get Ariel off the case. She could send as many King's Knights as she wanted, but I wanted her out of it. I still hadn't told my cousin about us, not that any of our ancient history mattered. But I needed to do something, otherwise, she was going to get caught in the crosshairs, and I wouldn't forgive myself if she was hurt.

What about your actual fiancée?

Fuck. Ella. I needed to get her to safety, which meant far the hell away from here. Away from me.

You're poison. Everything you touch goes to shit. Just ask Billford.

There had been at least a dozen times in the last twenty-four hours that I had wished I was him. But then I'd had that selfish thought that if I'd been the one at the hospital, then how was I supposed to protect Ella? And if someone was trying to punish me, that meant that Ariel was in the line of fire too.

Except no one knows about you and Ariel, so maybe that's safer.

That was possibly true, but safer would be away from me.

I needed out. I needed to be away from the palace. I needed air.

Behind me, I could hear Trevor's constant footsteps. I swear to God, that *clack, clack, clack* on the marble was like my very own telltale heart following me around everywhere. I could always hear it, even in my sleep.

"Trevor, mate, can I get a minute?"

Trevor's brows snapped down. "Your Highness, I am sorry, but no. If you would like to go down to the basketball court or the tennis courts, we can do that. If you'd like to go down the beach again, I'll change. I'll follow you down. We will need the Knights as well."

Fuck. The last thing I needed was more close proximity to Ariel. "It's fine. I'll just head down to the gardens."

He opened the nearest side door. "This way, Your Highness."

The fresh air did seem to help. I navigated my way through the Rose Garden and down to Majesty's Walk. It was the last wall before any trails and passageways down to the beach. It's the farthest I could get from the palace without actually being off the palace grounds.

The palace grounds included nearly two thousand acres of land. Buildings, monuments, gardens. The beach was technically still royal land, but only a part of it was private.

Just inhaling the air loosened some of the tension. I needed to figure things out.

If I made a misstep, someone was going to get hurt. Someone I loved.

Do you mean Ella or Ariel?

I'd messed up. I thought I had everything under control. I had to think this through. My plan hinged on me coming home, and everything hinged on the plan. But I hadn't anticipated these attempts on my life. What if they meant Max knew I was coming for him? What if whoever was trying to hurt me was on the Council? And my plan was on borrowed time. How the hell was I going to protect Ella when I couldn't even protect myself?

I rounded the corner toward the sports complex, and I saw a familiar face. Heading out of the tennis courts, bag over his shoulder...

Fucking James Gilroy. I had known I would have to see him eventually. I'd just hoped to put it off for a long time.

He stopped short when he saw me.

When he approached, I could almost hear the tension rolling from Trevor's shoulders, but I turned and waved him down. Gilroy wasn't dumb enough to actually do something to me in the open.

"Your Highness."

"Lord Gilroy."

"I'd heard you managed a way to wiggle your way back into the islands."

"It is my home. I belong here."

"Maybe I wasn't clear with you. You were not to come back," he spat.

"Yes, well luckily you weren't in control of that." I knew I shouldn't antagonize him, but bollocks to that.

"You managed to escape the islands before, and I couldn't touch you. You're back now, but my daughter is not. You are responsible for that. I swear to God, I will find out what you did to her."

"For fuck's sake, Gilroy, I didn't have anything to do with your daughter's disappearance. I don't know where she went or why she disappeared, but I'm not to blame."

"You knew how she felt about you. You strung her along with your texts and letters." He sniffled. "You toyed with her emotions. That poor girl."

"I don't know why you'd think that, but I'm not responsible for her disappearance. You can't put that on me. And to attempt to block me from coming home because of your misguided suspicions is bullshit. You have no proof."

"No, I'll tell you what's bullshit. A member of the royal family thinking he can get away with anything. You belong in high exile, just like your brother. If I had my way, I would shove you in a deep dark hole where no one would ever find you."

"Well, good news for me is that you don't have any proof that I did anything."

"We'll see about that. There are other ways to make you hurt. And I will find one. You should have stayed the fuck away from the Winston Isles."

"You know what? I'm fucking sick and tired of people keeping me from my home." I stepped in close to his face, and I could hear Trevor behind me. I stepped even closer. "I'm a grown-ass man. I will not be afraid. So, if you have something that you actually can do, go ahead, do your worst. I won't be going anywhere. Too much has already happened to keep me away."

And then I very deliberately shoved by him. I was sick of it. I was tired of being afraid. For years I had been afraid of my own home, and then I'd been afraid to come back. But not anymore. If Lord James Gilroy wanted to come after me, fair enough. He didn't have any proof, and I hadn't done anything to his daughter. I felt for the family, but that had nothing to do with me. I was done listening to his threats. Ashton had been lording threats over me for over a decade. I wasn't going to take shit from the bullies any longer. Not Max. Not Ashton. Not Gilroy. If they wanted to come for me, they were free to do so, but I was ready for them. I would swallow the fear. I would do what I had to do. Maybe it was time that they all started to fear me.

Later that night, my brain was still thinking about what happened with Gilroy as I worked with Lucas.

"So, are we going to pretend that didn't happen today?"

I was trying to master a sleight of hand trick that he had shown me, but my hands were still too big and too clumsy.

"What didn't happen?"

He effortlessly rolled a coin backward and forward over his knuckles. "Today's meeting. You and Ariel. I sensed tension there."

"No tension." I was trying to slide a stupid card behind my fingers and forward, but for some reason, of all the maneuvers like the brushes, the silent lifts, this was the most difficult for me. And this was the one I might have to employ. Leave that to be my luck.

"You're chasing windmills, mate."

"*You're chasing windmills, mate.*" He mocked me. "I know what I'm seeing. Even if everyone else was oblivious, I felt it. You two are boning. Which, far be it from me to judge, but what are you telling Ella?"

I stared at my cousin. He was far too astute for his own good. "We are *not* boning."

"Oh, but you want to. So what does that mean for the pretty fiancée?"

I wasn't ready to answer any of these questions, and I hadn't bargained on anyone asking them. Hell, Ella had taken off for a job, which was for the best right now. When she wasn't with me, she had her own security team, so I figured she'd be okay as long as she stayed away from me. "Ella and I are good. Solid. Nothing has changed."

"Okay, if nothing has changed, then does she know you want to bone your knight in shining armor?"

"I don't want to bone her." I craved her touch. Totally different.

He laughed. "Lies. You totally want to bone her."

I shook my head. Why was it that the one person who was so difficult to lie to was also the one person who had seen my truth?

"Look," Lucas said in a serious tone. "I've been friends with Ariel for a while now. She's sharp as a tack. She puts up with no bullshit and is fucking badass."

"You sound like *you* want to bone her." I attempted to deflect.

"You know what, I would if I wasn't already in love with Bryna. If I had paid attention and noticed her, I might have just boned her. But we're not talking about me. I'm a rogue. I have been, as they used to say, a manwhore, or at least a reformed manwhore. I'm just trying to figure out when you two would have even met?"

I tried the card again. It fumbled out of my fingers just like every other time. "Is there any chance you'll stop with the questions?"

Lucas leaned back on the couch, hands clasped behind his back and legs spread. Total man-spread on the couch in my quarters. "Nope. Not going to happen. I have seen it, the *we are so going to bone* look, and I've fought it myself. So, the question is why Ariel? Why now? I've already said Ariel is dope, so I understand *why* Ariel, but I want to know why her specifically, because your fiancée is a fucking supermodel-turned-actress. There is no reason in the world you should be doing this snap-crackle-pop tension thing with Red."

My brows snapped down, and the truth tumbled out before I could stop it. "You know she hates that nickname, right?"

Lucas lifted his head and pinned me with a dark gaze. "Oh, you mean being called Red? I know. The question is how do *you* know?"

Fuck. Fucking fuck.

I clamped my jaw tight, working the muscles to keep my lips from moving. I just couldn't keep my goddamn mouth shut. If I kept it shut, there would be no problem. But oh no, blabbity-blab. "I just figured, red hair, just like big guys hate to be called Tiny or Big Guy."

Lucas shook his head, for once completely serious. "Oh my God, you already *have* boned!"

"No, we haven't." My voice was tight, and it came out more of a growl than anything.

Oh yeah, way to go. Way to throw him off the scent.

"Oh, come on, cousin, you can tell me. I'm a vault as you know. Or we can wait until Sebastian and Roone catch a whiff of this. And then there will be no rest for the wicked."

I groaned. "Lucas, can't you just let it go?"

"Nope. As long as it doesn't have anything to do with whatever you need to learn the sleight-of-hand stuff for," he waved his hand in my general direction, "I need to know. She's your Knight now. She's literally your bodyguard. I mean, I think you *want* her guarding your body, if you catch my meaning." He winked.

"Oh my God, shut it. We are not having this conversation."

"Oh, we are, or should I call Sebastian to come down here and ask all the questions?" He grinned at me. It was pure evil. And he had me dead to rights. He was helping me. He hadn't asked any questions about why I needed to learn sleight of hand, or why I might need to become the perfect thief, or what I needed my new skill set for.

Not one question, and he'd kept his word. He hadn't said anything to Sebastian or Roone. Hell, I didn't even know if he'd told his fiancée he was tutoring me. But this, this was just too interesting for him. He wanted answers, and he wasn't going to stop until he had them. "Nobody knows, Lucas."

"Even better. A secret I can lord over people."

"No. There will be no lording over anyone, or I won't tell you. It doesn't matter who you call down here. I won't say a word."

He groaned. "Fine. But that's just because I love gossip."

I scrubbed my hand over my face as my fingers tried again to force the card to slip and hide. No luck.

"I met Ariel by mistake, actually."

"When?"

"Ten years ago... nearly eleven."

His brows drew up. "What?"

"I was home from boarding school for the summer. My dad saw that I couldn't stand being at the palace."

Lucas frowned at this. "What? I mean, I knew that you went to boarding school most of your life, but you were around sometimes. You grew up with Sebastian and Ashton."

"Only on occasion. Ashton and I didn't get along." That was the understatement of the century.

"Yeah, because your brother is a turd. No offense."

"None taken. He is. He's the worst kind of filth."

Easy does it. No need for him to see anything we don't want him to see.

"Okay, so you met Ariel one summer."

"Yeah. She used to work at this old tiny movie theater. I don't even know what possessed me, but I'd been trying to get out of the palace. I needed a way to hide. I had slipped my guard—"

"Something we have in common."

"Yeah. So anyway, I'd slipped my guard and just went out. I was more conspicuous with a guard than without them. I went to go and see a movie, and she was there. She was so cute. Flaming red hair, green soulful eyes... I liked her right away."

"I can see why."

"Anyway, I asked her out. And I don't know why we've kept it quiet. It's not like I had anything to hide. I don't know, I think I wanted something for myself. Something private. It's not like my father would have objected. And she was best friends with Penny, for the love of God. She was already allowed on the palace grounds. But I don't know... I didn't want her tainted by any of it. And I liked having her to myself."

"Makes sense."

"It was going great. We were... I don't know, dumb. In love, I guess. I was supposed to head back to school, back to Eton to finish my A-levels, but it was the last thing I really wanted to do. I wanted to be with her. And I had my wild dream of a team picking me up. I'd been playing in the under-18s, and I had been doing well. School got in the way a lot, but that was important to me, so I made it work."

"I mean, seriously, you were a killer. I've seen the videos."

I shrugged at that. "Back then, I think it was more natural talent than actual work. But Ariel, she was... my whole world. Or maybe she offered me a different world than the one I'd been used to."

"So what happened?"

"We made a dumb plan to run away together. Instead of going to do my A-levels, I was going to go off and do trials for teams abroad. And she was going to come with me. We were just going to strike out on our own."

Lucas chuckled low. "A loose plan, at best."

"I know. I had a definitive plan, at least. I did have trials scheduled to see if I could be on any warmup teams. I was still meant to go back to school though. And I did absolutely want Ariel to join me. She was supposed to come out and visit, see if she liked it. And if she did and I made the trial team, we planned to live together, that whole thing."

Lucas frowned. "But she was barely sixteen."

"I know. Kind of dumb. But that was the plan at the time."

"And?"

"And well, I fucked up."

"No, you need to tell me more than that."

I tried to let go of the emotion of it. "Okay, fine. I got offered a spot on Madrid's team. No trial. Their forward, Ian Tellman, had injured himself. Ian and I had played in the under-18s together. We had a similar style. He went pro before I did. He was just always that much faster, that much better. But then suddenly he was injured, and I had a shot."

"Wow. So, instead of going back to school, you went pro?"

I nodded. "Yeah. Just like that."

"But that doesn't make any sense because she still could have come visit."

"I know. I had to leave pretty suddenly, and I left word for her to meet me. I left it for her in the place we always used to meet. Ashton was a real dick, so texting wasn't always the most reliable thing."

"He knew your password?"

"I changed it so many times. One time I even got a burner to stop him from hacking my texts."

"Yeah, sounds like Ashton."

"I didn't know he was seeing someone in Intelligence, and that's how he was getting access to all my messages."

Lucas winced. "God, I mean, he must have been what, two years older than you? So, twenty and far too old for such adolescent bullshit. But you know what? That does absolutely sound like him."

"Yeah, anyway... so he intercepted my message to her to go to our spot, and as far as I could see, she never made it. She never showed up in Madrid either. When he gloated about how cute it was that I thought I could run away with her, I knew he'd interceded in some way. Still, I wrote her a million letters. I knew he was watching her phone, so I couldn't call her. But I wrote her letters, and she didn't answer any of them."

Lucas winced. "Shit. Think she was pissed that you left?"

"Undoubtedly. She'd wanted to escape this place as badly as I did."

Lucas frowned. "Okay, knowing her dad, I can see why she wanted to escape. But why did *you* want to escape so badly?"

I shook my head. "You didn't know him. Ashton was a special kind of hell."

Lucas frowned. "Penny told me some stuff. I'm sorry he was such a dick."

"Yeah, thanks. Hallmark should really start a *sorry your brother was a dick* line of greeting cards."

"So because of him, you two were like ships passing in the night."

"Yeah. But like I said, I wrote to her and she never wrote back. So that's the end of that. I hadn't seen her in ten years until she basically turned up on my doorstep a couple weeks ago."

Lucas whistled low. "Jesus. How is Ella taking it?"

I frowned. "Taking what?"

"Oh, I don't know... the love of your life showing up again?"

"Not the love of my life. It was just a kid thing. We didn't know anything."

He blinked at me. "Uh-huh. Just a kid thing. And that's why you two were busy eye-fucking each other in the meeting?"

"I was not eye-fucking her."

"No, you were ready to blatantly fuck her. And she was very much giving you the *I hate you but I still want to bone* face."

I threw the card in his direction, and it actually landed dead center on his chest. Lucas looked down with a grin. "Hey, card throwing. I never even thought to teach you that."

"Yeah, well, if I could actually hide the thing, I would be happier."

"So..." his voice trailed as he studied me. "What are you going to do about Ariel?"

"I'm not going to do anything about her. I'm with Ella."

Lucas nodded slowly. "Sure you are, until you're not. You don't strike me as the kind of guy to try and juggle two women. I've got to tell you, it's not a good idea."

"I wouldn't do that to either one of them."

"Well, the look you're giving Ariel is clear to me. It's clear to her. And it will start being clear to someone else, so you might want to talk to Ella."

"Ella understands what we have. She isn't the problem."

"Well, she isn't the problem until she is. Women and jealousy don't work well. And if you don't resolve your Ariel issues, it's going to come back to bite you in the ass. And Ariel, she's family. She shouldn't have to share you."

I cleared my throat. "You and I are in complete agreement. I wouldn't do that. I wouldn't ask that. And I'm not that guy. She's not a problem because I have Ella."

Lucas sat back, toying with the card, flicking it, making it vanish and appear again. Those words rang absolutely false to the both of us.

"Sure, she isn't."

FIFTEEN

ARIEL...

"How are you holding up?"

"You know... fine."

Penny raised a brow as I paced in her office.

"Fine? You're wearing a pattern on my hardwood."

I glanced down. "Sorry."

"Just sit down and talk to me."

"No. I mean, it is what it is, right? I just... you know, didn't anticipate it being this hard."

"Look, just let me tell Sebastian. He'll understand if you only assign the other knights."

"No. This is my duty. I agreed. And he is a member of the royal family, so he deserves the best."

"Well, you are doing the best. You're the best hacker on the team, clearly. So, you can just keep doing that. You don't have to torture yourself."

I ran my hands through my hair, gently massaging my scalp and trying to release some of the tension. "No, it's fine. Everything is fine."

"You sound like me now."

"Well, didn't this mantra thing work for you?"

"You saw how well that worked for me. I made myself crazy. I mean, honestly... you guys have got to come to some common ground. Has he at least stopped being a dick?"

"Yes, mostly. We don't talk."

"That can be awkward. No one else on your team has noticed?"

"You know, not really. Jax made some snide comment about how insanely professional I was. And well, neither Zia nor Tamsin say anything. And Jameson is always quiet. So, who knows? She may have noticed something, she may not have. I have no idea. Trace is the only one who would outwardly say something and call me out, and he hasn't been on duty with me yet. So right now, it's fine."

Penny released a clip and her curls sprang free. "Babe, I'm so sorry. I wish I had a better solution I could suggest."

"No, you have done everything you can. I'm the one who just needs to get over this. Did you know I had to sit down and endure dinner with him and Ella the other night?"

Penny frowned. "I don't know what to make of her."

"Yeah, tell me about it. She is certainly an ice princess, but she doesn't deserve me lusting after her man."

"So, you *are* lusting?"

"Penny, not helpful."

"Sorry. No. She doesn't deserve that, but that's not on you. That's on *him*. *He* should never have kissed *you*."

"Yes. I agree. It was just that much worse watching them at dinner, leaning in and exchanging little whispers."

Penny shook her head, her curls bouncing in her face. "God! But you know what's weird, though? They hardly ever touch."

It was my turn to frown. "What are you talking about? They touch all the time."

Penny shook her head. "No. They don't. Remember the other night at game night, right? Sure, they sat right next to each other, and they leaned-in to whisper a lot, but he didn't even so much as touch her knee."

I had been resolutely ignoring him. I was going to skip that game night, but I'd been on duty, so there was no escaping it. I had just deliberately *not* looked in his direction. The whole damn night. My neck still ached from the force of me holding it perfectly stiff and never allowing it to crane in his direction.

"I didn't notice."

"I sure did, because I was watching them. I was trying to figure out what he saw in her."

"It doesn't matter what he sees in her. He put a ring on it, so I'm out."

"Fine, you can be out. But I'm still going to observe and snark."

I had to laugh at that. "Thank you for forever having my back and snarking on my behalf."

"What are besties for? But honestly, it's weird. If there is a camera or if it's something public, something in front of the Council, or if there was any dignitary or a friend of Sebastian's around, something that could be... I don't know... public record, then they touch. But even then, they never kiss. It's only hand-holding."

"Jesus! You've spent a lot more time observing them than I have."

"Trust me, I keep watching for a reason. I would love a reason, any reason, why he's jerking you around."

"There is no reason. You're just going to make yourself crazy.

There is zero reason why he's doing this. Either he's confused or he's a dick. Whichever way it falls, I've given way too much mental space to this."

She shrugged. "Or he's truly conflicted. I mean, you guys didn't resolve anything. I'm just saying, watch them. They never touch. When they do, it's just the hands. They never kiss."

"How does that help me?"

"Well, maybe everything is not as it seems. Whatever is going on, that's not a couple that's in love."

"It doesn't matter. I don't care about excuses. I'm not going to do that."

"I know. That's not who you are. And that's not who I want my bestie to be, either, someone who's getting scraps. I'm just saying, maybe an open line of communication is what you guys need, because clearly, there is unresolved shit there."

"Yeah, well, that's not going to happen."

She sighed. "Well, okay. Then maybe we, you know, double the focus on Ian."

My phone vibrated then, and I glanced down. "Speak of the devil and he shall appear."

"Oh yeah? What's he saying?"

She leaned forward. "He's asking for another dinner. I know he asked for another date, but I just didn't know when we'd both be available. And with us on rotation schedules on Tristan now, I don't when I'll have time."

"Well, invite him to the gala."

I blinked. "Are you insane?"

"Maybe, but the point is your whole team is going to be there. Tristan will have more than enough coverage. And you obviously should be there as well. It's a good opportunity to get to know Ian better. And Tristan will see you with him, so he'll know that he can't just jerk you around."

I frowned. "That feels... I don't know... icky."

"Well, remember when I didn't want to use my assets to get Sebastian's attention?"

"Yes, but that was dumb because you were single and he was single."

"Ah, wait, I wasn't exactly single. I was still dealing with Robert and hadn't quite broken up with him."

"Yeah, you know, *details*."

"Well, I see our first breakup as when he didn't turn up for my birthday, so..."

"Yeah, he did it to himself."

"But I understand what you're saying. Look, Ian is super cute. At the very least, if Tristan does still have feelings for you and he won't talk about them, at least this will prompt him. If he sees Ian all over you, he will lose his shit, and he's going to be forced to confront what the hell he's doing with, you know, Ice Princess Ella and stringing you along."

I don't know why, but I felt the need to defend him. "He's not stringing me along. I'm a grown up. It was one kiss. I'm probably blowing it out of proportion because we haven't talked or settled anything, so the wounds still feel all fresh and oozy."

"Well, you know how to fix that."

"Yeah, but every time we get within a foot of each other, we're fighting."

"That's because you want to fuck. Maybe if you weren't so desperate to fuck, you guys could have a rational conversation. So get the lead out with someone else, and then you can talk to him."

"Oh my God, your solutions need work."

"What? I thought it was a great solution."

I shook my head. "You do have a point. I should ask Ian to the gala, because truly, the only way I'm going to be able to tell if I really like him is to spend more time with him."

"Are you going to be able to get over the whole *he ordered for you and invited someone else on your date* thing?"

I groaned. "You just had to bring that up, didn't you?"

"I'm just saying, it's a viable reason to not go out with someone again. So don't go out with him just because you're like, 'Well, this one. This is the only one I can make work.'"

"I'm not doing that."

I was totally doing that.

"Yes, you are. But I'll allow it because he is very cute and totally smitten with you, so one more date won't hurt. Besides, it's a really good excuse to get all dolled up and feel extra pretty. If someone else happens to notice who is at the gala, you know, far from me to complain."

I rolled my eyes. "Oh my God, you're forever going to be the matchmaker, aren't you?"

"Well, I love love. And what Tristan's got going on right now isn't love, so I'd like to get him to sort that out. But you are my priority. I just want you to be happy. So go on the date. It's certainly not going to hurt you."

She had a point. I went to my text and hit reply.

Ariel: *How would you like a date at the palace?*

His response was immediate.

Ian: *Absolutely. Basically, any reason to see you. Do you want me to come now?*

I laughed.

Ariel: *Not now, you goof. There's a gala on Friday night. Would you like to be my date?*

Ian: *Fantastic! I look amazing in black tie. You're going to find me irresistible.*

Ariel: *Who knows? Maybe it's you who'll find me irresistible.*

Ian: *I already do find you irresistible. I know the jury is still out for you. So, black tie it is. You don't stand a chance.*

I rolled my eyes, and then I lifted my gaze to Penny, who was watching me. "He's making you smile, so that's a good thing."

"Only because he is crazy. But it's done. I have a date."

Penny sat back. "Well, the good news is that at the end of this date, you'll know exactly how you feel about Ian. And you'll know exactly how Tristan feels about you."

I knew how Tristan felt about me. He hated me but couldn't help wanting me. Which put me right between a rock and a very, very hard place.

Ariel...

TWO BIRDS WITH ONE STONE. Okay, I was totally cheating. But when Ian had called asking for our do-over date, I'd invited him to the gala. It had been just over a week since I'd been back on Tristan's service, and I was going out of my mind.

Ella had come back for two nights. I'd been forced to watch them have dinner. I'd stood by, watching them whisper together, and I wasn't at all jealous. Or so I'd told Penny. She hadn't really believed me, but maybe she'd allowed me my delusion. She had a point though. I never saw them touch unless there was a camera present. Then there was much handholding. They never kissed that I could see.

I kept trying to tell myself I wasn't trying to prove anything by digging in with Ian. That I needed to give it one more go to see if I was actually interested in being with him. I hadn't really thought about the gala much, but it was the perfect venue. Technically I needed to be there, but I was just managing the team, so I could have a dance or two. Besides, if I waited on having available time in my calendar, it never would happen. And I wouldn't be able to make my final decision unless I actually went out with him again.

No, you can make your decision. You already know.

The thing was I'd been playing it safe my whole life, deflecting with humor and snark. Ian was a chance for something real. So what if he insisted on ordering for me? He was just a little old school. I'd just mention to him that I really did not like wine. See? Problem solved.

Uh-huh.

My inner self was not having it. Tonight, of all nights, she was in full bloom and taking no prisoners.

Well, her and Penny. "Okay, so let me get this straight. Tristan is here. Home. He's kissed you."

"Yes."

We were in Penny and Sebastian's quarters. She insisted I should get ready there, of course, instead of letting me get ready in my guest quarters.

"Okay, so Tristan's here. By the way, I never really noticed just how hot he was, but he is totally smokin'."

I rolled my eyes. "You only think that way because he looks a little like Sebastian."

She grinned at me. "Well, I mean, my husband is gorgeous."

I laughed. "Don't shove that in anyone's face, okay? It's already hard to like you."

"What? I'm easy to love."

"You are. You're adorable. And more likely than not have paint streaks on you somewhere. It makes you endearing."

"Shit. Do I have paint streaks on me now?"

I studied her closely. For once, she was paint free.

"No, you're good."

"Okay. Back to the important thing. So, you had a date with Ian which Tristan crashed. Maybe if we can pick apart every aspect of it, we can figure out what they're both thinking."

I thought back. Why did it already feel like eons ago? "Well, it wasn't entirely Tristan's fault because Ian invited him to sit down."

Penny frowned. "Yeah, I'm still mad about that. Who does that when you're on a date? He should have been like, 'Hey, I haven't seen you in a while. Let's catch up later over drinks. Right now, I'm with this hot date. Check out this piece. Isn't she sexy?'"

I snorted a laugh. "Oh my God, you doing that impression is one for the ages. Has Sebastian seen these impressions? Because I think they're awesome."

Penny paired her impression with trying to form a guy slouch, shoulders hunched, kind of sloppy.

I snort-laughed. "That's epic."

"Hey, I've seen it before. I'm just emulating."

"Yeah, so he... you already know this part. He basically invited Tristan and Ella to sit down."

"And Tristan did. Then he was playing footsie with you under the table, right?"

I frowned. "It wasn't exactly like *footsie*. It's just that I could feel him, you know?"

She waggled her brows. "Oh, I know."

"What's that supposed to mean?"

"Well, it means you still have feelings for Tristan."

" I have no feelings. My feelings are dead. *All* feeling is dead."

"See, that's the problem. We need you to feel something in your pants."

I snorted. "Penny."

"I'm sorry, but one of us needs to be you in this relationship. And right now, my bestie is taking a vacation. If this situation was reversed and it was me, you would be like, 'In your pants. Bone both. Bag and tag.'"

She was right. I would say that to her. I was not the bag and tag type, and neither was Penny. But she'd needed encouragement for such things. I needed no such encouragement because as outrageous as I was half the time, when it came to love, I still played it safe.

That's because you were hurt.

"Look, it's fine. When Tristan kissed me, I felt nothing."

Penny lifted a brow, and that's all she had to do. She knew I was lying.

"Okay, fine. I felt something. The point is I'm not going to act on it because he has Ella. He is engaged, and he has no business kissing me."

She nodded. "We are in agreement there. No closer to finding out why he's so hot and cold with you?"

"I don't know. He's a douche?"

"He's not a douche." Penny shook her head. "You know that's outside of character. Tristan is the... I don't know... sweet and sensitive one. He is actually really soft-hearted."

"I'm not sure soft-hearted is the right word. Are you sure you know Tristan?"

"Well, he might be going all alpha-caveman with you right now, but usually he's a good guy. And he hasn't kissed you since then?"

"No. But he did tell me not to go out with Ian. Asshole."

"Well, that's just a jealous guy thing."

She stepped back, surveying her work. She'd put me in a moss green jumpsuit. It brought out the color in my eyes. It was strapless. It made my tits look amazing. And I had hidden panels for my weapons, which made my day.

"Ah, you look dope."

I turned, staring at the glitter in my ears. "Penny, what the hell are those?"

"Well, I had those, and they have just been laying around, so I figured you should wear them tonight."

She'd slipped massive, dangling ruby earrings in my ears. Knowing Penny, they were real. "Jesus Christ. How much are these things worth?"

She shrugged. "You know I don't really care about that shit. I have no idea. You could tell me they're from one of those teen accessory stores we used to frequent all the time, or you could tell me they're the crown jewels. I wouldn't know the difference."

I rolled my eyes. "How is it you ended up as queen?"

She laughed. "Maybe because I don't care. Who knows?" Then she stepped back.

I had to admire her too. The girl was my klutzy, geeky best

friend and partner, but standing before me, she looked every bit the Queen of the Winston Isles. She was wearing white, like a crazy person. But it had a hint of ice blue woven throughout the sleek skirt of the dress. She was a little more daring. The bodice on her dress dipped down past her boobs, shoving them up under her chin. It would be a wonder if Sebastian let her leave that dress on for ten minutes.

"Okay, you look perfect. Are you ready to do this?"

"I guess as ready as I'll ever be?"

"Then let's do this. You're going to make both their eyes pop out of their heads."

"I only care about Ian, remember? Only Ian."

Penny giggled. "Sure. You keep telling yourself that. But when you're dealing with me, you speak the truth. You want Tristan to trip over himself."

I bit my tongue to keep the truth inside. But she didn't need me to say it because she already knew. I wanted him to eat his heart out.

Ariel...

"YOU LOOK ABSOLUTELY RAVISHING." I couldn't help but preen slightly at the compliment.

"Thank you, Ian."

"I mean it. I... wow. And thank you for the invitation to the palace."

"Well, it's the least I could do for not being available all last week."

"Oh, we'll make it up. Besides, this is not a bad date."

"Except I'm working."

"Are you working? I'm pretty sure we can escape to the gardens for a glass of champagne."

I giggled. "Well, I might be able to steal away, but I'll need to stay on comms."

Ian frowned. "Comms?"

I tapped my ear. Thanks to Blake Security, we had communication devices that were so small you could barely see them. "We don't anticipate anything will happen to the prince here, but better safe than sorry."

He frowned. "Is Tristan in trouble?"

I smiled beatifically at him. I wasn't about to discuss what I was doing. Just that I was here and I was acting as guard.

"You know I can't tell you that."

"Right. Right. Sorry. It's fascinating. I'm obviously super curious about what you do."

"It's easy really. I'm a business owner. I don't do anything that special."

He laughed. "Oh really? Is that why when I say your name a certain circle of people literally quicken and/or go instantly to fangirl status? I had dinner with a mate last night. He's an athlete I'm trying to recruit. He's local. I mentioned that the girl I'm dating invited me to the palace. He asked me who I knew that had that kind of clout. I said your name, and his eyes just went wide, talking about how you brought home the lost princess practically single-handedly."

"I had a lot of help. It wasn't just me. Roone, her fiancé, was also on the team."

Ian laughed. "But weren't you leading that team?"

I nodded. "Yes, I was. That part is true."

"That's pretty amazing."

I shrugged. "I'm just doing my job. I was just the lucky person who happened to keep her safe and bring her back. That's all we did."

"You're so taciturn. You won't give me anything about that?"

"While most people know that we found Jessa and brought her home, we can't actually talk about the mission."

"Virtual fight club, I guess."

I smiled at him. "Exactly."

"Well, either way, I think it's fantastic. Whatever you can tell me, I would love to hear. I want to know all about you."

It was sweet really. I wasn't used to that kind of attention. At least so far that evening, he hadn't tried to order for me or tell me what to do, so I supposed that had been an anomaly.

Or someone had warned him of the error of his ways. Or he thought I was a badass and that little-woman thing wasn't really going to work with me much longer. Either way, he was a perfectly delightful date.

Except he's not Tristan.

I needed to stop. I kept telling myself I was only aware of the prince's location because I had to be for my job. But that was a lie. From the moment I had walked into the ballroom, I could feel his stare on me. His deep, penetrating gaze, not leaving me. I also sensed his complete and utter fury when Ian showed up. What was he playing at? He was engaged. Was I supposed to sit around my whole life and wait for somebody who was never going to show?

I did my best to ignore him.

At ten o'clock, one by one my team checked in. I could see where they were in the ballroom. Trace was at the table with Roone, and Lucas, and they were having an uproarious time. Jax was on the door. I'd managed to get his fiancée, Neela, an invitation as well. She was enjoying herself. Their adopted daughter, Mayzie, was busy keeping Queen Mother Alexa entertained.

As soon as they'd arrived, the Queen Mother had run up and collected the baby while glowering at Sebastian and Penny for not giving her grandchildren yet. Zia, ever watchful, was dancing with Tristan. Every time they turned the circle, his gaze met mine and narrowed.

Well, let him eat his heart out. I wasn't his property.

Jameson had opted to stay at the office. She was manning our other projects. All in all, my team was doing exactly what they needed to do, and so far, it appeared that the prince was in no danger. But that didn't mean that we were any less watchful.

Everything went well until I felt a warm hand press up in my lower back. "May I have this dance?"

I stiffened. "Your Royal Highness, it's not appropriate that I dance with you."

"Are you sure about that, because Zia already did, as did Tamsin."

I had to remember to kill them later. "I came with a date."

"It's just a dance. I'm sure Ian won't mind."

"I warn you, I never learned to properly dance."

I was desperate for any reason to not have his hands on me. Any reason at all. I would have paid cash money for that reason to materialize, but it didn't. Instead, the music changed to something slow and jazzy, and I had no choice but to take his hand.

Wrapped in his arms, I knew immediately I should never have said yes, because there he was smelling like an Armani commercial, dressed the part, looking every bit the roguish prince. And I had no shield for my heart. "You look beautiful," he whispered.

"Thank you," I managed to force out.

He chuckled low. "Is that all you're going to say to me?"

"Tristan, maybe we should just stick to dancing."

"We could do that, or we could talk."

"I don't think it's a good idea. We tend to escalate quickly straight to fighting."

He nodded. "Yeah, that's true. But I couldn't let the night go without telling you how pretty you look."

I flushed under his gaze. "Does Ella know you talk to me like this?"

He sighed. "Look, Ella, that whole scenario—"

"You know what, I don't need to know. Whatever arrangement you guys have, I don't need to know about. It's not my business."

"Ariel—"

"No, seriously, it's not. I'm not going to judge you for whatever it is you think you're doing because it doesn't affect me. It doesn't matter. And it shouldn't matter to you what I'm doing."

"If I told you it does matter to me, what would you say?"

"I would say that is your problem. You walked away, so it doesn't get to matter to you anymore."

"Is that what you really think? That I walked away from you?"

"Isn't that what you did?"

"All this time, that's what you thought? That I just walked away, that I *could* walk away? You thought I was capable of that?"

She clenched her jaw. "No. I thought that I would be meeting my boyfriend and we would be taking a trip together. But he was a no-show."

"I had a really good reason, Ariel. I left you instructions on how to find me. You knew I couldn't call you. Ashton had access to my phone records. That put you in his crosshairs."

"Oh, I remembered what you used to say about that. But the whole point is it doesn't matter anymore. That was a long time ago. We were two different people. Those people don't exist anymore."

"Are you sure about that?" He watched me closely.

"So, you're saying that you somehow magically left me instructions to follow you?"

"Yes, that's what I'm saying."

"Where would you have left these instructions?"

His brows furrowed. "In our place, where we always left messages."

"You're full of shit. I went there. I went looking for you, hoping you had left me some kind of message, something to tell me, 'Hey, I had to leave early,' or 'I'll meet you somewhere,' but there was nothing. Instead, I found your brother."

He cursed low. "Fucking Ashton."

"Yeah, fucking Ashton. I'd always known he was a piece of work, but he took special joy in watching me crumble. He told me you had never planned on taking me anywhere. He was in *our place,* and he told me you'd told him all about it."

"And you believed him?"

"Well, I'm not an idiot. How else would he have known I'd go there? But there was no message." I shook my head. "Stop. None of this matters anymore."

"It does matter. You and I... you were my end game."

"Well, that's not how it worked out, is it? It got all fucked up. Extra messy. And not at all how we'd planned. So let's not pretend that we can go back in time because we can't."

His hand tightened on my lower back. "Are you sure about that?"

"Well, maybe that's a question for your fiancée." And with that, I stepped out of his hold. It was Ian who found me as I was making my escape to the balcony. "Running away already?"

I whipped around, the breath whooshing out of my lungs. I just needed to get out. I just needed air. "Yeah, I just got really hot in there."

"Hey, are you okay?"

I nodded and marched blindly toward the Rose Garden. I just couldn't. Not for another minute. I didn't want to hear anything Tristan had to say. I didn't want to think about the lies or the crushed hopes of the sixteen-year-old me. I just wanted to go.

Ian took my hand. "Okay, you don't look so good. Come with me. I found this spot in the garden when I was walking earlier."

I recognized where we were going. The path to the left led to the main path toward the north parking lot. But we were in the Rose Garden where the residences were. "Thanks for getting me out of there. I was just... I don't know. Maybe I'm not cut out to be so close to the royal life after all."

"Are you okay? You and His Royal Highness seemed to be having an intense conversation."

Did he suspect? God, this was already too complicated. "Um, yeah, we used to know each other, so we had lots to catch up on, I guess."

He nodded slowly. "Yeah, you know, I used to know him too. I know how those acquaintances can sometimes turn out in the end. I know what it's like to think he's on your side and then... well, he's not."

"Yeah. Sorry, this is the last thing I wanted to talk about on our date."

"Don't worry, I'm getting a make-up date, anyway. This is just some cool thing I get to do. The girl I'm seeing invited me here."

"So, now I'm that girl you're seeing?"

He laughed. "Well, yes. There is something I've been meaning to do."

As the moon lit us, I glanced up and felt better. A little distance from Tristan helped. I didn't doubt myself. I didn't overthink. I saw things clearly and for how they really were instead of how my teenage brain wanted them to be, because Tristan was *not* my boyfriend. He was a prince, and he'd already shown me once that he didn't want me. "Oh yeah? I'm more than willing to try."

Ian leaned forward, pulling me close. He cupped my face. "This."

He dipped his head, sliding his lips over mine. His kiss was fun. Warm. Pleasant. And he was certainly skilled. He knew how to kiss. He pulled me close, pressing his body into mine, and I wanted to lose myself. I wanted to let go. I wanted to feel free and wanted and desirable. Unfortunately, all it felt was pleasant. What the hell was wrong with me?

He's not Tristan.

Well, Tristan or not, he was the guy I had. My body needed to get on that because I did not want the prince. The prince was not good for me. From now on, I was only doing things that were good for me. I looped my arms around Ian's neck and kissed him back, throwing everything I had to give into that kiss. Still, it was just pleasant. And I was pretty darn sure that *pleasant* was not the feeling I wanted.

When I drew back, Ian was grinning down at me. "I am so glad we did that."

I smiled back at him, and he took my hand gently. "Let's go back. You can dance with me and tell me what it was like to grow up around royalty."

One of the rooms on the second floor lit up. I wondered whose it was. It could have been anyone's, and I wasn't sure what it was, but something assured me that it was Tristan's room. And all he had to do was open his blinds, lean out, and see me kissing another man.

What, do you care?

That is not for you to worry about because, for one, you won't be kissing Ian again, and two, you won't be kissing Tristan either.

"Right, let's go back. I need to check on my team, anyway."

I hoped he would accept the deflection, because unfortunately, as much as I liked him, there just wasn't enough chemistry between us. Not the kind there should be. And as unskilled as I was in relationships, even I knew that much.

SIXTEEN

TRISTAN...

She was mine, and that motherfucker had his hands all over her.

I recognized that I was being irrational. In fact, I recognized that Ariel hadn't been mine for *years*. It didn't stop the surge inside, the need to break something. In particular, Ian's face.

I had gone back up to my room to take a call from Ella. Max had called her, so she was feeling particularly vulnerable. I'd been on the phone when I'd seen them. Ian Tellman with his hands on Ariel, cupping her face and doing his best to knock her fucking socks off.

All I could think the whole time was, *mine*. She was *mine*. I didn't care what had happened between then and now, she was *mine*. And I needed to remind her of what we were to each other.

One little problem... she thinks you're engaged.

Or I could just fucking tell her. She was a King's Knight. She was used to keeping secrets. She could keep this secret if I told her the reason. I wanted to tell her so we wouldn't have this shit hanging over us, and we could have a goddamn conversation.

But can she handle it? Can she accept the truth? What if she doesn't love you enough?

Could I take that? Could I handle it if she'd just changed her mind? The lance of heat over my heart burned. I couldn't tell her even if I wanted to. I still needed to protect Ella. I'd promised her that no matter what it cost me, I would protect her, and she deserved that. No one had ever been there to protect her. And no one had ever been there to protect me. We had that in common.

There was a time Ariel protected your heart.

Yeah, but that was a long time ago.

Maybe I couldn't have her yet, but I wanted her as much as I had wanted her then. Just as long as Ian didn't have her, which was ridiculous because Ian was a friend. We'd come up together. It had been one hell of a shock to see him in the Winston Isles, but that didn't mean we weren't mates.

Still, I didn't like him playing with my toys.

She would skin me alive and painfully sew it back on if she even knew that was what I was thinking. But I couldn't just sit back and watch.

When I stepped back to the ballroom, it was Lucas I saw first. He nodded at me as he held Bryna in his arms. I'd teased him about the long engagement because I thought it was his choice to delay the wedding, but it was Bryna's. She wanted to wait until she was finished with her masters. That still hadn't stopped my cousin from putting a giant gravity inducing rock on her hand. It was a wonder she could lift it to do any work.

Lucas's gaze skittered over to Ariel, where she was dancing

with Ian. Then his gaze slid back to me along with a cocky smirk.

Asshole.

I didn't need his knowing smirks. As far as I could tell, he hadn't said anything. Penny hadn't barged in, and Sebastian hadn't taken me to task, so Lucas was as good as his word, which was surprising for a former con man.

Sure enough, my shadows were there immediately. Trevor, obviously, had been right behind me as soon as I'd gone up to my quarters. But Zia, Jameson, and Trace were more difficult to keep an eye on. They wove in and out of the crowd. Never too far though. Never too far.

When Ariel was finally free, I stepped through the crowd and gently took her hand. The jolt of electricity was immediate and powerful. With startled eyes, she gasped then asked. "Is something wrong?"

"Yes."

I pulled her out of the ballroom. I didn't care who was watching. Chances were they would assume—oh, who gave a fuck what they would assume?

I tugged her through the short hall and pushed a panel on the wall into one of the tunnels that led back to the Rose Garden. Back to where she'd kissed him right in front of me.

"What the hell do you think you're doing?"

"You know, I could ask you the same question."

She tugged her hand free. "Your Highness, is there something you need in particular? Perhaps I can get Zia, or Tamsin, or Trace. Trace is good with crazy."

"I'm not crazy, you know that."

"Do I? I don't know anything right now except you're dragging me out of the gala."

I stopped her exactly where she'd been. She glanced around. "What do you want?"

I stared at her, angry words ready to barrel out, gearing for a fight. But instead, I said, "You look beautiful."

"You said that already. Earlier." A flush tinged her cheeks, and I had to smile. She was so beautiful and had absolutely no idea what she was doing to me with her every movement. I couldn't even breathe just looking at her.

"What?"

"You look beautiful."

"You dragged me publicly from the ball to tell me I look beautiful again?"

"Well, if there was ever a reason to drag a beautiful woman out of the ball, wouldn't this qualify?"

She sighed. "Jesus Christ, what's going on?"

"I saw you."

Her breath hitched. "Saw me do what?"

"I saw you kiss him, right *fucking* here. Right under my goddamn window."

Her lips trembled, but she lifted her chin. "I feel like we have covered this. You are engaged to a beautiful woman. You don't get to torment me."

"I'm not trying to torment you."

"Aren't you?"

"There are things I *can't* explain."

"You know what? *I don't care.* You can have things you can't explain all you want. It's your business. I don't have anything to do with it. I don't *want* anything to do with it. But this game has to stop. You can't decide you're pissed off about something, kiss me, and then walk away and tell me to stay away from you. Then repeat. It's not fair. It's not going to work for me."

"I'm not trying to be a dick."

"Are you sure? Because you are doing a remarkable impression. Does that run in your family?"

I winced. I reminded myself that there was no way she could know the depth and levels of the depravity of my brother. She was angry, and I *was* acting like a dick. "I'm sorry. I just—"

"What?" She threw her hands up. "I am tired, Your Highness. I just want the night to be over so I can send my men home, give Sebastian his debrief, and go home myself."

I'd clearly lost my mind, which was why I was even bothering to ask. "Alone?"

"You know what? Fuck you, Tristan. Or better yet, call Ella to fuck you. Because I'm not interested."

Fury snapped out of me so quick and so strong, I wrapped my hands around her upper arms. I didn't hold on tight enough to hurt her, because that was not what I wanted. I just needed to make her see that I was hanging on by a thread. "You fucking kissed him right here. I watched him with his hands on you, trying to think of all the various ways that I could kill him."

"Screw you."

"You know what? Fuck it, I don't care." I slammed my lips on hers. She tasted like honey and wine and heaven. And I was going to lose my shit.

At first, she held herself stiff, refusing to mold her lips to mine, and I almost pulled away. Just as I was about to pull back, she whimpered. Tentatively, I slid my tongue over her lips and she gasped, allowing me entrance into her mouth. God, my blood roared, drowning out all possible rational thought.

Her. This one. Always her.

The chant increased with blooming intensity with every stroke, every slide of my tongue that hers met. I slid my arms over her shoulders and into her hair, gently cupping her face. And her hands went into my hair, sliding in underneath, tugging, pulling me closer. We were a clash of teeth and tongues and moans and frustrated whimpers. God, I had kissed the girl, but this was the *woman*, and the excitement level pushed it up twenty notches. All I could do was keep tasting her. My cock was still in my trousers, and the soft curve of her breast pressed against me made me quickly analyze every flat surface around us, so I could get her damn clothes off.

I slid one hand from her face down to gently cup her breast. She moaned into my mouth, arching her back, silently asking for more. I wanted more. So much more. But there were sounds, other people walking along the path. We were in plain sight of everyone.

It wasn't even as if we were holding to the garden maze. Nope, just there on the walkway, making out like two teenagers who were about to learn the definition of a quickie.

Jesus.

Ariel started to pull back, but even the sound of other people approaching didn't stop me. I couldn't let her go. I gave another quick, furtive swipe of my thumb over her nipple, and she gasped and tore her lips from mine, the fury in her gaze evident. "Stop it. Don't touch me again."

"Ariel."

"No. I mean it. If you come near me again, you're going to lose your life."

"Are you sure about that?"

"Oh, absolutely sure." And I could only watch as she stormed away, knowing full well I had fucked everything up.

SEVENTEEN

ARIEL...

My lips burned. My heart hammered against my ribs. I couldn't breathe. I couldn't fucking breathe. The heat still spread through me where his hand had been. My nipples still tingled, pissed off at the loss of his touch.

What the fuck was wrong with me? There was something seriously wrong with me because the one man I could not have was the one I felt like this about. As opposed to the one who had been eager to kiss me before, who I'd been lukewarm about.

I wasn't looking where I was going, and I stormed around one of the maze's hedges and bumped straight into Zia.

"Shit. Sorry. Fuck." Somehow, I'd gotten turned around. "Are you okay?"

Zia slid her gaze sideways. "Yes. I'm fine. Um, I was obviously on Prince Tristan's tail. But I guess... you had your eye on him."

Oh, fuck me. She'd seen us. "Zia—"

She held up her hands. "None of my business. At all. But you might want to fix your lipstick before you go back inside."

Quickly, my hands went up to my lips, gently touching them. They still burned. "I—"

"Again, none of my business. And I won't tell. Trust me, I know what it's like to want the person that you shouldn't have."

"Zia, it's not—" What was I going to say? *It's not what you think. I'm not a home wrecker. I don't really want him.*

All lies. Every last one. Because I did want him. Just now, if I hadn't heard those voices, I would have let him strip me there in the moonlight. I really would have. That's how desperate I was. That's how badly I could not function. God, I was such a mess. And he had a fiancée. I'd have to make sure I was not on his service anymore, because I couldn't keep doing this. I wasn't strong enough.

I'd thought I was. I'd thought I could function and just push through it. But no dice.

I checked my watch. "We've got another thirty minutes before we have to go."

She nodded. "Yeah, I know. You will need to see Sebastian before you go. Just to give him a debrief. But there have been no anomalies. Nothing, um, noted."

"Zia, thank you... you know, for being cool."

"Sure thing, boss lady. For what it's worth, I like you better than the ice princess."

"Shit. Does everyone call her that?"

Zia shrugged her slight shoulders. "Yeah. She's very cold and kind of a bitch."

"Yeah, but she's still his fiancée, so I think it's probably best if I stay off his service for a while."

She gave me a sympathetic smile and squeezed my hand. She held out her handheld device. "You go ahead. Get cleaned up before you meet Sebastian. I snuck a tracker on the prince's lapel. He's not getting away from me."

I blinked at her. And then I laughed. "You put a tracker on him?"

She nodded. "I figured it might be easier than trying to keep track of him in the crowd, especially if he was trying to lose us."

I frowned. "Do you get that impression? That he's trying to lose us?"

"I don't know. There have been moments since we've been on his service that he'll just vanish. And I don't know where he goes or what he does or who he's talking to, and well, it makes me nervous. So, I've started sticking one on him. I always remove it at the end of the day, don't worry."

"No, I'm actually impressed."

She grinned. "Happy to be of service. I'll see you in a little bit."

As it turned out, Zia was right. My lipstick was beyond smudged. Between Ian's kiss and then Tristan's full-on assault of my lips, any lipstick I did have left was smeared. I did a quick fix in the bathroom and tried to run my small travel brush through the rat's nest of my hair. Those loose waves had only increased in volume as Tristan had shoved his hands into it and tugged.

Then, there was a slight problem with my breast. I bruised easily, and when I adjusted my top, I could see a slight dusting of color just above my breast where he'd kissed down and rubbed his jaw. Jesus Christ. I was so screwed. Everyone was going to see.

No. Big girl panties. Concealer.

Oh yes. I did have concealer in my purse. I opened my cross-body clutch, pulled out the concealer, and quickly masked the evidence of what I'd been doing with the prince. God, how had this become my life? Back in my younger days, I had concealed many a hickey. I never thought I'd have to do it again.

When I got back to the party, Ian was looking for me. "There you are. Where did you vanish to?"

"Uh, you know, work. Sorry. Are you okay?"

He nodded with a grin. "Yeah. Fantastic. I'm making lots of connections." He studied me closely. "Are you okay? You seem... I don't know, off."

"I'm fine. I need to go debrief Sebastian though, and then we've got a team meeting after."

He nodded. "So, this is good night then?"

"Yeah, I guess so."

"All right, that's fine. But you know I'm going to get another kiss good night."

The smile tugged at my lips. Just as I was going to tell him thanks, but no thanks, Trace walked up.

"The king needs you."

I almost heard my sigh of relief, but I schooled my expression. "I'm sorry. I have to go."

He chuckled low. "Fair enough. I'll take a rain check."

"Thank you for coming with me tonight."

"It was fun. My favorite part didn't even happen at the gala."

I flushed deeply then. I knew exactly what he was referring to. Unfortunately, I didn't have the same feelings about our kiss.

"I swear, I'll call you tomorrow."

"Unless I call you first."

I was determined not to wince. That conversation wasn't going to be pleasant, but I had bigger fish to fry at the moment. When I followed Trace out, he grinned at me. "You looked like you needed a rescue."

"Sebastian doesn't need me?"

He shook his head. "I mean, I'm sure you're supposed to give him a debrief or whatever, but he didn't ask for you right now."

"Oh my God, I could hug you."

He opened his arms. "Ready when you are, boss lady."

I lifted a brow. "You know what, never mind."

"What, we're not hugging yet?"

"Nope. Still, team No Touching here."

He chuckled softly. "Anytime you need a rescue, call me."

"Who's got eyes on the prince?"

"Tamsin. He's gone back to his quarters."

"Okay, I'll meet you guys at the car."

It turned out Sebastian didn't need to be debriefed right away because, well, he had dragged Penny into one of the tunnels. The two of them hadn't even made it into their quarters before they were boning like rabbits.

They were very easy to hear in the hallway. So, I just shot him a text and said we'd catch up in the morning. There was no way I could look either one of them in the eye at the moment. Not just because I'd overheard them, or because of what happened with Tristan, but also because, well, I was mildly jealous. Which was fine.

I found the team waiting in the SUV and getting ready to head back to the office. Once we arrived, most of us immediately took off our shoes. I did a quick team round up, asking for status updates. Everyone checked in. No one had seen anyone who looked suspicious. No one was overly interested in the prince.

Everything was normal. But then Zia looked up from her tablet. "Actually, there is something interesting."

"Yeah, what's up?"

"I left a program running while we were gone to check

financials, unusual payments, money moving around in ways that it shouldn't, just to see if we could track anyone who might be after the prince for financial reasons. He doesn't have any gambling debts or anything like that, but he does make monthly payments, and then big lump-sum payments to the same accounts."

I frowned. "To whom?"

"To Ella Banks."

"Why?"

Zia shook her head. "Well, that's the problem. I don't know why. But it's been happening for three years. Monthly deposits for $10,000. Those are done by automatic transfer. And then every now and again, these larger amounts are deposited. $20,000 here. $50,000 there."

"Do those larger deposits correlate with anything specific?"

She nodded slowly and then met my gaze directly. She was quiet so long even Jax grew impatient.

"Well, Zia, out with it."

He was eager to get home. Neela had already taken the baby home an hour ago.

"Every time there's a big publicity event or they're photographed together, the next morning she receives a large lump-sum payment."

My stomach dropped.

Jameson frowned. "But why would he pay her for publicity engagements?"

Trace leaned back, his gaze on me. "Well, from my experience, I've been a bodyguard to a couple of wannabe socialites and starlets. When you got a fake romance, and you've hired someone to be your date, you usually pay them after the event."

Oh God.

My heart rate ticked up. *This is not happening.* But my mind kept replaying everything Penny had said about how they never touched and how they never kissed. Not once.

I didn't believe it. I didn't want to believe it. Because if that was the case, then he wasn't really engaged.

His words kept coming back to me. *'Everything is not the way it looks. Everything is not as it appears. I know I look like an asshole, but I promise you, I'm not.'*

He'd said that more than once. Oh God. I was going to be ill. The nausea swirled at my belly as the bile started to rise. I swallowed hard. "Okay, um, Zia, send me what you have." I had to swallow again and take a deep breath so that the quiver in my voice wouldn't betray me. "I'll look into it and see what else I can dig up. Also, I want to know everything about Ella Banks. I want you to dig back into what the Barcelona police had to say about her stalker. I guess I'll see you guys back here tomorrow morning. Trace and Jax, I'll put you on Tristan duty. Zia, you can help me filter through data. Jameson, I think you and Tamsin are off, right?"

Jameson nodded. "But if you need extra hands..."

I shook my head. "No, let's get you guys rested. We've been at this a while. And don't forget the Argonauts leave at four for their match in Chile, so I need everyone rested up. Tamsin you'll stay here, running solo, but I also need you to look at resumes for new recruits."

She nodded then pushed to her feet. "Copy that."

When Trace stood, he gently brushed my shoulder. "That new information is interesting. Whenever I saw someone in these fake relationships, they had a pretty ironclad nondisclosure agreement for all manner of reasons. So it's likely we didn't have that information because he might not have been able to disclose it, depending on the terms."

I nodded slowly. The way he looked at me, it was almost as if he understood or could at least see the struggle. But I wasn't going to crack. "Well, any other information you can think of, let's talk about it in the morning."

It wasn't until I was locked in my room that I let myself lean against my door and sink to the floor. Holy shit. *'I'm not the asshole you think I am.'* He'd been trying to tell me his relationship with her wasn't real. But for whatever reason, he needed it to *appear* real, which meant I didn't have all the information I needed.

It also means that he hasn't been cheating and you haven't done anything wrong. And you can have him.

That last thought... that was the most dangerous one.

Ariel...

I HADN'T SLEPT A WINK. Not after that bombshell last night. I kept trying to go through every interaction, every moment, trying to see what Penny saw. He was paying Ella, but why? What was he hiding? These scenarios only made sense if both parties got something out of it. So what was he getting? What was he hiding?

Do you really want to know?

He wasn't the person that I thought he was. Why wouldn't he tell me?

Because for some reason, he can't.

I had to assume that whatever he was hiding might provide

a huge clue into what the hell was happening with him. I just needed to fucking figure it out. What wasn't I seeing? I needed to know.

The rest of the team had their assignments for the day. Luckily, I was Tristan-free, so I could think for a moment, even though the first thing I *wanted* to do was run to the palace and demand answers, demand that he speak to me.

He's not even there. He's at practice.

Which made it a lot easier since I couldn't run to him like a disgruntled girlfriend, demanding to know why he was seen with a pretty blonde girl.

A chime sounded that let me know someone was at the door. And when I checked the security camera, I groaned. Fucking Ian.

But I plastered a smile on my face and greeted him. I held a cup of coffee in my hands, needing it to warm me from the inside. But still, it didn't matter. I knew I was going to have to do the thing that wasn't going to be comfortable.

"Ian. Come on in."

"Actually, can you come out here for a minute? I want to show you something."

"Ian, I—"

"Come on, get your shoes."

He was so perky and so excited, I almost couldn't say no.

Why? You're going to have to say no in a minute. You'll crush his little hopes.

Well, maybe he wouldn't even care.

"Fine." I went into my closet and slipped on my flats. Then we went outside. He had one of those old-school Rolls Royce convertibles. Powder blue. "I came to take you on a drive."

"Ian, I—" What was I supposed to say to that? "This is really sweet, honestly. But I can't. I have work to do."

"Come on, you're the boss. You can take a day off. Hell, take three hours."

"I wish I could." I actually did have work to do. And it was presumptuous as hell for him to just turn up. "I wish you'd called. I could have told you that it's impossible. I have a couple of client meetings scheduled, and there's another research thing I have to take care of." Yeah, because the mystery of Tristan's girlfriend was beckoning to me.

His face fell. "Oh, come on, Ariel. It's just a couple of hours. What's the big deal?"

"Well, the big deal is this is my job. I have to run my business. If you'd have just called, I could have told you that today wasn't good."

"Well, when would it be good?"

"I don't know. Let me look at my calendar." Also, let me never look at my calendar because we were not going to go out again. I should have listened to my original instincts.

"Yeah, check your calendar for more days when you don't have time for me."

"Ian, look, I like you. I think you're great, but I don't think we will work. Okay? Plus, you're super busy, and you work out of Miami most of the time. I know you've got that big deal that you're working with a football player here, but, I mean, you're going to go back. And that just doesn't make sense, right?"

"Well, I'm willing to try. Miami is only an hour flight."

"And I appreciate that, but that's the kind of commitment you make for someone that you really want to be with. And we just met."

"Well, I know how I feel about you."

I frowned. "And while I like you, I don't think we can move this forward."

His gaze bore down on me, and for a moment there was a shadow across his face. But then he sighed. "I came on too strong?"

"Well, a little. And what's more, I'm really not old school. I don't want someone ordering drinks for me. I don't want someone surprising me with things. I need plans, otherwise, I can't really function. I have people who depend on me. Right now, a whole palace depends on me."

He frowned. "You mean the prince?"

"What does the prince have to do with this?"

"Well, I noticed the way Tristan was looking at you."

I blinked rapidly. "I don't know what you're talking about."

"Come on. You think I didn't notice you vanished with him?"

"You know what, my job is protecting him. He had some questions we had to go over." Wow. I was a shitty liar. It was because I was almost always too honest. So when I had to lie, it just sounded terrible.

"Look, I get it. He's fucking royalty. I get the appeal, but I actually care about you."

"And I'm flattered. I am. It's just... This is terrible timing, and I'm just not necessarily in a place where I can—"

"Okay, look, I hear you. And maybe I come on too strong. I move too fast. I'm used to pushing for the deal, the sale, you know? So I get that. I'll back off, I swear. I just really like you. And the idea that I screwed up somewhere... I don't know. I hate that I might have fucked up with you."

"No, you're great Ian, for someone. I just don't know if there's enough chemistry here to really continue."

"Okay. Why don't we just be friends?"

I laughed. "Why are you so determined? Why do you want to be with me so badly?"

"Because there is a part of you that's really sad and vulnerable. And I don't know... it speaks to me, I guess."

I frowned. How had he seen that? I thought everything had been pretty surface with us. Or maybe I just wanted it to be surface. "I don't know—"

"Look, how about we have coffee at the end of the week? I'm going to Miami for a couple of days anyway."

"I swear to God, Ian. Okay, coffee. But as friends, okay? I just really can't do this right now. I have so much going on."

He held up his hands. "Friends. And then you can get to know me without any of the other stuff and see that I am not *that guy*. I'm not going to pressure you. I just think you're amazing, and I want to be near you. So, I can do friends."

"And I mean it, really friends."

"Of course." He held out his arms, and I almost pointed out to him that the obligation of a hug was probably just as bad as trying to force me to go on a date with him.

But I stepped in. "Thank you, Ian."

When he wrapped his arms around me, it was relaxed, friendly. He didn't try and hold me to him or anything like that. Maybe I had imagined that because it was easier.

He nodded and grinned. "See? I can do friends."

Suddenly, he was being dragged away from me, and things got chaotic. He moved so quickly, and I stuttered back several steps. But I regained my footing, and then I had my weapon out. Shit. My coffee. I placed my *I'd agree with you, but then we'd both be wrong* mug on the hood of the Rolls Royce, wincing a little, but keeping my weapon trained on whoever it was who'd dragged Ian off of me. Safety off. But then rapidly, I snapped the safety back on.

"Tristan?"

I glanced around, and sure enough, Jax was running up the drive. "Jesus Christ. He's fucking fast."

I rolled my eyes. "I thought Trace had an eye on him."

From behind me, Trace chuckled. "Well, I did have an eye on him."

I whipped around. "Oh, Jesus. Where did you come from?"

"Once I figured out where he was going, I came around the back. It was faster."

We all turned our attention to Tristan and Ian, who were both now basically snarling at one another with their hands on each other's lapels.

Tristan's voice was low and full of menace. "I believe the woman told you she wasn't fucking interested."

"And I believe the lady can tell me herself. You missed it. We agreed to be friends, which is a hell of a lot more than you'll ever be with her."

"Fuck you, Ian."

"What, pissed off that the little prince can't have everything he wants? You have a fucking supermodel fiancée. What the fuck do you want with Ariel? Leave some for the rest of us, would you?"

Tristan started to ease back as if he realized just how crazy he looked.

"Are your guys done yet?"

They both slid their gazes to me, Tristan's still full of fury, Ian's, confused. It was Ian who spoke first. "Yeah, I'm fine. It's not like Tris here has the real guts to go toe to toe with me."

"I will fucking kill you."

But Trace was on Tristan before he could release a hit. "Your Highness, that's not a good idea."

Jax had a hand on Ian's chest.

"Oh my God, everybody stop it. Trace, get the prince inside. Jax, get Ian in the car."

My men started to comply. But then Ian said, "Ariel, I'll take things as slow as you want. But last night's kiss will tie me over until I can get another one."

And then in a move that I hadn't seen since training, Tristan easily escaped Trace's grasp, and his fist snapped out, connecting with Ian's nose. The crunch was audible, and the snapping back of Ian's head was visceral. Even Jax was surprised.

Tristan turned to me. He didn't say anything, but his gaze said it all. I could feel it in my bones. *Mine.* He didn't have the look of a man who was engaged to another woman. He had the look of a man who was protecting his turf.

EIGHTEEN

TRISTAN...

Tʜɪs ᴡᴀs ɪᴛ. *Dᴏ ᴏʀ ᴅɪᴇ ᴛɪᴍᴇ.*

As I was preparing to depart for Chile, Ella took my hand. I glanced down at it, unaccustomed to her touching me on purpose. "You don't have to do this."

I was aware of being watched, so I softened my gaze as much as possible. "Yes, I do."

"Then at least let me be there?"

I shook my head. "You need to be elsewhere and constantly in the public eye. You leave tomorrow for LA, right?"

She nodded. "Yeah, but I mean, is this wise?"

"You go and prepare. You're an actress, and this will be the biggest acting job of your career. Act shocked and confused as to how this happened. Do you understand?"

"I know the plan, and I know my part in it, but I'm trying to talk you out of it because you might get caught. What if he's the one who's been trying to kill us?"

In my peripheral vision, I watched as Ariel came down the stairs toward the SUVs that were going to take us to the private landing strip. I pulled Ella forward and then kissed her forehead. She stepped back, startled. "I love you too," I said loud enough for anyone listening to hear. "I'll call you when I get there."

As she beamed a smile up at me, it was scary how quickly she could just slip into character. "I'll miss you."

"Me too."

I disengaged from her, feeling the hot sting of Ariel's gaze on my neck. When I turned, that shattered, hurt look I'd seen before was replaced with a different one. One that was quizzical and calculating, as if she was trying to figure out a problem. I knew that look. I'd seen it on her face dozens of times. Something was up.

Does she know? Does she suspect? I knew there was no way that she could. There was nothing she could do to stop me at that point anyway.

Lucas approached me. "Hey, cuz." He clasped my hand and pulled me in for a one-armed hug. "Your first game and I'm gonna miss it."

"Well, it's not a home game. That's next week."

"Can't wait. Remember I'll be right on the pitch. Ooh, do you think you can make me a referee?"

I rolled my eyes and laughed. "No. Absolutely not."

"What? I'd call it fair."

"You think the other team would really believe that? We're playing Ecuador. Those guys are brutal. We're gonna have to haul ass to keep up."

"Fine. I'll watch like a good little spectator. But you're not sticking me in the box."

"Got it."

"Break a leg or whatever."

I winced. "'They don't say that in football."

He laughed. "Fine, kick ass then."

"Yeah, that works."

Then he pulled me in for another one-armed hug. His voice was pitched low in my ear. "And that other thing that you're doing, the whole reason for the extra practices and extra work... I hope it goes well."

So did I. In my travel bag, I had my diplomatic credentials. I wasn't traveling with the team, thanks to my extra need for security. I'd never really used my diplomatic status before, preferring to stay with the team. But this time was unavoidable. Sebastian wouldn't have let me play, and as one of his subjects, he could have stopped me.

Luckily, he hadn't wanted to do that. He just wanted to make sure my travel plans were super secure, which made things a lot easier on me. Now the key was to time the travel with my plan for Max.

"Let's just say that I've enjoyed our practice sessions."

He nodded with a smile. "And you're ready for the big leagues now?"

I shrugged. "I don't know what you're talking about."

"Sure, you don't."

With another wave to Ella, who was chewing on one of her nails, I stepped into the SUV. Jameson was in the driver's seat. Zia was in the front passenger seat. Ariel was in the backseat with me.

In the follow car were Jax, Roone and Trace. With all the other Knights on duty, Trevor got a reprieve. Tamsin was staying behind to hold down the fort.

I had a veritable army with me. And none of them would be able to help me with what I had planned.

The flight to Chile was uneventful. I'd been given access to the bedroom in the back, but honestly, I didn't really want it. I just used the opportunity to pace back and forth, stretch my legs, stay loose. Everyone thought it was because of the game coming up, that I wanted to make sure I had no cramped muscles, but it wasn't for that. The soccer game I could take or leave. It was the game before that really mattered.

Ella kept texting me updates on Max's itinerary. She still had a friend in his office, and she managed to get itinerary updates under the guise that I maybe was looking for someone to manage my commercial endeavors. Someone other than my sports agent.

The assistant of course was all too willing to help. Max had tried to get me to agree to him managing my commercial endorsements way back when, way before I knew what an asshole he actually was, so it wasn't actually a stretch. When we landed, I forced myself to take a deep, long breath. This was what I had been working for the last three and a half years. I couldn't take back my life, but at least I could give Ella that gift. Now I was ready for it. Max Jacobson was going to wish he'd never laid a hand on her.

TRISTAN...

My mind raced as I tried to remember everything Lucas had told me. Be calm, be natural. Light fingers. I had to look at my fingers as intricate, tiny masseuses that were able to maneuver and move how I wanted.

I had what I needed in the pouch. I could do this. If I followed through, Ella would be free.

At least she *will be.*

I still had to contend with Ashton. But her needs were my priority. She needed me to be calm, and she needed me to make this happen. I checked my watch. Right on time. Actually, a little bit early. And because I wouldn't have to go through the normal customs procedure, that would save a little more time.

We disembarked from the plane. I'd left my bags exactly where they were. Someone else would carry them off.

Roone preceded me. And directly behind me was Ariel. I could feel her gaze on me, silently asking me questions that she couldn't voice.

I wanted to know what she wanted to ask. And why was she watching me so closely? For the most part, she'd been off my service recently. Maybe she thought I hadn't noticed, but I had noted that not once in the last week and a half had she been guarding me.

Maybe she just had a business to run.

We marched down the stairs and across the tarmac, and I was completely surrounded by the entire Royal Elite team.

It seemed like overkill. But hey, someone was actually trying to kill me, so there was that. Once we were across the tarmac and entered the building, the cloying heat was replaced by the stinging chill of air conditioning. I was glad I had on my blazer. Eventually, I would adjust to the temperature, but for the moment, Jesus, I felt cold.

We all handed over our passports, and they were checked meticulously. Roone and I had diplomatic stamps, so we were shuttled off to the left. I did my best not to look around. I knew exactly where the cameras were.

After all, I'd gone over the schematics a hundred times. Roone stepped aside to let me go first. I pulled my diplomatic pouch out. It mostly contained cash, something to make it look properly padded. I handed my passport over separately, and then I was patted down and sent through the metal detector, which was ridiculous, because anything I wanted to conceal would just be in the pouch. It didn't matter if it was drugs or something else, they couldn't search it.

They couldn't touch me. They could merely send me back to my own country, but only if they had knowledge of any crime that I intended to commit. On the other side of the metal detector, I was handed my pouch and my passport and welcomed to the country. I waited calmly for Roone to do the same. And we waited together for the rest of the Royal Elite team.

Knowing exactly where the cameras were, I gently shifted to talk to Roone so that my back was to the camera and Roone blocked the front of me momentarily. With my thumb and forefinger, I slid into the pouch, pulling out what I needed and tucking it into the inside pocket of my jacket.

Roone talked into his comm unit and placed a hand on my shoulder, making me pause.

In my peripheral vision, I noted Max and his team in the waiting area. I knew from my intel they were on their way back to the states, waiting to go out onto the tarmac. *Come on, come on.* Luckily, he had to get this customs procedure done first. Just 200 feet and she could be free, and I would regain part of my life back.

"Your Highness, wait. Ariel has to check all the weapons."

My gaze skittered to him. "What?"

"The weapons. She has to hand over all the paperwork."

"Seriously?"

"It will only take a few minutes."

I checked my watch. My window was shrinking to 15

minutes. And I wanted to be far the hell away before the commotion started. "God, do we really have to wait for all that?"

"It's safer if there are more of us protecting you. The cars are out front, but I'd rather we have you covered."

I shifted on my feet. "Right. Of course."

Come on Ariel. Make it fast.

But it wasn't her. When I glanced back over to the customs search area, I could see the holdup was the guy looking over the paperwork. He was on the phone, murmuring low to someone and holding the stacks of paper. And there were a lot of weapons and a lot of paper.

When I saw Max's team start to move, I tried to urge Roone on. "Listen, can we just go wait in the car? The car is bullet-proof, right? I don't want to just stand around here. I am getting cold. My muscles are tensing."

He frowned. "Honestly, waiting here is better. It's just another few minutes."

"Well, I mean, come on, mate. I'm going to be all locked up and stiff for the game because we have to wait for the paperwork to clear."

"Just give us another minute, okay?"

Roone was my mate. But my window was going to close if I wasn't careful. The airport was small and exclusive. Their private landing strip was less than a quarter of a mile from their main airport. And there were many businessmen on this side, all waiting to take some private jet somewhere.

Max and his team stood and walked out of the waiting room, headed straight in our direction.

No fucking way was Roone going to let me close enough. This was fucked. Finally, I just said, "Fuck it. Look, I'm going to wait in the car."

Roone's hand clamped on my shoulder, and I easily shook it off.

He frowned, and his eyes went wide in surprise at my ability to do that.

No use telling him that Frank had been training me for years.

I just waved behind me. "I'll be in the car."

"Your Highness, you have to wait."

I ignored him and just kept barreling forward, seeing my quarry, knowing what I had to do.

My heart thundered in that rapid-fire *te-ka-te-ka-te-ka-te-ka* beat. I couldn't even hear anything else. I knew Roone was coming for me and I had to move fast. I had to be faster than him, faster than Max, faster than Max's people, and faster than any of my guards who were now shifting on their feet.

It was then that Max really looked up. And his gaze focused on me. He skittered to a stop. "Tristan? Tristan Winston?" His voice was booming as if we were, in fact, old friends.

He seemed to forget that he'd told me that he would make me pay tenfold for stealing Ella from him. He'd said it publicly after a party. And I'd made it a point to tell him that he would never be seeing Ella again.

But now, he acted as if we were friends, all for show. There wasn't a single doubt in my mind as to whether or not he'd changed, because I didn't believe he was capable of changing. He put out his hand as if to draw me in close for a hug, and it confused me. Because that was not the plan. The plan was that I'd slide right by him and bump him.

But maybe this was better?

I moved my backpack to my other shoulder and reached inside my jacket pocket. I could feel the slide of a little plastic baggy between my fingers. When I palmed it, I grinned at him. Diverting his attention with one hand clapped on his shoulder. "Max. Mate, it's been a dog's age." And then I let him hug me. And just like that, with one hand clapping on his back, I slipped my fingers into his jacket lapel. And I deposited the drugs.

It was that easy.

Max frowned at me slightly as he pulled back, as if confused by my level of enthusiasm. But whatever.

I pulled back and grinned at him. "What's it been, a couple years?"

"Yeah." And then his smile hardened. "How's Ella?"

I forced my lips to tip up and to show some teeth. Just because I was showing teeth didn't mean I was smiling. "Oh, you know Ella. Tough that one. Busy too."

"Yeah, shame about that three-picture deal though."

It was hard work containing my snarl. "Yeah, you know, she did lose that one, but this new movie has Oscar buzz written all over it."

He frowned then. "Well, glad she's doing well without me. Independent films seem to suit her."

"Yeah, but I feel like she is poised to break into blockbusters again."

"Oh, God, I hope so."

As if. I could see it in his eyes. 'Over my dead body' is what he really meant to say.

Roone caught up to me easily. "Your Highness, I'll have to ask that you wait for the rest of the team." His voice was low, icy. He was pissed. It was fine. I didn't want any big to-do.

"Sorry Roone, I saw an old friend. Couldn't help but come say hi."

Roone nodded. "Max Jacobson, I know your work."

Max grinned at him, preening from the praise. "Always great to meet a fan." He clasped Roone's hand and shook heartily.

There was something in Roone's eyes that told me that he hadn't meant it as a compliment.

"Good man."

"Well, Max, I don't want to hold you guys up. You know, my Royal Guard is a little concerned about my safety."

"All right. I guess I had heard you and Ella had seen a spot of trouble."

"Did you? It hasn't really been public news."

"Well, you understand, I'm in the know when it counts."

I grinned at him. "Sure you are." He'd probably heard about Ella hiring more security, which was unavoidable, but still, he shouldn't know why. "Well, it was good to see you. I wish you luck on whatever endeavors you're pursuing."

"Well, you know, back to L.A. Ella's in L.A. now, right? I'll have to make an appointment to catch lunch with her."

Inwardly I thought, *Yeah, gonna be hard to do that from a jail cell.* But I smiled and stepped back. "Yeah, definitely. I'm sure she'll look forward to it."

Then I stepped aside, allowing Roone to direct me backward. His lips were tight with irritation. "You can't shake me, Your Highness."

"Great. Now you're calling me Your Highness?"

"Well, that's what happens when you're trying to slip your security."

"Sorry. I'm sorry mate, okay? My bad. Just let me go out to the car?"

"Fine. But I'm staying with you."

"Fair enough."

As we approached the exit, I held my breath. Waiting. Waiting for the dramatics to ensue. Max was going to have to go through customs. His handlers had his bags, and they were loading them through. I stopped and pulled out my phone. "Can we just stop here for one second? I just want to check in with Ella and tell her I ran into Max."

"You can't do that in the car?"

"It'll just take a second." After all, I had to be sure my plan had worked.

He nodded. I just had to confirm. It was too risky to just get in the car. I needed to see it happen, to make sure she was safe. I watched as Max handed over his passport and his paperwork.

And then the dogs were brought out. *Showtime.*

They sniffed each of the bags calmly, making sure there were no explosives, no drugs.

But there are drugs...

And then Max was patted down. Still nothing.

But then one of the dogs walked right up to him and sat down.

I could feel the tension crackling up my spine like one of those Fourth of July sparklers. *Pop, pop, snap.* Every guard in the place tensed. Two from the east side of the room stepped forward, one approached from the metal detector, and one moved away from Ariel and our crew and toward Max.

All I heard was Max saying, "What the hell is this?"

One of the guards asked him, "Sir, are you by chance carrying any illegal substances?"

Max gave a harsh chuckle. "No. Of course not."

"Then you'll consent to a search?"

"Of course."

It was done. Just like that. I turned to Roone then. "All right, let's go."

Roone pushed open the door, and all it took was three seconds before I heard the guard say, "Sir, can I ask you what this is?"

"But... that's not mine."

I heard the shuffle and clamor of the other guards moving in, and I knew it was over. It was finally fucking over. I stepped into the sunshine behind Roone and let the sun beat down on my face as I soaked in the freedom before stepping into the darkened interior of the SUV.

Ella was free. I had done it. And that motherfucker was going to jail for a very, very long time.

NINETEEN

TRISTAN...

I felt like I'd been beaten up.

My muscles were heavy, my head was foggy, and I was tired. Straight from the airport, I'd been driven to practice. The adrenaline was coursing through my veins, knowing that I'd managed to pull my plan off after all this time.

Three and a half years just to make our paths cross. To free Ella. I'd done it. And no one knew I'd done it. I couldn't very well text her, just in case anyone went looking, so I had to act as if everything was all right, as if I hadn't changed the course of her life forever. I'd also changed the course of Max's life forever.

I'd waited for it, the torrent of guilt, the remorse that came with changing Max's life for the worse. But it had never come. Instead, I'd arrived at practice feeling oddly, euphorically light. Later I'd realized that was strictly adrenaline.

Because by the time practice started I felt like crap. Utter shite. I was lethargic and tired. Coach had been screaming at me from the get go. By the end of practice, I had a booming migraine, and all I wanted do to was scrape the mud and muck off my brow and crash.

When I was deposited in my room, it was Jax who left me there. When my gaze met his, he studied me carefully. "Your Highness, are you all right?"

"Yeah. Nothing ten years of sleep won't solve."

He nodded slowly. "I'm not saying that you had anything to do with what happened at the airport, but if you did, I certainly hope that you know enough to keep it to yourself."

"What are you talking about?"

"Exactly. Because what reason would you, a Prince of the Winston Isles, have to do with someone like that? His bad reputation precedes him."

Oh, this was interesting. Had Jax heard something? "I only know him peripherally through Ella. I have no personal attachment to him whatsoever."

Jax nodded. "That's good. Plausible deniability if anyone should come asking. Of course, Ariel will make sure no one comes asking."

"She doesn't need to bother with that. Because there's no reason for anyone to come asking."

He smiled. "Well then, goodnight, Your Highness."

"Goodnight."

I closed the door. Once he was gone, I sagged against it.

Tired didn't even begin to cut it.

The shower was the best thing I'd ever done in my life. Still, I waited for the guilt. When it didn't come, I assuaged my lack of guilt by reminding myself that karma was acting through me. Yes, I was completely aware of how self-serving that was but I didn't give a shit.

I was out of the shower with a towel wrapped around my waist and heard a knock at my door.

For the love of Christ, the last thing I needed was someone

else checking to make sure I was in my room where I was supposed to be. I had an early morning tomorrow, and coach would not take kindly to me having another shit practice.

I checked through the peephole and saw the one person I didn't expect. *Ariel.*

I opened the door with a frown. "What's wrong?"

She blinked rapidly, and her gaze searched my chest. Everywhere her eyes tracked, I felt heat trace over me like a lover's fingertips. "What's wrong? What do you need?"

"Answers, for one."

I scowled at her. "What are you talking about?"

She didn't wait for me to invite her in, barging right past me. "You're up to something, Tristan, I'm worried it's going to get you killed."

"Ariel, is now the time?"

"When is the time? These days, we're never alone, which is probably for the best."

I hitched my towel tighter. And then I leaned against the desk in the hotel room. She wanted to do this, fine, we could do this. "You're going to have to be clearer about exactly what I did to you."

"It's not what you did to me." She frowned and started to pace, her teeth working her bottom lip just like she always used to do whenever she was working through a problem or trying to figure something out. *Careful, she'll figure you out.*

"Look, I don't even know what the hell that was at the airport. But something has been bugging me since before we left. For a week now, I've been sitting on this, trying to decipher it, doing all the research in the world. That guy today, that was Ella's former manager."

I opened my mouth to say something. But what was I going

to say? After all it wasn't a question. She already knew the answer, so I kept my mouth shut and watched her. She didn't need me to say anything, she was on a roll. "And they parted ways about six months into you dating her."

Again, not much for me to say. So I just waited.

"Did you have anything to do with that?"

I shrugged. "If you're asking if I told her to leave him, no."

She lifted a brow. "But that doesn't necessarily say that you're not the reason."

"I would never make her leave her manager. That's business."

"But if there was a reason to leave him..."

I shrugged. "Ella made a change all on her own. I just backed her play."

"See, right there. It's what you're *not* saying. The things that are being said between the lines, not using words but using evasions. Why did she leave her manager?"

"I—"

She held up a hand. "Okay, you know what, let me tell you what I know."

I threw my hands up. "By all means. You barged into my room, wanting to tell me all about my life. What the hell do you know?"

"What I know is you've been paying Ella. For every public appearance she makes, you pay her $20,000. She's amassing a small fortune from you."

"I'm not paying her. Look at it as perks."

"Perks? She gets a monthly stipend from you."

"Again, perks. I have it, why not give it to her?"

"Right after she left her manager, she was blackballed. Couldn't get a role for a year. She couldn't get a gig. Not a single one. But you, as soon as you became a couple, you started getting all these endorsements. The two of you were labeled the 'it' power couple. She was always on your arm. And she's a great actress, so she played the part to perfection."

I crossed my arms. "Is there something you're trying to ask me in there?"

"Yes. There is. And all I want is the truth. No embellishments, no extras, just the truth."

"Yeah, I'm still waiting for a question." She was too close. She probably had already guessed on her own. She knew about the money. I was praying she didn't guess the rest of it. But what could I do? If she guessed on her own, it's not like I told her. But still, I couldn't betray Ella.

There's no more betrayal. Max is gone.

Semantics.

"Is your relationship with Ella real? Are you in love with her? Is she in love with you? Are you actually ever planning to get married?"

I opened my mouth to answer and then closed it. I needed to think this through. What was I going to say?

Finally, I said, "You already know the answer."

"You never touch. You talk to her but there's no, I don't know, intimacy. And when you do touch, it looks like a performance."

She knew. She already fucking knew. "You already have all the information you need."

"That's right. So let's say maybe you can't tell me. Maybe you gave her your word, and your word is your bond. So let's pretend that after ten years, you see me, and there are residual feelings on your side."

I lifted a brow. "On *my* side, okay." For the moment, I'd let that one slide.

"From the beginning, you tell me everything isn't as it seems. You tell me that you *can't* talk about your past, not that you won't."

I nodded slowly. "This going somewhere?" I hoped it was going very far away from where it was careening toward.

"Yeah. I think that the rumors I've managed to dig up on your friend at the airport, Max Jacobson, are true. There are all these underground rumors that he's been sexually abusing and exploiting his young starlets for years, *decades,* but that Hollywood has buried it. I think Ella was one of his rising starlets, and he did a number on her. I think that Max had the idea, along with probably your agent, for a marriage or relationship of convenience. You make each other look good. Both your cachets would go up. It's a tale as old as time, right?"

I crossed my arms.

"I'm not done. I think Max got a little jealous. Maybe Ella's fake feelings became real. Am I getting close?"

I shrugged. "You seem to have it all figured out."

"Fine. I'll keep going. But what I can't figure out is why today?"

I ran my hands through my hair. "Ariel, just let it go. Just know that I'm okay. My safety isn't an issue. And Ella's okay. She's safe. She's clear."

She shook her head vehemently. "No. You're going to tell me."

"I don't have to tell you shit."

"You owe me this. After everything, just tell me the fucking truth."

She was close. Too close. If I stood, her breasts would be pressed into my chest. Her pupils dilated, and I watched her sudden awareness of how close she was to me. She attempted a step back, but my hand snapped out and captured her wrist. Gently, but still, I wasn't letting her go. "You just can't let it go, can you?"

She tipped her chin up and glared at me. "No, I can't. You've been dicking with my emotions for weeks. Kissing me and then telling me that you don't want me, and then kissing me again and telling me that I belong to you and I am yours. Only to learn you're *not* in a real relationship. Or not a traditional one anyway. I just want the truth. Because something happened with Max today, and I think it had a hell of a lot to do with Ella."

I didn't let her go, and I could feel her anger and the turmoil and the need bubbling forth. *Ella is safe now. She never has to worry about him again.* "You want to fucking know?"

"Yes. Is your relationship a showmance? I just need to know if it's fake or not."

I searched her gaze, the need to tell her the truth making my chest ache. "Yes. It's bloody fucking fake. Are you happy now?"

She snatched her wrist free. And I blinked with the pride of how quickly she moved. "Jesus Christ." She wrapped her arms around her belly and stepped back three feet. "It was all a lie?"

I ran my hands through my hair and then scrubbed them over my face. "The relationship is not real. We're not in love. We never have been."

"But why? Why all this time? Why didn't you just tell me?"

"I gave her my fucking word. And that matters to me."

Her gaze met mine, fury laced in the green depths. "Your word? You pulled the wool over everyone's eyes."

"Yeah. To keep her safe."

She blinked at me. "From Max?"

She knew. "Fuck. Fuck, fuck, fuck."

"Just talk to me. I can't help you if you don't tell me everything."

"I don't need your help."

"You think you don't. But at some point, Max is going to put it together that you framed him. Then what?"

I glowered at her. "Shut up, Ariel. Do not do this."

"Well, why not? The truth's coming out anyway, so we might as well do it right."

I stepped forward. "Yeah. I planted something on him. You realize he tortured her for years. Tried to ruin her career. He threatened her. Repeatedly. When the media loved us and she started to outgrow him, he threatened to tell everyone we were faking it. He threatened to ruin her if she didn't leave me. She called crying, and I went to her place. When I got there, I found her beaten bloody. That asshole. He could've killed her."

Ariel recoiled. "Oh my God."

"Yeah. Oh my God. He'd been hurting her for years. He'd met her when she was seventeen, and he promised her parents he was going to make her a star. And he did. But he also tortured her. And I know a little something about that."

She stumbled back. "Oh my God. I—" She shook her head. "I didn't—"

"You didn't know? How were you supposed to know? We played our parts to the T. If I ever loved her, I loved her like a friend. And God knows she needed one of those."

"So you just what, put your life on hold for all these years?"

I shrugged. "I've been discreet and so has she. But yeah basically. We didn't work at a real relationship. I guess both of us are too broken. But it's never been real. I promised her that I would make him pay."

She covered her mouth. "You realize what they're going to do to him, right?"

"No less than he deserves. He tortured her for years."

Ariel tripped into a chair. "Jesus Christ."

"I considered killing him, but even I'm not that fucked up. Besides, that'd be too easy for him."

"They've arrested him. It looks like the state department and his lawyers are involved. He's going to be tied up in this for a while. He's going to spend some real time in jail down here."

"Yeah, that was kind of the point."

She studied me. "You did all this to save her?"

I swallowed and leaned back against the desk. "Yeah. She deserves some freedom. His other clients do too."

"But why? What do you get out of it?"

I shook my head.

"Oh, come on, don't stop the honesty train now."

"She was going to help me get some information from Ashton."

"You're brother? But by the time you guys got together, he was already in jail."

"Yeah, I know. He has some files that I'd rather not get out. He's been holding them over my head for years."

"What files?"

"None of that's important. Now."

"So is she going to get them?"

I shook my head. "No. Once I realized that maybe Max was her stalker, or that maybe he was trying to kill us, I stopped that. Whatever Ashton's got on me isn't worth it. I'd rather just make sure she's safe."

"If you tell me, maybe I can help you."

The anger surged to life again. "No. You are staying away from this."

"Why do you always do that? Why do you try to protect me? I don't need protection."

"You have no idea what you need. I know. I know exactly what I'm dealing with. I've kept her safe, and I'm keeping her safe, so just stay out of it."

"What the hell is your problem? Why are you like this? God, you can be so caring and wonderful and just like a real hero, and then you're just—"

"And then what? Yeah, I'm fucked up. The woman I loved never fucking showed up."

"What the hell? You're the one who abandoned me."

"Ariel, I wrote to you every day for a goddamn year. You never once wrote me back. So you don't get to peel back my skin, poke around, and act like I should be happy about it. No. You don't get to do that."

Lips trembling, her gaze met mine. "I never got a single letter."

And my heart turned to ash.

ARIEL...

What letters? What the hell was he saying? It was too much. Too much information, too much pain, too much goddamn hope.

Hope that it was possible, hope that I could have him. Hope that the last ten years had been some kind of dream and he could be mine again.

"What letters?"

He stared at me, pulling back slightly. "Stop it. Don't act like you don't know what I'm talking about."

"That's the problem. I *don't* know what you're talking about."

His gaze searched mine. "Stop. This isn't funny right now."

"Well, I'm not laughing. I'm trying to understand what the hell you're talking about, why you think I would've gotten any letters from you."

"Ariel, I wrote you. Daily for a while. Then weekly, then monthly. And then eventually once a year, and then I just stopped. It was too painful."

"I never got a single letter."

He ran his hands through his hair. "Stop lying."

"Why would I lie? What purpose does it serve for me to lie to you?"

"No." He shook his head. "No, no, no. I wrote you. And you just ignored them."

"I don't know what you're talking about, Tristan. Last I heard from you, I was supposed to meet you on the docks."

He actually did recoil then. "No, Ariel, I left you a note at the cabana. In our spot. Always in our spot. I told you what had happened. That I didn't have any time and had to leave. And it wasn't safe to call you. I left you a fucking ticket. One you never used, by the way."

My gut twisted and knotted up, as I suddenly felt light and heavy at the same time. My head spun, and I was hot, too fucking hot. I couldn't look at him. I had to look anywhere but at him.

It was just like you thought. Because he didn't want you.

No. He didn't want me. He hadn't wanted me. I had gone back to that cabana. There was nothing there.

I shook my head. "Stop. Stop dicking with me. It's cruel. Why be cruel when there's no need."

"I don't know what you're talking about. I'm not being cruel, Ariel."

"There was no note, no letter, no fucking ticket."

He shook his head as he ran his hands through his thick blond hair. "Stop it."

"Tristan, I'm not lying."

"Well, *I'm* not lying."

He sighed. "Okay tell me exactly what happened that night."

I didn't even know I was crying until the wetness hit my lip and I licked away salty tears. "I went to the docks just like we said. I was going to wait for the boat. Then you didn't show. I waited for two hours. Then I went to the cabana because I knew that's where we left notes. I looked in our shell. Just like always. There was no note in there. No ticket."

He was still frowning. "Then what happened?"

I rolled my eyes. "Then your brother found me in there. And he told me where you'd gone. That you'd abandoned me. That you left and you weren't coming back."

"Ashton was there?"

I nodded. "Yeah. I'd just finished searching the whole damn cabana in case you'd left a note for me somewhere else. But no luck. You were just gone. And there I was with my bags all packed like I was following you somewhere."

"Ashton was there."

"Yes, Ashton. Your brother. Asshole extraordinaire. You should've seen him. The look on his face. He was almost gleeful when he told me that you weren't coming back. That you'd abandoned me. I didn't know what else to think or say. All I knew was that you were gone."

With a sigh, he collapsed on the floor. Towel still on, shirtless, his head laying back on one of the legs of the desk. "Fuck. Fucking Ashton."

"What are you talking about Tristan?"

"He must've found the letter and the ticket."

"Really, Tristan?"

He nodded slowly. "Ariel, I swear on my life. I left you a letter that night. A ticket. I wrote you letters from Madrid."

"For the love of Christ, Tristan, I would've gotten them."

"I sent them to your house, Ariel."

I frowned. "You sent them to my house? With your name on them?"

"Yeah."

"Jesus Christ, Tristan... my dad."

"I mean, I didn't know what else to do. You never showed up."

"Because I was waiting for you."

"Fuck, Ariel. I'm so sorry. I don't know what to say."

I shook my head. I couldn't think. My heart was racing too fast. And God, my legs. My fucking legs. I couldn't stand. But no way was I collapsing in front of him.

I ran for the door.

"Yeah, that's it, run away."

"Tristan, I can't."

I yanked the door open and ran out. Like a coward, I ran straight for my room, blindly trying to work through his words. Trying to piece together all the things. I'd lost ten years. Spent ten years loving someone who claimed he hadn't tossed me aside. Ten years loving someone who claimed that he had wanted me with him. Ten years believing the worst of him.

I wasn't even looking where I was running. I just turned a blind corner and ran straight into Roone, my face literally bouncing off his chest.

"Ariel, what the fuck?"

I tried to dodge around him. But he held me steady.

"What's wrong?"

"Just let me go. I don't want to talk about it right now."

His eyes widened in alarm when they searched my face. Yep, Roone had never seen me cry. And like every man before him, he looked ready to bolt.

But instead of bolting, he grabbed me by the shoulder and tugged me into the nearest room. I looked around. It was his room. "Talk."

"What do you mean talk? I've said all I can say, all right? I mean I don't know what else to tell you."

"I mean, why are you so upset?"

"I don't know. I just I don't want to do this."

"Okay, fair enough. Do you want me to do it? Do you want me to tell you what's going on?"

"Roone, I'm too tired for this, okay? I just I want to collapse. I need a minute."

"Tell me. This isn't like you."

I shook my head. "I don't even know where to start."

"Well you can start with how you're in love with Tristan, he's in love with you, and you've been avoiding his service for the last week and a half."

I glowered at him. "I have not been *avoiding* his service."

He lifted a brow. "Really?"

"Oh, fine. I've been avoiding his service. I just, I couldn't."

"Then talk to me. What's going on?"

"He just... God, I hate him."

Roone chuckled. "Really? You sure about that? Because you don't look like you hate him. You look like you're in love."

"Shut up. I don't *want* to be in love."

"Yeah, that's not exactly how it works. Sorry to break it to you."

"God, why is this so hard?"

"Well, it's hard because it's love. Now tell me what's going on."

"I found out that he and Ella aren't really engaged. It's a showmance, or whatever."

He chuckled low. "Yeah, okay. Makes sense. Continue."

I glared at him. "That makes sense?"

He laughed. "How many times a day do you see me touching Jessa?"

I opened my mouth to argue with him, and then I snapped it shut. Good point. "Fine. Maybe I should've seen that it wasn't real."

"Yeah, also because he, in fact, spends half his time eye fucking you. You guys are pretty obvious. You can feel the longing. It's sad and emo."

"Thanks."

"Don't mention it, mate. What else is bothering you?"

"He says he wrote me letters. So many letters. I never got a single one. Supposedly he sent them to my house. There was this whole misunderstanding. We were supposed to meet and run away when we were kids."

He frowned. "Okay, we'll get back to that. But let me solve the problem first. What letters?"

"That's what I said."

"When did he write them?"

"He says starting from when he had to leave and go to Madrid."

Roone held up a hand. "Hold my pint."

"What are you doing?"

"I'm going to verify."

"How are you going to verify mail from ten years ago?"

"Well, you're almost forgetting that you worked in Intelligence. What happens to mail sent by any of the royals?"

I frowned. "Well, okay. There's the royal process so even if they're abroad it goes through—" I blinked up at him. "Oh God. You *can* track it."

He nodded. "Because even though Tristan was abroad, he was still a royal. So all his mail would have gone through inspection, then been delivered to its actual destination."

"Everything was monitored."

He nodded. "Yes, so there would've been a record. And they would've been kept and inspected by Intelligence before they were delivered."

"Jesus Christ."

"Yep. He would've handed them off to a guard who would've airmailed them to be reviewed first."

"And then delivered."

"So if they were never delivered..."

"Then someone tampered with them. But there would be evidence of them arriving."

Roone picked up the phone and called home. As he spoke in a low murmur with someone, my heart leapt. *Oh my God. What if this is real? What if he'd written me?.*

I could hear Roone muttering. "Starting about ten years ago. Anything that was maybe addressed to Lee Ariel Scott. She wouldn't have been a lady then. That's right, her home address, not guard housing but her childhood home."

He stood there quietly and waited.

When his gaze met mine, he was patient and cool. After fifteen minutes someone came back. "Okay, so the records were digitized then."

More silence.

"They were tampered with? Okay so you see a record of letters coming in from the prince. To whom?"

I waited, my heart beating too fast. God, all I wanted to do was sleep. Just crawl in my bed and sleep for ten months and wake up and find all this was a dream.

Roone was talking again. "Wait so you have records of them coming in, addressed from the prince, and it says final destination Winston Isles, but there's no address? So it was deleted?" He paused. "Do we have the actual physical copies of the mail? Yes, I want you to fucking go look in the archives."

HE WAS silent for another minute and then spoke again. "Great. When you find them, I want them delivered to Royal Elite Security, care of Lady Ariel Scott."

When he hung up and turned to me, he said, "Looks like the prince might be telling the truth. There were letters. From the records, it looks like over 100."

"Oh my God." He'd been telling the truth. He'd written to me.

Ashton lied.

"Do they still have them?"

"They're going to look in the archives, but I don't know. You'll have to speak to the prince."

My hands shook. "Oh God. I ran away."

Run back.

"Yeah, I know. Happens to the best of us. But maybe you take a minute for yourself to figure out what outcome you're looking for. Go grab a shower, get some sleep."

"Yeah. I'm going to do that."

"You going to be okay?"

"Oh, you know, I just have to reevaluate every thought I've had for the last ten years. It's going to take a minute."

He nodded solemnly. "Yeah I understand that."

When I left Roone's room, I only had one destination in mind. My bed. I just needed to sleep this off. When I woke up, I would know what to do

Are you so sure about that?

TWENTY

TRISTAN...

ONCE I HAD MY CLOTHES ON, I COULDN'T FIGURE OUT what to do.

I wanted to go after her. Every muscle in my body told me to go after her, make her understand, make her see that I would never have abandoned her. That Ashton must've interfered somehow. But I knew how it sounded. And after what I told her and what she'd seen at the airport, God, why would she even want me?

There was a knock at my door, and I ran to answer it without even thinking. I yanked it open, and Roone was on the other side, arms braced in the frame, with a scowl on his face. "Mate."

"Roone?"

"First of all, you didn't even ask who it was. Second of all, if you're dicking with her, I swear to God I will have your nuts."

My brows lifted. "Excuse me?"

"Mate or not, prince or not, if you dick with Ariel, I will fuck you up, you twat."

I squared my shoulders. "I'm not dicking with her. I fucking love her, you prat."

"She loves you too, you knob. So how are you going to fix it?"

It only occurred to me then that she must've told him, and I stepped back. Roone barged into the room, and I closed the door behind him, crossing my arms and glaring at him. "I wouldn't hurt her."

"I was an idiot who didn't really see it at first. But now after watching you guys for a couple weeks, it's fucking apparent."

"Yeah, well. What am I supposed to do? I love her."

"Yeah well I do too. She's fucking family to me."

Hearing this made the hairs on the back of my neck stand up. "Just family?"

Roone rolled his eyes. "Yes, just fucking family. I'm in love with Jessa remember? Gorgeous princess. A smile that can light the room. Basically looks like sunshine?"

My lips tipped into a smile. He did love Jessa. "Mate, I'm not lying to her. I did write her letters."

Roone nodded. "Yeah, I made some calls. The mail was tampered with. It seems that any letter you sent home, if it wasn't addressed to your parents, it never made it to its final destination."

"Wait... not just letters to Ariel?"

"Yeah. I have someone checking the archives to see if we can actually locate the letters. But anything not directed to the palace never made it out for delivery. They couldn't erase the incoming records, but they erased the final destination. So someone didn't want her to get those."

"Fuck Ashton."

Roone frowned. "Why would your brother care if Ariel got letters?"

"It was his whole goal in life to make sure that I enjoyed none of mine. He hated me."

"Fuck, I'm sorry."

"I'm even more sorry he continues to fuck with our world."

Roone narrowed his gaze on me. "What the fuck are you going to do about it?"

"What do you mean?"

"Well, she knows that that farce with Ella isn't true."

I winced. I guess Roone knew too.

"Look, let me think here."

He shook his head. "She didn't tell me, just so you know. I could see it."

"How?"

"If you're going to pretend to be shagging someone, you're going to have to touch them. Like a lot."

I frowned. "Right."

"Just saying. It shows when you're into someone and when you're faking it."

"Yeah good to know."

"Also, every time you look at Ariel it basically looks like you want to jump her bones and shag her senseless. So, there's that too."

"Ah, bloody fantastic."

"So, are you going to go get her?"

"There's nothing to say. It's been too long. A lot of pain. And anger, clearly."

"You're a twat."

"What?"

"You heard me. You are a twat."

"I heard you."

Roone lifted a brow. "Oh, you don't know what it means?

Well, generally it means you're a giant pussy. But since I don't want to use pussy in a pejorative sense, because it is my favorite thing in the world, I'll call you a wanker, a knob, an egit."

"Yeah, thanks for that. Why the abuse?"

"Because you don't see that she loves you and that she could make you happy."

"Yeah, but I don't think *I'd* make *her* happy. She deserves a lot better than me."

Roone grinned then. "You won't get any disagreement from me. But, you seem to be the one she wants. So you know, don't be an asshole. Fix it. Whatever it is, fix it. Otherwise you'll regret it for the rest of your life. And if I ever, ever see Ariel actually fucking cry again, I will kill you. Whether or not I'm sworn to protect you, I will kill you with my bare hands."

And with that, he stormed out.

"Christ." I stared after him. I needed her. I didn't want to be weak, but I did need her. I just wanted to talk to her. Really talk. Not that talk-shouting thing we've been doing at each other for weeks. I needed her so badly I could breathe it. My body vibrated with it.

Then go and get her. And make it count.

I just hoped to God she would let me in.

TWENTY-ONE

TRISTAN...

I WAS SCARED. I COULD ADMIT IT.

I ran down to Ariel's room and then stopped just short of knocking because I had no idea what the hell I was going to say.

What if she slammed the door in my face?

What if she told me she didn't want me?

What if she told me the lies were too much, and she was sick of it?

What if she told me she wanted someone else? Just the thought of Ian with his hands on her pissed me off all over again, and I had to work to quell my anger.

I wanted her. I just had to make her understand that I wanted her. That I had *always* wanted her. That I never would have abandoned her. I didn't know how I was going to do that.

Well you won't know if you don't knock. Finally, I just sacked up, lifted my hand, and knocked on the door.

It took her so long to answer, I was afraid she wasn't going to. When she finally did, her eyes were red-rimmed, and she looked tired.

"What do you want?"

"I'm sorry. I'm sorry for everything. I'm sorry I lied. I'm sorry my brother is a psychopathic asshole. I'm sorry you got caught up in our hate situation. I'm sorry that I ruined your life. I'm sorry for all of it. But I love you."

Her eyes went wide. "What?"

I nodded. And then I kept talking faster and faster in hope that she wouldn't turn me away. "I love you. I loved you from that moment I walked in and you tried to explain the benefit of action movies to me, a guy. But from like this completely philosophical, intelligent angle. About what they did for the release of endorphins in our brains. And then you proceeded to outline your favorite."

She shrugged.

"Die Hard, of course."

"Yes. But, I mean, I still argue that there are others. I mean, you have to reevaluate that whole list. John Wick is out now."

"Yeah, that's fair."

"Ariel, I bloody love you. And I'm sorry about the Ella thing, and I'm sorry that it seemed like I've been dicking with you. That was not my intention. I just... it's a mess and I never expected to see you again, and I didn't think that you would want to, and—"

She stepped forward and placed a hand on my stubble. "You love me?"

"Absolutely. Without question. I haven't been able to love anyone else." I almost told her that even when I was with someone else, she was who I thought of. But I didn't want to conjure up those ideas of me being with anyone else, so I kept my mouth shut.

"You wrote to me?"

"I did. God did I. I didn't know why you didn't come. I thought you'd had second thoughts or didn't want me—"

"Tristan,"

"Yeah, Ariel?"

"I love you."

The simple words flooded my veins with a mixture of relief and need. I couldn't even think at that moment as I crushed my lips to hers. I had everything I had ever wanted, and I never, ever, ever wanted to let it go.

My arms wrapped around her. It was impossible to think.

My tongue slipped between her lips and she moaned.

Fuck, she tasted good.

Too good. I never wanted to stop.

I stepped us both inside and backed her up against the wall as I growled low in my throat. I slid my thumbs over her cheekbones, and I nipped at her bottom lip. Ariel hesitated for only a second before her arms looped around my neck into my hair. When she twined her fingers into the strands, I groaned and deepened the kiss.

Fuck. She was going to light me on fucking fire from the inside. I couldn't think. All I knew was I needed more. So much more.

I braced her against the wall and urged her legs around my waist. We both moaned as that brought her heated core in contact with my pulsing erection.

I treated her mouth like a delicacy, tasted and tempted and teased her tongue into playing. Making sure she wanted this. Wanted *me*.

Before it had been sweet. Two kids in love. She'd been so innocent I hadn't wanted to push her too far. And with my shit, I didn't think it was fair, so we'd never taken things this far. But there was absolutely nothing stopping us now, and I intended to make up for lost time.

As I licked into her mouth with my hot tongue, I slid a hand up her stomach and ribs. I paused just short of touching her breast, and Ariel whimpered, arching into me.

So soft.

I skimmed my thumb over her breast, and she gasped, undulating her hips, grinding along my cock. With a muffled moan, I scooped a hand over her ass and held her tighter to me, pressing my erection against her.

Control. Get goddamn control. But I was losing it. She was rocking against me, and the pleasure... Christ the pleasure. I wanted to make this so good for her. This wasn't about me.

My dick had some other ideas about that at the moment with her heated center grinding against it. My tongue slid over hers, and I sucked her tongue into my mouth, her little whimpers spurring me on.

I tore my lips from hers and dragged in ragged breaths. Ariel forced her eyes open and met my blistering gaze. When I spoke, my voice was low, gravelly. "I'm going to make you come."

"Yes, fucking please."

I PICKED her up and carried her to the bed. I would have loved to sink into her there against the wall. To get that first desperate orgasm over with so that we could both take our time and bask in the pleasure, but for what I had in mind, I needed a bed.

Once I had her settled in the middle of the king-size bed, I wasted no time hooking my thumbs in her shorts and tugging them down her long, lean legs. I went to her tank next. I already knew she wasn't wearing a bra, but I needed her bare to me. I planned on paying proper homage.

I was going to lick them. Suck them... *fuck* them.

I loved everything about the way she tasted. Spicy, with just a hint of sweet. I'd been slowly losing my mind for weeks. And now she was in my arms and she wanted me. I looped her hands over her head and clamped them in place with one hand. I ran my other hand down her body.

Her lips parted on a sigh, and she relaxed her thighs, slightly opening her legs for me. My cock throbbed.

A tremor ran through her body, and I kissed her softly, still sliding my hand over her belly. At the juncture of her thighs, I dragged the back of my knuckles over her panties and she pulled in a shuddering breath.

"You're so responsive. I bet you're soft as butter too, aren't you?"

She mumbled something unintelligible, and I swallowed hard. My hand shook as my fingers traced the edge of her panty line. I watched her face intently for a hint of hesitation, but there was none. Only the same longing need that drove me.

I slid my finger just under the fabric, and she wiggled in my grasp. Her legs widened, and I held my breath. So damn wet. So hot.

I found her slick entrance, and I slid the tip of my finger inside her. Ariel tossed her head back and bit her lip. God, I could have come just from watching her, she was so beautiful. As I slid in farther, I bit back a curse. "You're so tight."

"Tristan... oh God."

I kissed her again, sliding my finger in deeper as I did. While I sucked on her tongue in time to my questing finger, I slid my thumb over her clit.

She bucked and tore her lips from mine. "Oh, oh, oh."

With another gentle stroke of my thumb, she flew apart in my arms, whispering my name as she milked my finger.

ARIEL...

Shudders racked my body.

Jesus Christ, the prince had a way with his hand. And I wanted more. *Needed* more. I slid my tongue over his and rolled my hips into his hand.

He released my hands and tugged his shirt over his head. I reached for him with frantic, trembling fingers then slipped his belt from its loops, and he growled low.

I watched him intently as I slid my hand inside his trousers. When I closed my palm around the scorching-hot length of him, he dropped his forehead to mine and cursed. I let my hand slide to the tip and smoothed the drop of pre-come over the head of his erection, then I squeezed him gently as I slid my hand to the root. His hips bucked into my hand.

"Bloody hell, I..." His voice trailed, and his breathing was heavy and labored. "Do you have any idea how close I am to losing it?"

I could do this to him? The feminine power went to my head, and I slid my palm over him again. This was why Tristan was so dangerous. His ability to make me believe I was sexy and powerful and a goddess.

He snagged a hand around my wrist, and my gaze snapped to his. I saw more than lust in his gaze though. I saw trust and love.

Tristan kissed me again, and my insides turned to liquid. I

slid my hand from his flesh, and he quickly shrugged out of his pants. He yanked a condom out of his wallet and sheathed himself with a quick efficiency that I marveled at.

When he turned his attention back to me, I shivered. To be the object of that kind of focus was overwhelming. He slid his hands over my thighs, his gaze on mine as his fingers grazed the lips of my sex. A shudder racked my body, and I gasped.

Tristan kissed up my body. When he reached my lips, his thumbs stroked over my cheeks as he kissed me. A move so tender in contrast to the way he'd previously devoured my mouth like a starving man.

Tristan lifted me again and I willingly wrapped my legs around him. I arched my back and he leaned forward, nuzzling one breast before suckling the tip. As he sucked, he palmed the other and tested the weight while teasing my nipple.

God, I could totally come this way. But I wanted him to make love to me. I arched into his palm, spreading my legs wider to make room for him between my thighs. Gently he teased my nipple, sending a spear of need through my core. "Tristan, c'mon."

With a chuckle, he positioned himself at my slick center. "Look at me," he whispered.

I disobeyed and let my eyelids flutter closed.

He pinched my nipple lightly. The moment I arched my back, looking for more, he ceased the action. "I said, look at me."

I dragged my eyes open. "Stop teasing me."

His lips tipped into a smile. "I want to see your eyes when I sink into you."

Inch by inch he slid into me, both of us holding our breath. I grasped on to his shoulders, digging into his flesh for support, while Tristan slid his hands under me, cupping my ass as he sank deep into me.

It was all too much, too intimate. I tried to look away. But with every shift, he met my gaze. There was no hiding from the intimacy between us, no running from it. No concealing the vulnerability.

The thick length of him rocked inside me then retreated slowly. The tension coiled deep inside me as I slid my hands into his hair. As he nuzzled into my neck, I tugged on his hair slightly, and he hissed, "Harder. I like that."

I was more than happy to comply as he nipped at my jaw, then my collarbone.

He stroked deeper, each thrust hitting both my clit and that hidden spot deep inside.

"Oh my god," I whispered.

"You feel fucking amazing. I've waited so fucking... so long... wanted you."

With whispered sex words muttered in the darkness, the shiver of bliss came on strong, snaking rapidly down my spine, the spasm racking my whole body and ending in my toes. But it wasn't until he lifted his head, kissed me deep, and slid a hand between us to stroke the bundle of nerves between my folds that I flew apart, unable to hold on to my illusion of control any longer.

"You're so sexy when you come." With another deep stroke, Tristan groaned into my neck, his whole body shuddering.

♛

I MIGHT WELL BE BROKEN.

I was pretty damn sure I was broken.

But Tristan wasn't. He held me close, gently stroking my back. Eventually, he got up, removed the condom, and helped clean me up.

When he came back to bed, I noticed he was still semi-hard. "Jesus, how can you go again?"

His smirk was immediate as he slid in behind me and pulled me close. "I've been dreaming of nothing else for years. I have built up quite the fantasy list to try out with you."

He went in for another kiss, this one hungrier. Bolder. "Tristan..."

"Yes?" He devoured my lips. I wiggled my hips against his hardening erection, and he hissed curses into my mouth. "You see, this is all your fault."

Gently, he turned me over, his thumb sliding over my cheek as he met my gaze. "You okay? Not too sore?"

I responded by lacing my fingers into his hair again and giving the strands a tug.

Tristan shuddered. "Jesus, Ariel."

Something deep inside me pulled. God, I still wanted him. My prince. How was that even possible? My limbs felt like noodles. Gently, I drew his hand to my right breast.

His eyes flared, and his lips parted as he whispered my name. I widened my legs, giving him the invitation he was asking for. He kissed me again, his palm curving around my breast and testing the weight. His thumb slowly circled my nipple, and his hips rocked against me, positioning his rock-hard cock at my cleft again.

I knew from experience just how good he'd feel. Knew I'd be climbing toward orgasm in no time.

Gently, he nuzzled the cleft of my breasts, and I whimpered.

Tristan bracketed my hands above my head again. "You're so naughty. Making me want you. How do you think I should punish you?"

His tone was stern, but his gaze was mischievous. Of course, I played along. "I'm not sure. I didn't mean to be naughty."

I smirked and tried to press him closer to me. I was so wet with wanting him. He could just slide in again, and we'd both be coming in moments. With every stroke and tug of his deft fingers on my nipple, my body softened.

Tristan kissed a path to my nipples and teased the puckered tips with his lips. His warm breath whispered over my flesh, and I shivered. When he closed his lips over the stiff peak, I slammed my eyes shut and moaned. His gentle tugging movements caused an answering pull in my core. I was dying for him. Needed him to fill me again.

He pulled back though, and with a hand on my hip, he turned me over. Oh, hell yes.

His hands ran gently over my ass. "I wonder. How does my girl feel about being spanked?"

I stiffened. "You will not spank me."

"You don't like it, or you're indignant?"

I paused to think about that. I'd never been spanked before, so I had no frame of reference. I was mostly indignant that he thought he could. The idea of it though... intrigued me.

"Indignant."

I could hear his smile. "That's what I thought."

The swift smack to my ass was more surprising than painful. "Did you seriously—"

Another one came on the other cheek.

Holy hell, I was wet. But still, I wiggled in protest. At least I thought it was protest. I was sort of angling for his palm again.

His breathing was ragged and his voice guttural when he spoke. "Still indignant?"

I cleared my throat. "Less so now."

"Hmmm, noted." He ran his hands over my ass again, and I shivered in anticipation. Gently, he lifted me up so my ass was in the air. I followed his lead. I'd have done just about anything if it meant he'd give me an orgasm.

I expected his palm again, but instead it was his tongue. He grasped my hips tightly and lapped at me from behind. "Do you know your ass is a thing of beauty? I haven't been able to keep my eyes off of it."

I tossed my head back as he licked and stroked my clit. With every flick of his thumb, I would get closer to ecstasy, then he would back off my pleasure button.

The stroke with his firm tongue was a shock as he licked the entire length of my slit. The second sure stroke was a promise. Every stroke of his tongue between my wet folds was a race to orgasm. The third lick was a seduction. He avoided my clit and teased around it, instead, sucking at my pussy lips and licking my slit. The tip of his tongue circled my opening, and he pushed it in as far as it would go.

I reached back and held on to his hair, urging him to go faster, to give me what I needed. But he continued at his own pace. When he slid one finger inside my tight entrance as he licked, I expelled a long breath. "Oooh."

He retracted his finger, only to reenter me with two. Finally, his tongue swept over my clit. With his teeth, he gently teased it, suckling the hot spot as he had my nipples.

My orgasm crashed into me with the force of a tidal wave. I hadn't known I was so close until he'd started in on my clit. I came—hard. As I came and came, he continued easy, lazy strokes. His fingers and his tongue showed no signs of giving me any rest.

When I'd tumbled down from my high, he continued to lick at me. Eventually, he stepped back from his feast.

I panted as I held onto him. He muttered nonsense words, crooning to me. Telling me how sweet I tasted, how beautiful I was.

Tristan reached over to the bedside table for his wallet and pulled out another condom. When he lined himself up with me, I arched into his touch, begging for more from him. He sank deep, his big body covering mine. His muttered curses in my ear. "I really, really wanted to take my time, but you're so damn tight. God, you feel so good."

He slid his hand into my hair, gripping loosely, careful not to hurt me, but he was relentless with his lips, his teeth, his dick. He slid his hands up my torso, bringing me upright against his body as he made love to me. He kissed and nipped at my neck and shoulders, whispering about all the things he'd dreamed of doing to me.

"You're so fucking tight... made for me... fit in my palms just right." He didn't stop talking to me, didn't stop making me feel as if I was going to be hit by a lightning strike of pleasure at any moment. But in the end, it wasn't the dirty words that had me careening off a cliff.

It was the simple ones he whispered as he started to come.

"I love you. I have always loved you."

And then I was lost, chasing him into the abyss of pleasure.

TWENTY-TWO

ARIEL...

I was sore. Like sore, sore. Like sore in places I didn't even know I could be sore.

Tristan still had an arm wrapped around my waist. Well, sort of wrapped around my waist. His big palm cupped one of my breasts. Every now and again he'd give it a little possessive squeeze in his asleep.

How was any of this possible? After everything? He was mine. All mine. I still had questions of course. Like what the hell would happen with Ella? And how in the world were they just going to continue the fake relationship? Although I supposed they didn't need to anymore. But how would that work? How in the world was *any* of this going to work?

I eased out of his hold carefully, determined not to wake him. He'd been, uh, *enthusiastic* the night before, and I knew he had a practice that day. If I was feeling sore and groggy and lethargic, I could only imagine how he was feeling.

I thought of the way I'd tried to beg off from another orgasm, and he'd still demanded one and given it to me. Then he'd pulled me against the hard length of his body and expected me to sleep. He told me I would be sore. He told me that he wasn't going to make love to me again because it would hurt and this morning I wouldn't be able to walk right.

But then I had been demanding and insistent. And now, I was pretty sure I couldn't walk right. He was so damn... big. And last night had been... Jesus Christ, I didn't even know what it was. All I knew was that I had never experienced anything like that in my life. And fuck, I wanted it more.

But what did it mean?

It means you have permission to be happy.

I wanted to ask all the questions, but I needed to stop. I was going to make myself crazy. I needed to just relax and enjoy this. Oh, and I also needed to call Penny and tell her holy hell, orgasms are the jam.

When I finally managed to escape his grip, I sat up in bed, pulling a sheet tightly around me and wincing as I headed to grab some water. When we got home, we were going to have to invest in a lube company. Also, it looked like I was going to need some Pilates or something to stretch the inner thighs.

Tristan thrashed in the bed. Moaning and mumbling under his breath.

I frowned. What was he saying?

"Stop. Please leave me alone. I don't want this."

Oh God. What was happening?

"Ashton, I'll tell Mom and Dad." He made this low keening moan, and I realized he was in the throes of some horrific nightmare.

I ran to the side of the bed and shook him hard. "Wake up, Tristan. Wake up for me." When he didn't, I put my hand in the water glass to wet it and then slapped him on the cheek.

That did the trick. He startled awake and jerked upright.

"Fuck." He blinked rapidly. "Forgive me if I'm wrong, but since when do orgasms warrant slapping?" he croaked.

"You were having a nightmare."

He paled. "Did I wake you?"

"N-no. I was already awake. But you scared me a little... It sounded bad. What were you dreaming about?"

"I can't remember. Come back to bed."

"No. I'm not coming back to bed. That looked really bad. You were mumbling your brother's name."

He blanched. "No idea why."

"Tristan, you were a having horrible nightmare about Ashton."

The horror on his face broke my heart. "What did I say?"

"I don't know. You tell me."

I reached for him, and he scooted just out of reach. "I don't want to talk about it, Ariel. Can't we just go back to bed and pretend the night was perfect?"

"Tristan, I don't want us hiding anything from each other. I don't want to pretend. I just want to be with you and share the good, the bad and the ugly."

"I promise you, you're not going to want me when you know the ugly."

"Tristan, my father was a traitor. It doesn't get any worse than that. Whatever is going on, you can talk to me."

His gaze snapped to mine. "Not about this. You were innocent. I..." His voice trailed. "I need you to let this go. Please. I just want to finish out the perfect night. *Please.*"

The pleading in his voice broke me. "Okay..." I dropped the sheet and climbed back into bed next to him. Only when I lay my head on his racing heart did I finally feel the tension start to ease out of his body. He was afraid. Something was scaring him.

But what?

He tucked me against his body, sliding his leg between mine. But he just held me, despite the thick erection throbbing between us. This wasn't about sex. He really did just want to hold me.

👑

ARIEL...

Eventually Tristan drifted back off to sleep, but my consciousness hung in that space between dreams and wakefulness. My mind played what he'd said in his nightmare over and over again. The distress. The fear. The child's voice.

His brother had done something to him. I knew it like I knew my own name.

I tilted my head and watched him sleep. A light etching of a frown told me his dreams still weren't entirely peaceful.

My phone buzzed on my nightstand, and I rolled to grab it. When I glanced at it, there was a message from an unknown number. Automatically, I swiped it to read the message.

Unknown: *You should have listened to me and not come back. Now you'll pay for your disobedience.*

What the hell? It was only then I realized I had the wrong phone. *Shit.*

I sat up. Who the hell was texting him? Not to mention threatening him? Quickly, I checked his breathing. He was fast asleep.

I scooted out of the bed and padded over the cool tile to my laptop on the desk under the window. The text had come in from an unknown number, but I'd set up a monitoring program to track calls that came to him or that he made.

Invasive yes, but that was actually part of the job. With his life in danger, privacy was a luxury he couldn't afford.

But you're about to hack his phone...and that's out of purview.

The guilt on that one stung more, but still I couldn't stop. I needed to know. Especially if it was a threat. It took me less than five minutes to get his password. It was the date we'd met.

Once I was in, my stomach roiled. There was a history of text messages from an Unknown number going back years. All threatening him with retribution and blackmailing him not to return to the Winston Isles.

I had a pretty good guess who they were from, but there was no way he had access to a phone.

You know the rules verify. Always verify.

I pulled up a program I'd made to track incoming signals and where they came from. When the program spat me out a location, my gut twisted. It was a bitch when you were right about things. And since I was right, it meant once again team Winston Isles couldn't trust anyone.

With another glance over at Tristan, I allowed myself one minute for my broken heart. He'd been hurt. And we had lost all these years together because of one person. And the fury it filled me with made me capable of all kinds of things in the moment.

I grabbed my phone off the nightstand, and I took it into the bathroom to make my call.

Penny picked up on the first ring. "Hey, everything okay?"

"I need you."

"Anything. You will be saving me from the monotony of palace appearances. What's going on?"

"We are going to do something that's probably going to get me arrested. And very likely, one of us might get maimed in the process."

"Sweet. When do we leave?"

"You don't want to know what it is?"

"Well, you're calling me *before* you get arrested. So that means that you need help."

"No, I don't need your help. I want you to talk me out of it."

"Not gonna happen. You know how this goes. I'm Thelma to your Louise."

"Are you sure I'm Louise?"

"Well, we can both be Louise. I really don't care. If you're into something, *I'm* into something."

"There a good chance someone is going to get hurt."

"Oh, fantastic! I have the perfect outfit for an ass kicking."

"Jesus, you're crazier than I am."

"And that's why you're my best friend. So, what's wrong?"

"I need access to Stanstit Prison. I know who's trying to kill Tristan."

"Awesome. When do we leave?"

To be continued in To Love a Prince...

THANK YOU

Thank you for reading RETURN OF THE PRINCE! I hope you enjoyed this installment from the Royals Elite Series.

Continue the saga about the mysterious Prince Tristan and the sassy determined Ariel? Find out what happens in the next book...To Love a Prince

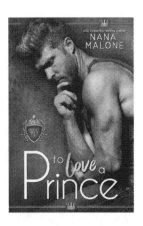

They said I'd **never come home again**...**they were wrong.**

There is one person **worth returning home for**. *Her*. One little problem. **She hates me.**

She should, **I left her behind**.

Now I'm back and I have a **score to settle.**

I'll do what ever it takes to to **win her back.**

Even if it means spilling my secrets.

Pre-Order TO LOVE A PRINCE Now>

Sign up for my newsletter to get new release alerts, exclusive bonus scenes and more: http://nanamaloneromance.net/newsletterlanding

NANA MALONE READING LIST

Looking for a few Good Books? Look no Further

FREE
Sexy in Stilettos
Game Set Match
Bryce
Shameless
Before Sin

Royals
Royals Undercover

Cheeky Royal
Cheeky King

Royals Undone
Royal Bastard
Bastard Prince

Royals United
Royal Tease
Teasing the Princess

Royal Elite

The Heiress Duet
Protecting the Heiress
Tempting the Heiress

The Prince Duet
Return of the Prince
To Love a Prince

The Bodyguard Duet
Billionaire to the Bodyguard

The Donovans Series
Come Home Again (Nate & Delilah)
Love Reality (Ryan & Mia)
Race For Love (Derek & Kisima)
Love in Plain Sight (Dylan and Serafina)
Eye of the Beholder – (Logan & Jezzie)
Love Struck (Zephyr & Malia)

London Billionaires Standalones
Mr. Trouble (Jarred & Kinsley)
Mr. Big (Zach & Emma)
Mr. Dirty(Nathan & Sophie)

The Shameless World

Shameless
Shameless
Shameful
Unashamed

Force
Enforce

Deep
Deeper

Before Sin
Sin
Sinful

Brazen
Still Brazen

The Player
Bryce

Dax

Echo

Fox

Ransom

Gage

The In Stilettos Series
Sexy in Stilettos (Alec & Jaya)

Sultry in Stilettos (Beckett & Ricca)
Sassy in Stilettos (Caleb & Micha)
Strollers & Stilettos (Alec & Jaya & Alexa)
Seductive in Stilettos (Shane & Tristia)
Stunning in Stilettos (Bryan & Kyra)

~~~

In Stilettos Spin off
Tempting in Stilettos (Serena & Tyson)
Teasing in Stilettos (Cara & Tate)
Tantalizing in Stilettos (Jaggar & Griffin)

The Chase Brothers Series
London Bound (Alexi & Abbie)
London Calling (Xander & Imani)

Love Match Series
*Game Set Match (Jason & Izzy)
Mismatch (Eli & Jessica)

Don't want to miss a single release? Click here!

ABOUT NANA MALONE

USA Today Best Seller, Nana Malone's love of all things romance and adventure started with a tattered romantic suspense she "borrowed" from her cousin.

It was a sultry summer afternoon in Ghana, and Nana was a precocious thirteen. She's been in love with kick butt heroines ever since. With her overactive imagination, and channeling her inner Buffy, it was only a matter a time before she started creating her own characters.

Now she writes about sexy royals and smokin' hot bodyguards when she's not hiding her tiara from Kidlet, chasing a puppy who refuses to shake without a treat, or begging her husband to listen to her latest hair-brained idea.

Made in the
USA
Columbia, SC